Patricia,
To My Dear Friend and
Fellow Trainer of our Nation's
Best Vampires!!
With Esteem!

VAMPIRES RULE!

ANDREAS JAWORSKI &
ROLF MOWATT-LARSSEN

Vampires Rule!
©2021, Andreas Jaworski & Rolf Mowatt-Larssen

All rights reserved. This book or any portion thereof may not be reproduced or used in any manner whatsoever without the express written permission of the publisher except for the use of brief quotations in a book review.

ISBN: 978-1-66782-161-0
ISBN eBook: 978-1-66782-162-7

DISCLAIMER

The Central Intelligence Agency (CIA) has conducted a thorough review of this book for sensitive material. The CIA has determined that certain facts and material in the book must be removed. The authors have agreed in the interests of national security to remove this content and it has been redacted accordingly. The redacted material has been blacked out in this book as received from the Publication Review Board. We do not believe the redacted portions of this book will detract from readers' ability to follow the story.

This book is a work of fiction. All incidents, dialogues, and characters are solely the products of the authors' imagination and are in no way to be construed as real. In instances where real-life figures do appear, those situations, incidents, dialogues, and events are entirely fictional and not intended to depict any actual events or to alter the entirely fictional nature of this work. In all other respects, any resemblance to persons either living or dead is entirely coincidental.

Given the assault on conventional understandings of metaphysical reality as described herein, we your humble authors anticipate your many questions and offer our unscientific responses in the back of this book in the section entitled "Vampire Physics and Frequently Asked Questions (FAQs)." We have answered to the best of our modest abilities many of the natural questions that are surely to arise—and some unnatural ones, as well—as you digest our testimony. The compilation of our observations and research is to prepare you to enter another world—the world of CIA and KGB Vampires!

INTRODUCTION

We strived to have some irreverent fun by creating a dystopian world in which the most dedicated, committed, and effective intelligence officers among us become so consumed by their mission, their cause, and themselves that they get carried away and things go terribly awry. We all know that never happens in the real world. Bear in mind that our characters are Vampires, not human beings. Please don't make unintended associations between the words and actions of our fictional characters, in their altered state of consciousness, to any persons past and present.

Do Vampires exist? Who really knows? It's complicated, as you'll discover. Our gothic-inspired, Vampire-themed description of the dark arts of intelligence is intended provide our readers a sense of the deep moral, ethical quandaries that inhabit our secret world. That much is real. Very real. If you are still disturbed by the characters and the depiction of our beloved profession, it might help to remember that humans alone, not Vampires, hold the power to destroy the world with the push of a button.

And remember: Vampires cannot rescue us from ourselves. We alone can **save the world.**

TABLE OF CONTENTS

INTRODUCTION vii
1. WALK-IN 1
2. EYES ONLY 11
3. THE LOYALTY TEST 16
4. FINDING ABEL 27
5. THE BLOOD OF YURIY ANDROPOV 34
6. THE NUMBERS GAME 43
7. VAMPIRE 3 52
8. CRISIS OF CONSCIENCE 59
9. VAMPIRES 4 AND 5 61
10. AGENT NUL 66
11. IN THE BELLY OF THE BEAST 74
12. VAMPIRE 6 78
13. VAMPIRE 7 83
14. AMERICAN VAMPIRES 88
15. THE TRUST 95
16. THE SYSTEM 103
17. A DEAL WITH THE DEVIL 107
18. WIRING THE WORLD 113
19. ACCIDENTAL ENCOUNTER 117
20. MOSCOW RULES 120

21. THE SERUM	124
22. THE MARK OF CAIN	128
23. MOSCOW LIAISON	134
24. FEEDING FRENZY	139
25. MAD SCIENTIST	143
26. FAREWELL TO GEORGE	147
27. SERGEY POSAD	151
28. THE DEAD HAND	157
29. THE QUEST	162
30. THE COMMAND CENTER	167
31. THE CHASE	175
32. MASKIROVKA	179
33. THE RACE TO SILO 747	188
34. BY HIS OWN HAND	198
35. BERIA'S OPERATION	206
36. THE MOLE HUNT	211
37. BORIS'S REVENGE	214
38. A PERSONAL AFFAIR	217
39. ODE TO THE CHIEF	226
40. THE SYSTEM STRIKES BACK!	231
APPENDICES	236
CONCLUSION	248

"The collapse of the Soviet Union was the greatest geopolitical catastrophe of the century!"

—Vladimir Putin, address to the Russian parliament, April 25, 2005

CHAPTER 1

WALK-IN

"**W**HY AM I HERE?"

Bucharest isn't exactly known as a hotbed of international espionage and intrigue. Within the ranks of the Central Intelligence Agency (CIA), the Romanian capital has a reputation for holding modest operational potential. But that's all about to change.

The CIA Station, as it's called inside the Agency, is a place where officers practice the black arts of espionage. CIA case officers are trained to hunt spies, and occasionally they recruit them. As a general rule, good spy potential combined with a less restrictive operations (ops) environment usually makes for a successful tour. If an assignment at this relatively obscure posting produces a good number of quality recruitments, a follow-on assignment to a real hotbed of espionage is almost assured. So, in the final analysis, Bucharest has always been and will always be a middling Station within the hierarchy of overseas CIA franchises.

At least that's what Deputy Chief of Station (DCOS) Aaron Janicke keeps telling himself. Aaron is at his desk in CIA Station Bucharest and about to leave the office to meet a new developmental, or prospective spy. This Eastern European outpost was not on Aaron's bid list of overseas assignments. Having been assured of a posting to either Berlin or Moscow, he was dispatched to Bucharest at the last minute without much in the way of explanation. He's now living on blind faith that this sea change of assignments was for a damn good reason. "So why the hell am I really here?"

Aaron has taken to muttering to himself whenever he gets frustrated with the humdrum pace of business. He, of course, has no idea just how important Bucharest Station is about to become to the future of all humanity. What an appropriate place to begin this story, given what civilization is about to endure.

The physical spaces that make up Bucharest Station can best be described as exemplifying the current standard in US Government style-neutered office spaces. These days, all Station office spaces follow the same cookie-cutter, politically correct template. The walls are a sterile blend of bland bureaucratic off-white, decorated with large USG-approved and USG-provided rah-rah slogans hardly noticed and thus utterly and legally incapable of offending anyone of any persuasion. Very corporate.

The sample adorning the walls of Bucharest Station include:

"Hang in there. You can do it!"

"Be bold. The prize is yours!"

"You were born to win. Go for it!"

Perhaps intended to inspire or motivate, these bile-inducing slogans actually ring from the walls like an annoying child's dirty hands tugging incessantly on your trousers, seeking attention.

Other wall hangings in the Station are a curious motif of random photos of US tourist attractions, such as the San Francisco Bay Bridge and an aspen grove somewhere in Colorado, mixed with disorienting posters of house pets caught in curious poses, mouthing pseudo-philosophical human words of encouragement.

"Some bureaucrat thinks we're gonna go native if we don't have this shit to remind us of the homeland," Aaron decries somewhat loudly.

No surprise Chief of Station (COS) Desmond (Des) George personally hung the house cat "Hang in There" poster in his office.

Station spaces consist mainly of XXXXXXX. A small office is dedicated to COS George and next to it is a small, if not tight, conference room equipped to seat up to twelve people: seven around a prototypical oval-shaped conference table, with the remaining five seated along the side and back walls. A large, forty-inch flat-screen TV with video teleconference hookup is affixed to the rear wall opposite the door. Both the COS's office and the conference room open up into a larger room where the Station staff – XXXXXXXXXXXXXXXX XXXXXXXXXXXXXXXXXXXXXXXXXXXXXXXXXXXXXXXXXXX XXXXXXXXXXXXXXXXXXXX XXX and DCOS Aaron work in an area configured into a newsroom-style open space. There are no partitions, just desks with faux wood tops arranged along the outer walls.

The bullpen is loud, interactive, and exactly the kind of engaging environment Aaron prefers—COS George, not so much. A compact disc carousel shuffles an eclectic mix of music, all donated by Station officers. Each officer has the right to veto the play of one disc per day.

In silent protest of the enforced political correctness and as a visual reminder of Station's real mission, a one-half-scale, inflated great white shark hangs suspended a foot and a half from the ceiling in the middle of the room, its large teeth exposed with eyes fixed solidly on unsuspecting prey. A three-inch-thick gray metal door provides the only entrance into the Station and opens directly into the bullpen.

A cold November rain is falling heavily in the city and has been for the past day and a half. Most Station officers are out on the street, doing their jobs and surely soaked to the bone. Aaron has just put on his parka and is about to exit when the phone connected to the dedicated outside line lights up. He stops, turns, and nods to Station officer Tom Burns, who picks up the receiver.

The caller claims to be a Russian volunteer. The volunteer passes his bona fides to Burns. His biographical information and claimed professional associations seem credible, at first glance anyway. During the short conversation, he gives a vague but tantalizing lead to the existence of a Russian mole within the CIA. Through his thick Russian accent, he claims to be a Russian Internal Intelligence Service (FSB) officer.

Good or bad, one thing is for certain: It's too good of a lead to pass up.

The FSB officer refuses to meet in the embassy and will not meet in Bucharest. "*Eto slishkom opastno!*" Too dangerous. Tom speaks passable Russian, but the caller doesn't test it. From the tone of Tom's voice, Aaron knows there's no way he'd be able to convince this guy to come into the safer sanctuary of the US Embassy, where XXXX prefers to meet unvetted volunteers. Strange, the normally reliable XXXXXXXXXXXXXXXXXXXXXXX failed to engage for this call.

The caller is well versed in the basics.

"One last requirement." The Russian waits for an acknowledgment.

"What?" Tom replies curtly. No case officer likes to be told what to do by a prospective source, not under any circumstances.

"Come alone. I will approach you and will ask about your father's health."

The choice of a verbal parole startles Tom. His father has been recently hospitalized with a chronic heart condition. Tom takes a moment to clear his throat and compose himself. His voice still cracks. "Okay. I'll carry a black bag on my left shoulder."

"*Ne nada*. I know what you look like."

Two days later and the rain has finally stopped, but the sky is still shrouded in a heavy gray overcast. Tom and Aaron, with Aaron at the wheel, drive several hours to meet the mysterious volunteer at a prearranged site in Transylvania.

They go over their plan several times. Janicke will perform countersurveillance while Burns handles the approach. Tom is to remain within sight the entire time. They joke about why the FSB officer will only meet in the village of Brasov, the Transylvanian town a short distance from Dracula's castle. Probably has a flair for the dramatic.

Aaron and Tom haven't ruled out the possibility the person they're going to meet is either playing a prank or mentally unbalanced.

"Great, just what we need, another nut bag!"

The vast majority of these unsolicited intelligence officer volunteers turn out to be bogus. But his claim to know what Tom looks like has the two case officers curious. He has them on the hook, and they know it.

Aaron waits at a distance from the meeting site while Tom moves in to make contact with the volunteer. Aaron watches the initial encounter between Burns and the Russian from a discreet countersurveillance location, through the dirty side window of a nearby long-abandoned metal storage shack.

He's kicking himself: this was perhaps too discreet of an observation point. It's hard to see anything. Janicke can only make out two shadowy forms as they recede into the background. He observes them approach one another under the corrugated metal awning that covers a crumbling, concrete loading dock attached to the side of a large, abandoned warehouse.

Inexplicably, they slip from view.

"Damn it, Tom! What the hell are you doing?"

Aaron strains to see something—anything—through his now useless binoculars. He's visibly annoyed by Tom's carelessness. "What the hell good is countersurveillance if Tom doesn't remain in sight?!"

Through strained eyes, Aaron thinks he sees shadows. Are they struggling? It's hard to tell one way or the other. Should he rush in? The last thing he wants is to interrupt the meeting unnecessarily. Can't risk spooking this Russkie bastard who might, at this very moment, provide Tom with critical information about a mole in CIA. How could he explain to Headquarters if this Russian source broke contact and ran off, all because DCOS Dumbass didn't have either the patience or the discipline to maintain his position?

Aaron has no choice but to wait for a sign of life. It's a fateful decision, as it turns out. Anxiety turns minutes into hours.

At the meeting location, the strange encounter between American and Russian spies continues to unfold.

Once he's satisfied they're alone, the Russian identifies himself to Tom matter-of-factly.

"Kruchkov, KGB officer!"

The normally self-assured American case officer is startled by the deep, raspy voice emerging from the shadows. He wipes some sweat off his brow. It's odd the leathery-faced Russian would use the term *KGB* to describe his organization, and not the current term, *FSB*.

Neither offers a handshake. They're wary of one another. The CIA officer nods to encourage the Russian to explain himself.

The Russian's buzz-cut, silver hair gives off a subdued glisten in the twilight. Tom is unable to avert Kruchkov's penetrating gaze. The Russian begins to speak. His speech is slow and deliberate, emanating in a deeply soothing, almost hypnotic tone.

"As you know, Gaspodin Burns, the KGB was replaced by the FSB and the SVR (Russian External Intelligence Service) after the collapse of the Soviet Union. I prefer to think of myself as a KGB officer. You will understand shortly."

Tom's eyes are held captive to the cold stare of the Russian's unblinking, snake-like eyes. He can't avert Kruchkov's gaze. "How does this fucking Ruskie know my real name?" the CIA officer whispers to himself, instinctively trying to break the Russian's spell. The two now communicate without one audible word exchanged.

Tom Burns is overwhelmed by confusion, anxiety. In a matter of minutes, the tall, hulking case officer has been rendered submissive to the short, wiry Russian. Tom can't move a muscle, but his mind has shifted into overdrive. Panic. Things are happening way too fast for him to process.

Kruchkov needs no words to unmask his true self to the trained CIA case officer. In his trance-like state, Burns is unable to comprehend the fact that the Russian with the piercing eyes has inched ever so slowly toward him and now stands one solitary inch from his face. Frozen in place, the American is oblivious to the danger directly before him. He's even unable to recoil from the strange, foul stench of Kruchkov's breath.

Kruchkov speaks Russian in a whisper. It sounds like gibberish to Tom.

The Russian need not explain himself to his helpless prey. It's all over with one swift bite delivered to the tender flesh on the back of Tom's neck. The CIA officer staggers forward a few steps. The veins in his neck are ready to pop. He grimaces, opens and shuts his eyes tightly in rapid succession. Tom struggles to summon the final vestiges of human free will and tries to arrest his transformation from a man into something neither dead nor alive. All for naught. Tom collapses in a heap on the ground and crawls into the fetal position. Within minutes, Tom Burns is dead. Mercifully, the end comes quickly.

Tom's exit from one world begins his reemergence into another. His eyes shut tightly as he lies motionless on the ground. A new life force wells up within his lifeless body. After several minutes he regains consciousness only to confront the awful truth. An alien creature is slowly occupying both his mind and body. This thing, whatever it is, is breathing life into him. Whatever now occupies his being isn't human! His eyes emit a brief flash of red. Kruchkov stands over him. An evil smile purses his lips. Satisfaction.

As Tom emerges from the twilight of his human existence to peer for the first time into the shadows of a new world, he instinctively feels a firm loyalty to his master, KGB officer Kruchkov. The American automatically kneels in front of the Russian, his head tilted downward in supplication. A strange metamorphosis has begun. One that irreversibly transfers the American's loyalties to the Russian side.

Tom—if he can still be called by his Christian name—senses a siren call from Mother Russia welling deep within his soul. He hears fairy tales from the great poet Pushkin, tales he learned years ago when he studied the Russian language. He tries to fight the changes enveloping his being, but his resistance is overwhelmed by the initiation of the intensely painful physical and psychological transformation into something inhuman.

Kruchkov gently strokes Tom's hair. His soothing voice sounds like that of a kindly father speaking to his loving son. The Russian whispers, "Welcome to the new KGB, my son."

Unable to speak, Tom exhales in a high-pitched moan, nodding his head in response to his master's orders. Kruchkov extends a hand to help Tom to his feet. "I will be your handler," Kruchkov explains matter-of-factly. "For your first task, you will bring out some Station files. Do not draw attention to yourself. Only bring documents you can carry in your black bag. I will make copies so you can take them back. The most important information is the identities of any CIA agents, especially Russian sources working with the CIA, now or in the past. Understand?"

Tom acknowledges with a spastic nod. His fleeting eyes betray the shock and bewilderment of his continuing metamorphosis into a Vampire.

"From this day forward, you will be called Maykov. You will be addressed by that name by those to whom you owe your allegiance. You are one of us. Now and forever. Congratulations, Maykov."

Their next meeting is scheduled in one week's time. Kruchkov orders Maykov not to tell anyone what's transpired. The Russian need not worry. The transition has been swift. The CIA, even his good friend Aaron Janicke, are the fledgling Russian agent's sworn enemies.

Kruchkov gives the CIA officer some humdrum FSB documents, called feed material, to pass on to CIA Headquarters. This will satisfy their desire for intelligence information and help establish Kruchkov's bona fides as a new source. At the KGB officer's initiation, they shake hands and part ways slowly in opposite directions.

There's no enthusiasm in Kruchkov's voice. His calm, deadpan speech helps soothe his victim's agitated state of mind. The old pro has worked up an appetite. He's looking forward to celebrate, to bragging about his new agent conquest, complete with a toast of fresh blood.

Aaron Janicke has seen none of this. He's worried. Upset, actually. This meeting has taken much longer than planned. Questions torment him. Is Tom under threat by the Russian? Should Aaron break countersurveillance at the risk of interrupting the meeting?

DCOS Janicke nervously strokes his closely cropped black hair. He steps outside the metal shack to see Tom emerge from the shadows, briskly walking in his direction, seemingly okay.

Tom reaches his Station mate, now standing several feet outside the shack, but studiously avoids eye contact. "Let's go."

"Is that it? Why didn't you stay outside as we agreed? You don't know this guy. Tom! What the fuck happened?"

Tom doesn't acknowledge Aaron's questions. He continues to walk in the direction of their car, still hidden from view.

Tom is suspiciously quiet on the long ride back to Bucharest. Aaron can tell something's wrong. His friend's demeanor is completely out of character. Normally an enthusiastic if not effusive prankster, the portly Burns practically lives to regale his Station colleagues with jokes and anecdotes drawn from the archives of his Eastern European sources. He's the Station dirty joke referent. Aaron tests him a bit on the drive. He tries a joke about how Tom is at the top of the ten most wanted list of the world's sheep farmers. Tom doesn't respond. His face is blank, ashen. He looks morose.

Aaron decides to further test Tom, seated in the front passenger seat of their black Jeep Grand Cherokee, dark shades on, staring straight ahead. He tries to elicit a response. "How'd it go?"

"Good. Looks promising." Burns is impassive.

"That all? C'mon, Tom. What'd he say? What'd he give you?"

"Ah, you know... He's cagy, like they all are at first. Gave me some SVR docs. I got some names of local Russians. More next meeting."

As they approach the outskirts of Bucharest, Tom crumples forward in obvious pain. He looks nauseous. Aaron shoots a glance at Tom and notices what appears to be a thin smear of dark blood on the front of the passenger seat just below the headrest. Janicke resists a feeling of panic. He recalls his training. *Never ignore an indication something is amiss during an operation.*

Tom's description of the meeting doesn't sit well with Aaron. His colleague's positive assessment is betrayed by a lack of details. Not enough there to justify a second meeting. His responses to questions are vague, even evasive. The Russian walk-in didn't provide any solid information and nothing to help confirm his bona fides, yet they scheduled another meeting a week from now? It just doesn't add up. WTF!

Aaron's also preoccupied, perhaps distracted, by feelings of guilt for having missed the initial encounter between Kruchkov and his colleague. What happened after they disappeared from view? Why didn't Tom follow the plan to stay in sight?

Tom's front channel cable report offered some leads supposedly provided by the Russian volunteer. His assessment concluded the Russian "needs further assessment as a potential source during the next follow-up meeting."

This doesn't wash with Janicke. Back at the office COS Des George doesn't contest or even question Tom's decision to meet the Russian volunteer a second time. Despite his gut feeling something's off, Aaron's input is muted as he doesn't want to have to explain to his COS why he was in a poor countersurveillance position and failed to adequately back up his colleague. One uncharacteristic lapse in judgment, and something weird happens. "Just my freakin' luck," Aaron thinks to himself. Hopefully everything will work out.

CHAPTER 2
EYES ONLY

The next day, Aaron consults—or attempts to consult—with COS George regarding his concerns about Tom's mysterious encounter with the Russian walk-in, FSB officer Kruchkov. A sleepless night has convinced him to fess up to his own lapse in judgment and share his concerns about Tom's meeting.

A search or trace of Station databases reveals no information on Kruchkov. A complete lack of information on a senior Russian intelligence officer is unheard of and only adds to Aaron's palpable feelings of unease.

Des George is intently playing putt-putt golf on a narrow length of green indoor-outdoor carpet extended across the floor of his office. The short, nearly bald chief grunts and exhales loudly as he tries to assume the correct putting posture. His gloved hands wrap and unwrap around the handle of his golf club as his chunky hips sway humorously from side to side. White golf balls litter the landscape of the floor, with only one resting in the simulated cup.

Normally, George's antics are comic relief from the tedium in Bucharest, but today Aaron's not amused. George is about as good at golf as he is at being a case officer, referred to in-house as a C/O.

The best officers want nothing more than to be acknowledged as being among the artists at what they do, which is to recruit and handle spies. This gives Aaron pause to reflect on his chosen profession. The world—his world—is changing. Sadly, classical espionage is no longer valued as much as it once was, even in-house.

The pudgy COS's main goal in coming to Bucharest is first and foremost to not make any mistakes. Famously risk averse, George stopped doing ops as soon as he made it into the management ranks. Better safe than sorry.

George avoids direct eye contact with Aaron, who's standing near the entrance of the golf ball–littered office. The chief is jealous of the young, dynamic officer. Aaron recalls his COS's oft-repeated motto, "No flaps on my watch," punctuated with the point of a stubby index finger and the word "Capisce!" The COS's large bullfrog-like double chin expands and contracts when he talks.

George is a relentless suck-up to his senior supervisors at CIA Headquarters in Langley, Virginia. As a result of this and in combination with his lackluster professional skills, he's lost the respect of his Station subordinates. Fortunately for George, his consignment to relative obscurity has rendered a need for professional validation unnecessary. Station officers wonder aloud how this empty suit could have survived as a C/O, much less in the coveted position of Chief of Station—"The Freakin' COS!"

Morale at Station would be bad were it not for the fact that the dozen or so officers at the US Embassy in Bucharest have bonded well, in part to get things done in spite of their boss.

Perhaps not coincidentally, they're all in the prime of their careers. They've found success and are refreshingly idealistic. Working undercover overseas, recruiting spies and stealing secrets isn't a job, it's a calling. And great fun to boot!

Station officers have gamed how to work around their COS, who has long figured out how to credit himself with his subordinates' accomplishments. The disturbing aspect of the situation is how seniors back at Headquarters haven't seemed to notice the chasm between the rank and file and management.

After another disillusioning encounter with Des George, Aaron heads back to his office to check on the day's incoming cable traffic. Chief of the Central

Eurasia Division (C/CE) Rainer Wolf has just sent DCOS Janicke an Eyes Only note addressed to Aaron personally. Janicke is directed to return to Headquarters for consultations immediately. Excellent. He keeps his excitement to himself. Someone is listening after all!

Wolf has been a mentor for Aaron since the young officer entered on duty (EOD). It bears repeating that Janicke's assignment to Bucharest was something of a surprise. The native German and Serbo-Croatian speaker sought an assignment to either Berlin or Moscow, but the C/CE made clear that could wait. Wolf wanted Aaron Janicke in Bucharest. It's practically unheard of within the DO to turn down a directed assignment. CIA officers tend to have the same "can do" spirit as their elite military unit colleagues. At least the good ones do. Aaron was no different.

Since the fall of the Berlin Wall and the collapse of the Soviet Union, Bucharest has evolved into a modest hub for the pursuit of Russian intelligence-related activity in the region, an emerging crossroads of espionage. To the Kremlin, Romania remained well within its backyard and, therefore, within the Russian sphere of control, complete with heavy-handed interference in Romanian internal affairs, albeit exercised behind closed doors.

Unfortunately, Russia has dimmed in stature since the Cold War. Many Washington policy makers dismiss Russia as an "Upper Volta with missiles." These policy wonks have no idea just how far off base they really are. It is, however, shocking that some of the Agency's senior leadership actually share this myopic view. They seem to have conveniently forgotten one critical fact: Russia is the one country in the world with the capability to annihilate the United States with nuclear weapons. And vice versa, of course. The threat of terrorism may peak and subside, but the threat from Russia will always remain. The US and Russia are eternally tied to one another in a geopolitical Gordian knot.

Rainer Wolf, known simply as "the Chief," is himself on the fast track in the Directorate of Operations, the DO. Graced with height, gray hair, and a distinguished bearing, the salty field soldier previously served as COS XXXX, COS XXXX and as the chief of the Counterintelligence Center (CIC), where he led the hunt for moles (Russian spies) in the CIA.

Aaron is well aware that to his detractors the Chief is too intense, even somewhat of a loose cannon. But those who've served with him love his laser-like mission focus. Mission above all else. In fact, his closest friends call him Kurtz in honor of the iconic rogue character Colonel Kurtz in Joseph Conrad's novel *Heart of Darkness*.

One thing's for sure: Wolf is one lucky bastard. Everything he touches turns to gold. Much in this profession often depends on luck, but great case officers have an uncanny ability to make their own luck. Aaron hopes to one day team up with Wolf. In many ways they're much alike.

With the Eyes Only cable clutched firmly in his hand, Aaron races into George's office. He's professionally obliged to request George's guidance commensurate with his upcoming temporary duty (TDY) status. "Des, did you see the cable from the Chief?"

"Which Chief is that?" George asks churlishly. He lines up another attempt at a long putt across the room. The attempt fails. The golf ball comes to a rest about nine inches to the right of the cup. George's focus remains on the golf cup at the other end of the green stretch of carpet.

George answers his own question. "Go meet the boss, Aaron." He sighs dismissively. "Give Rainer my regards. Bring back any juicy gossip. I've heard big changes are a'comin.'"

Aaron's determined to get George's attention. "Chief, I plan to express my concerns about the Kruchkov volunteer op. This just doesn't feel right. I think the Russians have inside information. My gut says they're springing some kind of trap."

Des isn't interested in Aaron's assessment. "An op is an op, Aaron."

George tries to turn this into a teaching moment for his junior colleague. "We get credit for following up with this walk-in, whether he turns out to be good, or not, crackpot, super spy, or bed wetter. What's not to like? I don't see a downside."

"Des, you read Tom's cable. There's no basis for a follow-up meeting, nothing remotely tangible." Aaron can scarcely hide his contempt. "The Russian gave him no damaging information. His bona fides are sketchy. We can't even validate whether he is who the hell he says he is. Don't you think it's strange that we're meeting someone who claims to be a KGB officer and we've never heard of the guy? And why did he say he's KGB? The KGB no longer exists. Who does this guy think he is? You gotta admit. This is more than a little disturbing on many levels."

George looks up briefly, feigning contemplation before returning his gaze to the grip of his golf club. "Janicke, if I didn't know any better, I'd think you were jealous of Burns's opportunity to get a scalp. Maybe if you spent more time on the street instead of in my office, you'd get on the scoreboard too."

Aaron's face is flush red. He wants to punch his bloviating COS in the mouth.

Still avoiding eye contact, George concludes his pointless efforts at golf, removes his gloves, and for some unknown reason tucks them into his right back pants pocket—the fingers stick completely out. He then walks into the bullpen and stands near the open doorway to the Station conference room. George's gaze is drawn to the oval faux wood conference table. He's staring at some errant crumbs at the far end. Annoyed, he announces loudly for all to hear, "Keep your clammy paws off of my jelly donuts—Capisce?"

CHAPTER 3
THE LOYALTY TEST

A ARON JANICKE RETURNS TO HEADQUARTERS AND REPORTS TO RAINER WOLF'S OFFICE. Jet lag has given way to anxiousness and adrenaline. "Shit, I really hope this goes well."

It's late Friday evening and the Chief is alone in the Central Eurasia Division front office suite in Langley. His efficient and meticulous secretary, XXXXX, has departed for the evening at her ritualistic, punctual time of 7:00 p.m. Aaron notices her tidy desktop and the large white coffee cup emblazoned with the words "National Museum of Art" placed in the usual perfect order. Wolf is the third division chief for whom she's served. Given her overly protective nature, XXXXX humorously refers to herself as the Chief's "moat dragon." No one gets to see the Chief or onto his calendar without going through XXXXX first. Save for Rainer Wolf, the front office suite is deserted.

Wolf gestures for Aaron to come into his office and shuts the door. His large executive desk is clear of papers. Two black leather accent chairs sit vacant on the opposite side of the desk. A keyboard and darkened computer screen are perched neatly on the sideboard. The room is comfortable and nicely appointed. In the manner of a big game hunter showing off his trophies, the walls are adorned with a mix of arresting photos and artifacts taken from exotic locations worldwide. An expensive silk Persian rug, a gift from the head of a Middle Eastern intelligence service, spans the distance between the Chief's desk and a seating area comprised of a black leather couch, two matching chairs, a rectangular coffee table, and a sidebar with a cabinet. The flat screen TV mounted on the wall closest to the desk is set to CNN. The sound is muted.

As Aaron approaches, Wolf stands and walks around to the front of his desk. After the customary handshake and greeting, he motions for them to sit in the two chairs opposite the desk. Given the recent turn of events in Romania, Janicke is glad, if not relieved, to be summoned back to Headquarters. He hopes to finally get the hearing he didn't get with his inept COS.

Several rounds of small talk peppered with elements of locker-room humor ensue. On one level, they are two case officers working with one another. Aaron hopes the Chief's Eyes Only cable is a precursor to news of a new assignment, far away from George and sleepy Bucharest, as long as it isn't back at Headquarters. Anywhere in the field is preferable to the sentence of answering cable traffic from people who are actually out in the field doing ops.

"Aaron, I called you back here to talk about the walk-in, the one Bucharest Station met last week. Tom's reporting cable struck me as—well, as a bit odd. It doesn't add up. I want to get your firsthand account of what actually happened at that meeting."

"You saw it too, Chief!" Aaron feels his heart racing. "I tried to tell Des George something wasn't right. We're meeting a guy who gave us a name that doesn't check out and little else. But that's not the half of it. The meeting didn't go down as planned."

"What do you mean?" Rainer's eyes squint.

"Tom didn't follow protocol. He was supposed to remain visible so I could counter-surveil the meeting. Instead, he disappeared into the shadows for about ten minutes."

Aaron stops just long enough to inhale. He feels guilty for dissing his colleague. He knows he failed to keep close watch over the meeting. This is his confession. He needs to get it off his chest. "I thought I saw a struggle. I didn't want to interrupt the meeting. Didn't want to spook the walk-in. Afterward, Tom was strange. Not himself. I'm concerned something really bad happened."

The mood is tense as Wolf listens attentively to Aaron's story about Burns and the mysterious Russian walk-in. Aaron has talked nonstop for about a quarter of an hour when the C/CE asked him to retrieve two cold beers from the mini refrigerator out of sight in the corner cabinet. It's an old tradition in the DO to knock back a few at the end of a long, hard week. Unfortunately, given the current trend of overzealous displays of political correctness, many new age managers have prohibited such "unprofessional behavior."

"Let's raise a glass to the more professional officers in our ranks who refuse to dull their senses by imbibing at the end of a long, hard week."

Wolf is uncharacteristically sarcastic, a side of him Aaron hasn't seen before. At Wolf's gesture, he stands, walks the distance to the sidebar, and leans over to open the right lower cabinet containing the mini fridge. Once he's distracted with his back turned for several seconds, he hears the C/CE speak in a low, serious voice. "You have joined The Trust, and The Trust will make you proud."

Aaron has no time to react. Wolf's mysterious remark catches him off guard. Rainer Wolf silently closes the distance between them and bites down hard on the tender flesh on the back of Aaron's neck. The young officer is stunned and confused, and he has a hard time registering what's just happened.

He trusted Rainer. How ironic. Both served as Army officers before joining the Agency, Janicke in the Special Forces. He has never lost the self-discipline of an elite soldier. The ex-soldier still keeps himself in impressive physical condition and has a certain contempt for those who let themselves go mentally or physically. The intelligence business is just too important to entrust to anyone who doesn't take it seriously. One mistake can cost a spy his life. Even their career paths meshed well in the CIA. They both are sons of immigrant parents, and both learned English as a second language. Aaron is overwhelmed with questions now flashing through his mind. *Why did Rainer do this to me? What does Wolf want? What just happened!? WTF! WTF?*

He rises from the Persian rug cushioning him from the hard floor and grabs the back of his neck. Dark red blood, partially coagulated, smears his hand. Powerful and overwhelming new feelings of strength, heightened senses, and visceral urges emerge from deep within. The pain is excruciating and exquisite all at the same time. His lips can no longer form words. A grunt-like whimper is all he can muster to protest what's transpiring in the core of his being.

In the absence of all logic and reason, Aaron is left with the surging instincts of the beast into which he's mutating. His mind takes him on a journey through a long, dark tunnel toward an uncertain destination. Feelings of confusion and betrayal are mingling with strange euphoric sensations. The once proud CIA officer will emerge as neither man nor beast, but as a Vampire! Aaron senses the existence of a new world order, the dark presence of a much bigger picture. His eyes pulse on and off with an amber glow. He feels a raw power surging through his veins. The newborn Vampire stands unsteadily.

Wolf speaks slowly. His voice is calm, soothing, hypnotic. "I'll explain everything, Aaron. This is your loyalty test. I trust your unconditional devotion to our country, to your duty. You'll soon understand why I chose you for this calling."

The apprentice Vampire would like to say, "Fuck you, Rainer Wolf." But he can't. So he bows his head.

Wolf takes Aaron for a walk on the narrow, tree-lined path around the CIA compound, late at night. A few lights still glow in windows behind which officers are intensely responding to night-action-required (NIACT) cables from around the globe. But otherwise the compound is completely in the hands of the guard force. The Chief relates a story about an intensive mole hunt when he was the chief of the CIC.

"Aaron, let me explain why we're here tonight. As I searched far and wide for traitors in our ranks, the decisive lead came from a Russian intelligence officer walk-in to Bucharest Station three years ago named Sergey Deniken. The volunteer, an FSB counterintelligence officer, met with DCOS J. Oliver Reed in a Bucharest safe house. As you know, Oliver was your predecessor."

Janicke nods to acknowledge he understands the connection Wolf has just made between the Deniken and Kruchkov Russian walk-in cases.

Wolf continues. "Sergey Deniken had quite a story to tell. He claimed to have a colleague in the FSB named Boris Smertsov. Sergey and Boris were childhood friends from a small town in Siberia. They joined the FSB at the same time and went through training together.

"Boris told Sergey he'd been sent personally by Vladimir Putin to kill him. He didn't know what Sergey had done to merit a death sentence directly from the Russian president. But it didn't matter. No one questions an assignment to carry out a wet operation (assassination). Boris warned Deniken to flee Romania at once. If Sergey didn't disappear, he'd be hunted down and killed. Boris claimed powerful forces were at work inside Russia. In an effort to convince Deniken of the seriousness of the threat to his life, Boris confessed to being a Vampire.

"Sergey Deniken's astonishment at this revelation from his friend Boris seemed genuine as he offered up this information to his debriefer. C/O Reed kept listening, although he'd written off the walk-in as a kook, or as Reed put it later to his colleagues, 'Bat Shit Crazy.' He did, however, continue to take copious notes. 'At least this'll make for a good story over a few beers at Friday vespers.'"

As Wolf continues to relate the origins of Russian Vampire penetrations of the CIA, Aaron feels like his head will explode. The emerging Vampire's enhanced awareness of the true nature of time is rapidly expanding. He has a sudden insight that the past, present, and future form parts of one greater reality accessed through folds in space-time. Time travel through the mind? "Impossible! Absurd!" Aaron tells himself. He's about to learn how wrong he really is!

Sensing his protégé's unsteady mental state, Wolf grabs Janicke by the shoulders with both hands and, with a penetrating stare, peers directly into his eyes. It's a form of Vampire hypnosis, a sort of mind meld in which Vampires can travel to the same point in space-time together. They're soon transported back in time to the CIA safe house in Bucharest where DCOS Reed met the walk-in FSB volunteer, Sergey Deniken. The scene plays out in Aaron's mind like a grainy video recording. He hears their voices. He sees the two men huddled around a plain table in a sparsely furnished sitting area. Neither can sense the invisible presence of the Vampires Aaron Janicke and Rainer Wolf. They're locked in conversation.

"Can you imagine? He said he is a real Vampire!!"

Sergey Deniken was shouting at DCOS Reed, who by now had stopped taking notes. The CIA officer sat staring at the Russian in disbelief. The meeting had started with such promise. How unfortunate it took such a bizarre turn. This kook sure did a good job of appearing sane. "Of course, I thought Boris had gone mad," Sergey admitted, lowering his voice.

Sergey's voice was a whisper as he carried on, wary of presumed listening devices in the room. He leaned over to get closer to C/O Reed, who fought the urge to pull back beyond arm's length. "Boris must have sensed my doubts. He demonstrated his Vampire powers to convince me of the truth of this awful thing he had become."

Reed motioned for Sergey to go on as he took notes in order to avoid eye contact.

"I got up one morning and found myself sitting across from Boris… at the small kitchen table… in my tiny Bucharest apartment."

Deniken began to hyperventilate.

"Go on."

"Boris was waiting for me when I came into the kitchen for morning coffee. He was just sitting at the table, motionless. My friend looked directly into my eyes. I suddenly felt very cold. My body began shaking uncontrollably. All color left the room. All I could see was black and white. Shadows seemed alive, dancing on the wall, on the ceiling. I tell you, I was staring into the face of pure evil."

"What do you mean… the word 'evil'"? Reed felt goosebumps. This was getting creepy.

"Boris's lips didn't move, but I heard him say, 'Now about that rat problem.' The kitchen turned pitch black. I could see nothing at all until the lights returned. When they did, Boris was holding two large, disgusting, rats, squealing loudly."

Sergey paused. The boyish-looking, blond-haired Russian's voice was completely drained of emotion. He looked hard at DCOS Reed. "I know you don't believe me, 'Mike,' or whatever name you're using. But take good notes, please. You must deliver me from this evil. Don't take my word for it, but do your job. Check me out. Tell the CIA my story."

DCOS Reed shifted in his seat. The young officer swiped his thick mop of hair to the side of his forehead, absentmindedly looking down at his notes. Finally shaken by this vivid horror show, he could use a stiff drink.

Deniken took the CIA officer back to the scene with his friend Boris. His voice was shaking with fear. "In my own kitchen, I sat there and watched Boris bite one rat, then the other on the back of their necks just below the skull. I had to shut my eyes in horror. When I opened them I saw Boris devour the lifeblood from those rats. It made me sick. I lunged for a trash can and vomited."

Deniken's face turned a ghostly white. Reed noticed thick beads of sweat running down the walk-in's forehead. A drop of sweat landed with a muted splash on the open page of his notepad, causing ink to form a small pool on the letter B. Deniken pulled himself together. It was time to wrap up his story. He was on a mission. The CIA officer was his last hope.

"This, believe it or not, was followed by something even more incredible. There was a horrible noise, a commotion coming from inside the walls. Boris told me to look out of my kitchen window to the street below. Rats, hundreds of them, were running away from the building. They ran away in every direction."

Reed wiped some sweat off his brow. Deniken had finally unnerved him with the graphic description of his delusions. The C/O struggled to maintain his composure. "Please continue."

"Boris stood up and walked over to me. I couldn't move a muscle. He put his arm on my shoulder and gave me one final piece of advice. 'Take the rats' advice and run for your life—now!' I tried to thank Boris for sparing my life, but I couldn't speak. All I could do was give him a hug in gratitude. He was cool to the touch, not warm like you or me. Before he left my apartment, Boris warned me not to go to the CIA for help. 'Know this. They cannot protect you because Vladimir Putin has a Vampire mole buried deep inside the CIA.'"

Deniken knew his warning was dismissed by the CIA debriefer but was determined to finish his testimony. "As he walked toward the door, I asked my wretched friend Boris, 'What will become of you?' Boris was quiet. At long last, he said to me: 'The System now rules Russia. They will eliminate me if they so much as suspect I spared you. So you see, my friend, my warning to you is not altruistic. You must get as far away from Russia as possible—and from the CIA. If they find you among the living, I will die along with you.'"

As Boris's last words of advice to his friend trail off, Aaron recovers from his Vampire-induced trance. He's back in the present, walking the narrow, winding path through the woods of Langley, Virginia, with Rainer Wolf.

Wolf grabs Janicke's arm. "Yes, Aaron, can you imagine my astonishment when I discovered Sergey Deniken wasn't crazy? The Russian walk-in spoke the truth. There really was a Vampire mole in the CIA! Fortunately, Reed duly sent a cable detailing a full report of this meeting for the record. The cable naturally went into a dead file. All further contact with the volunteer was dropped on the basis of Reed's assessment that he was deranged and mentally unstable. Not uncommon, as you well know."

Wolf chuckles at the irony of finding the initial leads of a Vampire penetration of the CIA in the "dead" file. "Aaron, it was the walk-in's good fortune the Agency dismissed him as a nutcase. Had he been taken seriously, he would no doubt have come to the attention of the Russian mole within our ranks and mercilessly killed."

"What caught your eye about Reed's reporting? No one could have believed Deniken's story. Everyone knows Vampires don't exist except in movies!"

Wolf was pensive. "I pored over the cable traffic. In his effort to convince Reed he was lucid, Deniken provided some odd clues—physical characteristics that distinguish Vampires from humans. These subtle clues led me to the Russian Vampire penetration inside the CIA. I had a hunch who the mole was, but more on that in due course."

Wolf recalls the insight that led to his discovery of the identity of the traitor within the CIA. "You see, Aaron, when you sent your Eyes Only cable, I knew Kruchkov was a Vampire. The behavioral anomalies you described reminded me of the Deniken reporting. It was no coincidence Kruchkov walked in to the same city where the Vampire Boris Smertsov was sent to liquidate Deniken. Kruchkov's mission was to recruit a Bucharest CIA officer, or, rather, to bite a CIA officer! Then the Russians made their second mistake: Kruchkov used his Vampire calling card when he identified himself as KGB not FSB. I adopted the Russian mindset to complete the nonlinear pieces of different puzzles into one: KGB mole in CIA. Deniken walk-in. Kruchkov walk-in to Bucharest Station. Sloppy bit of tradecraft on Kruchkov's part to reveal his true KGB affiliation—his link to the past."

Wolf pauses to allow his apprentice to absorb this implausible story. He loves playing CIA-FSB chess with the Russians. They're unmatched in the counterintelligence game. But even the FSB chess master occasionally tips his moves. The CIA has also won its fair share of the many espionage matches over the years. Wolf eagerly anticipates the prospect of matching wits against them once more, but this time as a Vampire!

"Chief, why? Wuh, wuh, why are the Russians so desperate they resorted to using Vampires to recruit spies? What's wrong with the human factor? The old Spy versus spy?"

"Aaron, hold that thought. What you missed during the encounter between Kruchkov and Burns was the death of our colleague and his return as a Vampire. The Russians need to replace their penetration in the CIA. Our one advantage is they have no clue that their plan is compromised. But we have to move fast to reverse what they've done. And remember: so far, you and I are the only pieces on our side of the chess board."

Aaron is dismayed. Has he been reduced to the role of a pawn in Wolf's Vampire chess game? For a fleeting moment, he's envious of his contentedly oblivious COS George. Aaron knows what Wolf is about to say. He wants to cry. Vampires don't cry, do they?

"We must eliminate Tom Burns and the KGB Vampire Kruchkov. You are the action officer. I'll advise you when and where this'll be done after you return to Bucharest. These are our first moves to challenge the Russians."

Wolf sighs sympathetically. To keep his protégé from fixating on his own personal plight, he pushes Aaron relentlessly forward.

Aaron's legs move like wooden stilts. He's unable to speak in full sentences. Physical sensations spread through his body while cool blood rushes through his veins. His heart pumps at an unsustainable rate while his body adapts to the inhuman physiology of a Vampire. He's unsure which fate he'd prefer if given a choice: to be dead, lying peacefully undisturbed in his grave, or to be a Vampire.

If Aaron had only been in a better position to observe Tom Burns, none of this would have happened! He fights panic with denial. "This isn't so bad. I can do this." His college philosophy class finally seems relevant to him after all these years. He now knows what Descartes was thinking when he uttered, "I think therefore I am." Will human awareness of one's existence have any more meaning for a Vampire than it does for a human being?

Rainer Wolf has a formidable task before him: to teach his new deputy that being a case officer Vampire is way more than anything he could ever have imagined as a human. A Vampire's unique ability to sense tremors of geopolitical instability can be compared to sensing the earth's magnetic poles or to feeling the slightest tremors in seismic or magnetic forces as they shift within our planet. Vampires can sense the slightest changes in the strategic balance between the United States and Russia. Aaron begins to sense those imbalances. In a halting voice, the protégé asks his mentor if he'll indulge him with one question, Vampire to Vampire.

The Chief nods.

"How the hell did that idiot George get to be COS Bucharest?"

Rainer laughs. He admires Aaron's spunk.

"That's another story. George's last promotion is long past."

"So, Chief, does this job come with a Vampire sign-up bonus?"

"Janicke, don't press your luck."

The emerging Vampire yearns to hear his own familiar voice again. He's suddenly aware of his swollen tongue. His mouth feels numb at the corners. He strikes a theater actor's pose. Words spill out with a lisp. "My journey will continue in this afterlife. What of this rebirth? Is it second life? And what of my old self? What's left of me? I feel stinging white hot flashes. What the fuck is going on?"

Rainer smiles affectionately. "Channeling Hamlet? Okay. I'm good with that."

Wolf is relieved, even amused. It seems Aaron the Vampire still enjoys Shakespeare. He hasn't lost his trademark sense of humor. Rainer wraps his arms around his mentee and gives him a Vampirely hug. But there's no sugarcoating what happened here today. Aaron Janicke is dead. He's resolved to embrace his new destiny as a Vampire, whatever that means, but he's also intent to preserve as much of his human self as possible. "Not quite the new assignment I was hoping for. At least I'll be back in the field and away from Headquarters."

CHAPTER 4
FINDING ABEL

T HE NEXT DAY THE CHIEF REVEALS THE IDENTITY OF THE MOLE. The Russian spy inside the CIA was, undeniably, Remington (Rem) Philbin, a good officer and friend, someone highly regarded with whom Rainer served in Moscow. The Chief never suspected Philbin was the traitor he'd been hunting for years.

Even with the benefit of Deniken's leads, at first Wolf refused to believe his colleague and close friend could be a Russian spy. However, the result of his investigation left open no other possibility. The only person to whom the evidence pointed was his old friend Rem. The spymaster might be forgiven for not putting the puzzle pieces together sooner. The only reason Philbin managed to remain unmasked for so long was because he wasn't human. Being a Vampire gave him a significant advantage over his mole hunters.

Although Deniken was unable to identify the Russian spy during his meeting with C/O Reed, Boris Smertsov told Deniken that the CIA Vampire turncoat was given the pseudonym "Abel" by his KGB handler. Sergey also provided some tidbits on Abel's background as well as sketchy information about his habits and interests. Ironically, Reed had taken copious notes of his meeting with Deniken in order to discredit the walk-in, not to use the leads to help find a mole in the CIA.

In the course of pursuing his solitary hunt for spies, Rainer Wolf discreetly pulled the personal files of CIA officers past and present and reviewed them for possible matches with behavioral characteristics that might distinguish Vampire spies from human spies. Lacking direct evidence in this regard, Wolf drew liberally from the Vampires of fictional lore. A strong preference for darkness and aversion to light. A disgust for fully cooked food. Uncontrollable drooling at the sight of blood. A Russian Vampire penetration of the CIA would presumably display little patience for office politics, human ineptitude, social norms, and political correctness. All clues to unmask the Russian Vampire mole hidden within the CIA's ranks!

Truth be told, if it had been anyone except Rem Philbin, it wouldn't have taken Wolf so long to catch on to him. In this case, Wolf's legendary CI mind betrayed him. He simply couldn't imagine the possibility his trusted colleague and friend was a Russian spy. Even now, it is difficult for Wolf to admit how wrong he was.

"My case against Philbin was entirely circumstantial," he admits to Janicke. "I needed a confession. I went to his home. Rem was lying in bed, hours from death. I had to act before Rem sensed I was there to unmask him as a Russian spy."

Aaron is so absorbed with the testimony that he trips over a crack on the trail and falls face first onto the ground. Wolf helps him back to his feet.

"I had to confront Rem right there, on his deathbed, with the truth. My slim chance was to provoke him to confess. You see, Aaron, Rem's only son, Harold, is also a CIA officer. Harold has no idea of his father's treason and it must remain so. He's a fine young man who deserves the opportunity to build a life of his own. It would destroy him to learn the awful truth, that his father was a traitor.

"I had one handle to play, one vulnerability to expose in my bid to induce a deathbed confession. I knew Harold was completely devoted to his father. He loved Rem so much he joined the Agency only to please him. Young Philbin actually wanted to be an architect. Poor kid, ill suited for the craft of espionage. Rem knew his son didn't have 'it,' but didn't have the heart to tell him he'd be much better off in the civilian world. He loved his son more than anything in the world, or so I hoped."

"Did Remington Philbin's love for his son trump his loyalty to the Russians?"

"I'll get to that, Aaron. It's complicated. I was willing to gamble that Rem's dedication to the Russian System didn't equal a father's love for his only son."

"C'mon, Rainer. Did you really think that ploy would work? A man… I mean… Vampire who'd betray his country would surely betray his son."

"Oh, it was a desperate gamble, but I counted on a Vampire's emotions to take over Rem's sensibilities. I needed to provoke him to bite me so I could become a Vampire myself!"

Wolf twitches in recollection of the pain he suffered on that fateful night. "I had to persuade Rem to bite me at the precise moment when his emotions were most susceptible to manipulation. I had to introduce a psychological wedge that would cause Philbin to rationalize he could do something for the CIA, born out of love for his son, without compromising his loyalty to the Russians. He had to believe he could serve two masters. I knew my pitch was a long shot, but what choice did I have? I knew if I didn't succeed, all would be lost—at least for me."

"So, Rainer, when I sent the Eyes Only cable describing Kruchkov and the scene at the walk-in meeting, you put two and two together. You realized Kruchkov was a Vampire. The Russian Vampire was on a mission to bite Tom Burns to replace Philbin as a KGB penetration in the CIA. But that didn't help you three years ago when you confronted Philbin. You had nothing. What made you think you could get a committed spy to confess to treason, much less do your bidding?"

"I had no idea if it would work, Aaron. I went to Rem's house and confronted him with the truth. I hoped it was a truth he couldn't deny—or wouldn't deny. Not long into our conversation, I knew I could help him in his final hour. My old friend craved recognition for his secret life as a spy. Who better to confide in than a peer, someone who could fully appreciate his 'greatness'? I knew Rem. I was confident he'd revel in being able to confirm he'd beaten me at my own game. No one can better appreciate the art of your craft than another artist."

Rainer Wolf stares deeply into Janicke's eyes. His concentration is intense. Several minutes pass until time stops. Janicke levitates, at least in his mind. Wolf stands next to him, suspended in a gray mist. He guides them through a wormhole toward a light on the other side. The two American Vampires are transported into the past at the time when Wolf appeared at the home of a traitor to confront him with the fact of his betrayal and gain a deathbed confession.

Rem's ex-wife Noreen escorted Rainer Wolf upstairs and left him alone at the door of Rem's bedroom. The dying CIA officer was lying in the middle of a king-sized bed that almost filled the tiny room. Heavy curtains were drawn and the lights were off. An unpleasant odor of death filled the room. Philbin's extended family members were gathered downstairs, on death watch, waiting for their patriarch to pass. Once Wolf closed the door, he sensed the old spy was waiting for him. Lying in wait.

Rainer took a seat in the tall-backed wooden chair placed next to Philbin's bed. He was struck by how the chair looked so out of place, as if it was displaced from an antique Elizabethan-style dining room table set. With his two hands, he gently grasped his dying colleague's folded hands for the last time. "I miss the good old days, Rem. But we had a good run, didn't we?"

The dying Vampire was utterly still. His face was a ghastly white.

"I'm sorry I came without my customary single-malt scotch. I figured you might not be up to it, you old dog."

Without opening his sunken eyes, the dying Vampire responded in a clear, low voice. He was surprisingly lucid. "Would that we could have one more sniff of Oban together, old friend. I'll raise a glass in your name in the afterworld to the good old days. And none of that 'goodbye, old friend' bullshit!"

Wolf cleared his throat. He spoke in calm but firm voice. "You want no bullshit, old friend. I'll give you no bullshit. Here it is, you son of a bitch. I'm going to expose you as a Russian spy. I'll disgrace your reputation. The publicity will devastate your family. That's the way it's gonna be. Before you die, I want you to know that we beat you. Checkmate. Game over. Oh…and I'll tell Harold the news personally. He's downstairs, you know."

Wolf sensed his target was wavering. Breathing patterns became erratic. Philbin tried to control his breathing in an effort to conceal the betrayal of his emotions. His eyes remained shut. The standoff lasted for several agonizing minutes. The old pros understood the value of contriving calculated periods of silence in a recruitment pitch.

Philbin's eyes opened a slit to gaze up at the ceiling fan, which was spinning softly. "What can I do, *stariy protivnik*, so you'll let me die in peace, with my honor intact—at least in the eyes of my son?"

Wolf was prepared for this moment. "Old friend, there's only one thing you can do to make things right."

"What makes you think I have to make things right? I like the way it turned out, Rainer. I'm lying here in the knowledge I've beaten you. What more could a man die for?"

"A man, or a Vampire?"

"Come on, Rainer. Why so bitter? Does it really matter if a spy is a man or a Vampire? Every form of existence on God's great earth is only a means to an end, no? What makes humans so special?"

"Rem, we went our separate ways, and that's too bad. I don't want to know why you switched sides. I don't care. I'm asking you to join forces with me for one last hurrah."

Philbin closed his eyes. His breathing slowed. The annoying wheezing sound coming from his nose suddenly stopped. He looked strangely serene. The heavyset Vampire's thick jowls, deep-set eyes, and severe expression seemed less intimidating now. His thick white hair was matted in knots. He was ready to die his second and final death.

Wolf knew he'd lose his target if he didn't play the full deck, and fast. "Rem, listen to me. I know you're still with me. You've done things no other CIA officer has done. And now I'm giving you a chance to do something no Russian or American case officer has ever done."

Philbin shifted under his blanket, a signal for Wolf to continue his pitch.

"Rem, you can become the father of a new bloodline of Vampires—CIA Vampires. You'll live on through them forever. The best service you could gift your Russian masters is to provide them with a worthier adversary. Great warriors are defined by their *glaviny protivnik*—their main enemy. In better times, you and I shared our disdain for the amateurs of our craft. We expressed a mutual admiration for *seriozhniy chilovek* (serious person). There aren't enough serious people left in our profession, are there? There's time for one more chess match between us. You can control it from the afterlife. Let's put ourselves up to the test. I came here to prove I'm a serious person. Are you? Are you a serious person, Rem?"

Philbin slowly opened his eyes. They emitted a faint, pulsating crimson glow. He turned over on his side and propped himself up on his arms. Wolf was surprised his adversary had that much strength left in him. "I'll bite, Rainer. If I decide to play your game, what are your rules? What is it you would have me do? And what would I get in return?"

"Bite me!"

Wolf said it emphatically. He waited for a reaction.

Philbin's face went blank. Those were the last two words the dying Vampire expected his enemy to utter. After a long pause, the old Vampire grunted. "Why the hell would you want me to do that, Rainer? How would becoming a Vampire serve your cause?"

"Rem, we reach our full potential only when we're tested by the best among us. How can you not accept my game-changing challenge? May the best Vampire win! Think carefully. You have the fate of your family to consider. Think of your son. You can die with your reputation and legacy intact. A hero in Moscow and in Washington. Your secret will remain safe. My entry into your world will assure my eternal discretion, in case you harbor any doubts."

"No, Rainer! You don't always get what you want. You're an arrogant SOB, but I've never doubted your integrity. You've always been truthful. Some of your most annoying qualities, actually. As usual, I need to know exactly what's up your sleeve." He grunted bitterly. His voice was now raspy, his speech labored.

Wolf banked on the influence of his target's ego, the inexhaustible vanity that led Rem Philbin to betray his country. He had to pique his target's interest in being something greater than he'd ever imagined as a CIA officer or a Russian Vampire. "What do you have to lose, Rem? If I prove unworthy, I'll die, simple as that. Or I'll be brought over to your side. But if I survive and emerge as a Vampire, a Vampire who remains loyal to my country, what harm is there in that?"

"And why would you trust a trusted agent of Russia to act in good faith, my dear Rainer?"

"Because I know you're true to who you are, even if your betrayal disgusts me. Is there honor among Vampires, or have I misjudged you? Well, Rem?"

With much effort, Philbin pushed himself up and into a sitting position. He eased over to the edge of the bed and placed both feet flat on the floor. Rainer helped him stand as he firmly grasped the Vampire's ice-cold, shaking hand.

"Rainer, I'm near my end. May I impose on you to go over to the bedroom window and describe the view for me?"

Rem had the last laugh. Literally. The old coot offered up a bit of tawdry humor, something to the tune of how this is usually the time the pretty, young wife next door likes to sunbathe topless.

Wolf was momentarily distracted. He partially drew the curtains and peered out through the window, half hoping to see a nude sunbather. Silently, Remington Philbin leapt forward, practically flying at his unsuspecting but willing prey. It all happened in the blink of an eye. Rainer Wolf felt Philbin's teeth sink deep into the soft flesh on the back of his neck.

"For my dear son Harold."

"Aaron, those were the last words I heard as a human."

CHAPTER 5

THE BLOOD OF YURIY ANDROPOV

AFTER CIRCLING THE CIA COMPOUND THREE TIMES, THE TWO AMERICAN VAMPIRES RETREAT ONCE MORE TO THE CHIEF'S OFFICE FOR A SHORT BREAK IN THE ACTION. Headquarters is deserted. Wolf's office is pitch black, as he prefers. With a wry smile he retrieves a bottle of Johnnie Walker Black Label and two plastic cafeteria cups from the bottom left drawer of his large executive desk. Aaron is offered his first stiff drink as a Vampire, complete with an encouraging salutation. "A toast! It tastes better, and the effects wear off faster."

After settling into their oversized chairs, the two Vampires are transported again into the past and back to the scene where a dying Vampire has just given birth to a new Vampire.

The uncertain transformation of Rainer Wolf had begun. The old friends stared blankly at one another for the first time as Vampires. Neither knew what would happen next. Wolf walked slowly, agonizingly, over to the mirror in the bedroom and opened his eyes, revealing a faint glow of amber light.

Philbin exulted. "So, my old friend, are you finally ready to announce who's won this game?"

Wolf instinctively resisted the effects of becoming a Vampire. Doubts, buyer's remorse. What had he done?! His limbs were racked with intense pain. His mind was clouded in confusion. What about his identity? Did he still have a soul? He sensed twinges of an emerging consciousness. In a fight to suppress gut-wrenching pain, the stricken victim fought to stay connected to his human identity. Rainer touched his arms in a desperate test to see whether his mind was still connected to his body.

In his metamorphosis, Wolf knew it would take time to know whether he was independent of the bonds that bound Philbin to his Russian masters. He gambled on a pact made in good faith between man and Vampire. To gamble his life on such a flimsy theory was impetuous, if not reckless. Nonetheless, Wolf wasn't willing to allow the Russians to gain the upper hand over his unsuspecting CIA without a fight. For all his idealism, he was still too cynical to believe a dying Russian spy would enter into this pact with the devil simply for the sake of his son. In his experience, traitors are narcissists. Self-justification is necessary to rationalize their betrayal. The Russians really did their homework in targeting Remington Philbin.

Rainer Wolf was willing to risk his life on the proposition Philbin was so consumed with the need to achieve some form of immortality that he'd see this Faustian bargain through. Philbin's love for his son would hopefully add the necessary element of distracted confusion in order for Rainer to remain free of any dependency to Philbin's Russian overlords. Wolf's greatest fear was that his own loyalties might turn to Russia. As insurance, he was resolved to kill himself before his transition was complete. And exactly how do you kill a Vampire?

"Either way, there's no way out now." Wolf was staring absentmindedly at the ceiling. "What the fuck have I done?"

The Russian Vampire snickered in a subdued display of arrogant satisfaction. He enjoyed the spectacle of watching his old friend suffer the pangs of rebirth. As he drew in his last breaths, Philbin fully expected Wolf's loyalty to transfer to Russia as his had turned when he was bitten by Kruchkov. Buoyed by the assumption he had the upper hand over his bitter foe, Philbin felt the urge to share more of the details of his recruitment by the KGB.

"Rainer, I've honored your request. Now, please indulge a dying Vampire one last request."

"What is it?" Wolf's voice sounded foreign to him.

"For the remainder of our time together, please refer to me by my KGB code name, Abel. I've lived in this life as Abel, and I shall die as Abel."

Wolf sat on the chair next to the traitor's bed. Bent over in pain, he held his head tightly between his hands.

Abel was motionless on his back, staring upward, eager to reveal the secrets of the Russian Vampire KGB collective. "Rainer, it's my turn to comfort you. Rest while I describe the exclusive club you're about to join. As you know, I served in Moscow Station during the 1991 coup attempt by the Soviet military and the KGB against Mikhail Gorbachev. The coup failed. It brought down the USSR. I was recruited by the KGB after the coup during a meeting with an SVR general. Like you, I was bitten. Can you imagine my shock? Of course you can, now. My recruiting officer, Badanov—yes, that's his name—revealed to me that he was a Vampire. He gave me the code name Abel to use from that day on. My mission was to penetrate CIA Headquarters. I have willingly served my new masters with gusto, I must say, for the past fifteen years."

"How the hell could you allow yourself to be run by the Russians?! Like a dog!!"

"Now, now, Rainer. No need to get nasty. Like a Vampire. With honor!"

Abel's voice dripped with sarcasm. "You're always right, aren't you, Wolf? Better than the rest of us. We'll find out how good you really are, won't we? I won't go on unless you accede to my request. Address me as Abel. You're in no condition to dictate terms to me. I've honored your request, now honor mine."

Wolf wanted to kill the Russian Vampire right there on his deathbed, but was in no condition to do so. No time to allow raw emotions to take control over him. "All right. Please go on… Abel."

"It didn't take long. My Russian soul gradually eclipsed all that was American within me. I gave no more thought to who I was in my prior life. You know something? I don't miss anything about my old human life. The CIA is dead to me. Badanov gave me new life!"

"How could you say that? What the hell happened to you, Rem?"

"Rainer, you're old school. Obsolete. A dinosaur. The agency doesn't need you anymore than they needed me. You just don't know it yet. Take it from me. If you want the truth, you'll find it at the origins of deception. So let me take you back to the origins of *our* deception."

Abel nodded his head and made no attempt to suppress a smile of open satisfaction. In some ways intelligence officers are like middle school kids on a playground. They absolutely love gaining the upper hand over one another.

"As the last great Soviet leader, Yuriy Andropov, lay on his deathbed, the KGB was desperate to halt the fall of the Soviet Union. They would do anything to turn back the clock. Reformers demanded youth and change. Mikhail Gorbachev emerged as a leading candidate to become the next secretary-general of the Soviet Union. Even then the KGB didn't trust him. Wasn't cut from their cloth."

Abel wheezed. He lay motionless for several minutes. The Russian spy was milking his last act. Rainer moved to check Abel's pulse. The dying Vampire spy picked up where he left off, without missing a beat.

"It was an act of desperation. KGB chairman Vladimir Kruchkov ordered Soviet biological weapons researchers to develop a serum to revive Andropov. He was gravely ill. They would do anything to revitalize him, to bring him back to life. Their orders were clear, and impossible to fulfill. It was November 1982. The KGB gave the order: 'Get five years out of Andropov and we'll save the USSR!' They weren't so lucky. He lasted fifteen months. A brilliant young microbiologist by the name of Volkov began experimenting with dangerous pathogens and bioweapons developed in top secret Soviet facilities. He was determined to succeed even after the doctors said nothing more could be done for Andropov."

Wolf leaned in closer to Abel's face, straining to hear his words. The tenor of the dying mole's speech slowed. Up close, Rainer could see traces of his own bright red blood still smeared on the Russian Vampire's fangs.

Abel continued. "One day Dr. Volkov burst into the Kremlin chamber where Yuriy Andropov's lifeless body was stretched out on a metal gurney. Three KGB guards, a nurse, and Andropov's personal physician were in attendance. The body was covered head to toe in a white sheet, prepared for whatever happens after death. The biologist was jubilant. He proudly held up a vial containing some sort of liquid serum. The scientist claimed to have found a cure, an elixir that would bring Andropov back from the brink of death. Despite the obvious grave doubts from those in the room, no one dared utter a word in opposition to Volkov's gleeful pronouncement. After all, it couldn't hurt, could it? At gunpoint, the KGB guards ordered Volkov to stand down while they consulted with their superiors. It didn't take long, perhaps a half hour, before Kruchkov himself appeared on the scene accompanied by two other KGB generals. Volkov was by now pacing back and forth restlessly.

"The biologist gave them a short briefing, just enough to convince them to proceed. On order, a nurse quickly set up an IV. The crowd stood back when Volkov stabbed the needle directly into Andropov's arm. The needle was huge, something like what a veterinarian might use on a large animal. Everyone was mesmerized at the sight of the fluorescent yellow serum passing into the lifeless leader's body. No one said a word. Time passed slowly. The witnesses stood in stony silence, awaiting any sign of life. No one recalled for certain exactly how much time had passed. After maybe an hour, maybe two, Andropov began to stir. His eyes suddenly popped open violently."

Abel shut his eyes tightly. His head jerked back and forth. Some minutes passed. He and Rainer were transported back to the scene to experience firsthand the night Andropov died a second death.

"Andropov began to stir. He looked around with wild eyes. He looked confused at his arms as if they didn't belong to him. Then it began—all hell broke loose. He tore that massive needle right out of his arm, sat up straight, and shrieked. The nurse at his bedside screamed and tried to run from the room. She got no farther than the locked door. Andropov's cries were not of this world. His eyes were blood red, full of confusion and fear. It took the three guards and the doctor to physically subdue him. He convulsed violently for about thirty seconds.

Then he died. Or at least he was motionless. The KGB guards made the mark of the cross on their chests, convinced they'd just experienced something unholy."

Abel suddenly opened his eyes widely, which spooked Rainer so badly he fell off his chair. Momentarily amused, Abel returned to the story.

"Yes, Rainer, you're right. It was unholy. Witnesses to this inhumane experiment were given strict orders to never speak of it, under penalty of death. But that wasn't the end of it. Oh no! Not by a long shot.

"Seven years later, the KGB conspired with the Soviet military to overthrow Gorbachev. Kruchkov was alone in his office when he received word the coup had failed. His military coconspirator, Marshall Ahkromeyev, committed suicide. You know him. Planned the invasion of Afghanistan. Great man. An honorable man. Real pity."

Abel nodded in tribute to Ahkromeyev.

"Okay, you're far enough along. Now concentrate; continue with me to experience firsthand the rest of the story. Come with me. Let's go now."

The two Vampires formed an invisible presence in KGB Headquarters at Lubyanka Square in Moscow, USSR. It was a warm, sunny day back in August 2001.

Alone in his cavernous office, Chairman Kruchkov was desperate. He stared at the white granite bust of Yuriy Andropov peering down at him from his venerated perch, high above on his bookshelf.

"Yuriy, all is lost. What would you do now if you were me?"

About then an aide knocked on his door. The young KGB captain bowed in respect as he entered the office. "Sir, is there anything I can bring you?"

"Poison, perhaps, double dose."

Kruchkov was inconsolable. Then came an inspiration. The chairman sprang to his feet and raced out from behind his massive oak desk. He barked orders in quick succession as he threw the heavy red velvet curtains open to allow in some sunlight.

"Captain Petrov, we must urgently convene a session of the General Staff. Summon that scientist, the one who tried to cure Andropov. What's his name? Volkov! Tell him to *bring me the blood of Yuriy Andropov!*"

Kruchkov returned to his desk. He pulled open a drawer and took out a pen and a pad of paper on which he wrote a short list of names. He handed the list to his aide.

"Petrov, contact these officers immediately. Instruct them to attend a meeting in the chairman's conference room at 2200 hours tonight. Advise them they are to tell no one about this meeting. Top secret. You will report directly to me and to no one else. Understand?"

"Yes, Sir!"

That night, the KGB general staff gathered around the large, highly polished table in the chairman's conference room. Kruchkov was in complete command, invigorated.

"You who are seated here today represent the vanguard of those who will one day rule Russia. Only the KGB is sufficiently reliable and capable of responding to a clear and present danger, a danger to our country. We must save Russia from our enemies, internal and external. We must take the crown jewels with us after we clean out our desks and leave this place for the last time. Take the files of our most valuable agents so they are not compromised! Repossess our precious national assets, to borrow an American word, from the carpetbaggers who would enrich themselves at Russia's expense! In our tireless efforts to take back Russia from the thieves who would steal her in the night, we must act in the spirit of our Chekist forefathers."

A general spoke up, no longer able to contain his exuberance. This general would later become known as the Vampire Iron Feliks.

"I'm in, Sir! With my life, I serve Mother Russia!"

All stood at attention. As one, they repeated the Chekist motto.

"Clean hands. A cool head. A warm heart!"

"Henceforth, we will be known as The System: *Systema!*"

Rainer found himself back in the present, in Abel's room, now consumed by the acrid stench of death. *Is he done?* Always the case officer, Wolf wouldn't rest until he squeezed everything he could out of the dying traitor.

"Abel, you're not finished. What about Andropov's blood? How does Putin fit into the picture?"

"Ah, yes... Vladimir Putin."

Abel dragged out the moment, savoring Rainer's anxiety. He saved the best for last.

"It turned out the chairman had a special surprise in store for his select group of KGB officers. On queue Volkov was escorted into the room. You could hear a pin drop. At Kruchkov's command, the group listened incredulously as the scientist animatedly related the story of Andropov's final moments of second life after receiving the experimental serum."

Abel and Wolf returned once more on a flight to the past to find themselves in the KGB chairman's conference room in Moscow. They watched as Kruchkov questioned Volkov as the other attendees sat in stunned silence.

"And what did you do after Andropov died, Dr. Volkov?"

"Sir, I drew blood from General-Secretary Andropov and preserved it for further study."

"And what have you learned from your research, Dr. Volkov?"

"Sir, I have refined the serum. I can vouch for the fact it is ready for use in human subjects if the need were ever to arise."

"Well, there is most certainly a need now, Dr. Volkov. We must summon forth all the advantages of this earth and beyond to restore Russia to her former greatness. We need a volunteer to take this serum. Who's willing to volunteer in the name of Mother Russia?"

No one raised a hand. They all sat stone solid, not daring even to blink. After all, these senior KGB officers were skilled at assessing people. They knew a madman when they saw one, and Volkov was, in their minds, absolutely stark raving mad.

Kruchkov banged his fist hard on the table.

"Find a volunteer, now!"

Wolf returned to Abel's bedside to witness the moment of truth. A delicate breeze from the whirring ceiling fan provided a moment of distraction.

"Rainer, I'm sure you've surmised the identity of the intrepid volunteer for Volkov's Vampire-creating serum."

"Abel, don't play games! You can't expect me to believe that…"

Abel cut Wolf off in mid-sentence.

"Yes, Rainer, the nondescript KGB lieutenant colonel who volunteered to take the serum was none other than Vladimir Putin. Yes, you see now, don't you? Putin is Vampire Zero. He received a transfusion of an enhanced version of the serum from the Andropov experiments. Vladimir Putin received the blood of Yuriy Andropov!"

Abel might have stopped there, but the dying Vampire couldn't resist seeing Wolf's reaction to the awful truth he was about to disclose.

"You see, Rainer, Vladimir Putin controls *Systema*, the Vampire leadership collective that rules Russia today. There are ten who share Vampire Zero's bloodline. I, Abel, am proud to have served among them. You have finally met your match, Rainer. It's a pity I won't be there when you meet your inglorious end at their hands. *Dosvidanniye, stariy drug!*"

Those were Abel's last words.

The scene returns to Rainer's office in CIA Headquarters as the light of day approaches. It's been a very long night for Rainer and his new Vampire protégé.

"And this, Aaron, is why I need you. We have our work cut out for us. We are no match for *Systema*."

The Chief puts his hand on his protégé's shoulder in an attempt to provide some comfort. Aaron wants to describe how badly he feels trapped in this existential battle between good and evil. He wants desperately to explain how he now sees the world in shades of life and death. He wants Wolf to hear him say that the distance between life and death is not as far as he thought when he was human. The Vampire Aaron Janicke is still unable to express such profound thoughts, so he sits in anxious silence.

CHAPTER 6

THE NUMBERS GAME

A FTER A LONG DAY OF MIND-NUMBING PAPERWORK, AARON IS PROPPED ON THE SOFA IN THE LIVING ROOM OF HIS BUCHAREST APARTMENT. Unfortunately, one aspect of his job hasn't changed since becoming a Vampire. Even Vampires have to contend with the mature bureaucracy. How freakin' ironic. He still hates the drudgery of all that redundant paperwork. Supposedly things were different in the good old days in CIA. At least that's what the old guard, those colorful characters of yesteryear, have told him. Aaron talks to himself. "Very soon paper cuts may well be the most dangerous part of the job. First aid kits stationed by every printer complete with annual certification requirements."

The hour is late and the apartment is completely dark. Aaron's reading the most recent COVCOM messages from Rainer, the Chief. A wet, sticky snow has been steadily falling for most of the day. The wind has picked up and enters the apartment along the edges of the poorly insulated living room window like an unwanted guest. The night's temperature plummets to a few degrees below freezing, which renders it near impossible for the building's old communist-era construction to retain much in the way of heat. These are but a few of life's inconveniences that no longer bother the Vampire. In fact, he feels invigorated by the sharp arctic blast.

Aaron's laptop computer is perched on the coffee table before him. He can read the text even though the screen is turned off. He's taken to reading in darkness. It helps exercise his Vampire eyesight. Of all the physical changes, his sharpened visual acuity is most exciting. How the resolution of objects appears so sharp against the magnificent blackness is astounding. Even the faintest light is superbly amplified. Bright colors are now a bit harder to distinguish than when he was human, but shades of gray are precisely, immeasurably defined.

Shadows come alive. Shadows speak to him. The dark is ablaze with subtle images and color. The experience of continued evolution, the emergence of new powers, the discovery of his new self is intoxicating. He's arriving at the point of transcendence as his body continues the transition of becoming a Vampire.

Janicke can't forget the first COVCOM message received from the Chief. Rainer Wolf confirmed what Aaron feared: Bucharest Station officers were hand-picked to become part of CIA's Vampire syndicate, colony, or whatever the hell we decide to call it. It wasn't by mere coincidence that so many exceptional officers were dispatched to Romania just to work for such a dolt of a COS!

When the time is right, Wolf plans to send piecemeal the names of each case officer hand-selected to join their group. In the interim, Wolf will work with his deputy to overcome emergent psychological obstacles and physical growing pains, for they must establish themselves as a viable force before the Russians become aware American Vampires exist. Aaron's ability to execute Wolf's orders will not only establish the seniority of each American Vampire, but determine the collective strength of the group based on each individual's contribution to a greater whole.

Janicke slowly reads each word of Wolf's message. "Our purpose is to counteract instabilities in the global geopolitical order and to restore humanity to its natural evolutionary cycle."

The apprentice Vampire has no idea what the hell that means. The rest of the message, however, is clear. The Trust must remain politically independent, as the CIA has throughout its existence. Not Democrat or Republican. Not conservative or liberal. The role of intelligence is to inform policy and thwart threats to national security. The purpose of Russian intelligence is to ensure internal order and implement the leadership's plans and intentions through control, influence, deception, and manipulation. Russian intelligence ensures the perpetuation of the authoritarian system by any and all means, at home and abroad. American intelligence strives to ensure the democratic governance model remains free and open in a transparent society. If they fail to uphold this moral distinction between the role of intelligence in a free society and the purpose it serves in authoritarian regimes, the Trust will be no better than the System. Aaron hopes his role in this high-stakes conflict will play out without any acknowledgment of his participation. Human or Vampire, intelligence officers embrace anonymity. To not seek credit for one's accomplishments is a virtue in the intelligence profession.

Wolf's covcom message informs Aaron of the existence of a strict set of Vampire rules that must be obeyed in waging this war between the Trust and the System. The Russians may have no more than ten Vampires, not including Vampire Zero (Putin). Any change plus or minus ten will destabilize the System and reduce their collective power. There's also a set limit of seven American Vampires with the same negative effect should that number not be strictly maintained. Rainer Wolf doesn't know why this balance of power exists, except that it does. His theory is the 7:10 ratio establishes order in global stability without which chaos will ensue.

Aside from pondering conspiracy theories about what this mumbo jumbo means, Janicke is pleased by the simple rules of the game. There can only be seven American Vampires. Our seven will confront their ten. What more does he need to know?

As a Vampire, Aaron has developed a knack for numbers, something the liberal arts major never had as a human. Numerology fascinates him. Prime numbers. The significance of the discovery of the number zero. The concept of infinity. He finds himself memorizing pi out to several thousand decimal places in his spare time.

Janicke is given a jolt by the last part of the Chief's message.

"Before we can build up the Trust, you must eliminate Kruchkov and Burns. To be clear, you must kill them both as soon as possible. Let it be tonight! Our existence is imperiled each day they continue to breathe."

There's no turning back now. Aaron briefly hopes he'll awake from this bad dream, but that's clearly not going to happen. So he's determined to see this through, wherever it leads. He's actually much better prepared for this mission than he anticipated. Acting on emotion is dangerous for any intelligence officer, but especially for a Vampire. The arrow of Vampire calculations points forward, never backward. Vampires rarely reflect on what has happened. They focus on what is happening and what will happen. Their ability to eliminate distractions and to shed emotions gives them an edge over their human counterparts. It's going to be a wild ride, that's for sure!

Later that evening, Aaron stealthily makes his way to Tom's apartment. He enters the small, one-bedroom seventh-floor apartment through an unlocked window after scaling the outer brick wall of the building unseen. His ascent up the wall of the building is effortless. A heavy snow is falling. He stops between the sixth and seventh floors to take stock of the situation.

People pass by occasionally on the sidewalk below, trailed briefly by footprints before being quickly erased by the falling snow. Aaron can hear conversations in the apartments on his left and right, above and below. He picks up strong, unique odors of individual tenants inside, warm and content. Such fortunate souls! Blissfully unaware of the fragility of their existence. What a rush!

Aaron/Vampire 2 is standing motionless in the middle of the darkened living room when Tom Burns emerges from the kitchen. He's wearing only dark gray briefs and a black T-shirt. Snow and ice melt from Janicke's clothing and form a small puddle on the faded, hardwood floor. Tom has just finished a meal of raw meat. Blood slowly trickles from the mouth of his beefy face.

Burns is startled by the shadow of Aaron Janicke standing before him in the darkness.

"Aaron, are you here to help me? Please tell me there's a way back to being the man I once was. Take me with you. Help me!"

Tom shakes with fear.

Vampire 2 spares no words. He's not open to a discussion about what he's there to do. He's there simply to do it, quickly and without making a fuss.

Tom reads the look on Janicke's face. He's resigned to his fate. "I know why you're here. Do what you came to do. I won't resist."

Vampire 2 crosses the room to within an arm's length of his target.

"Wait, Aaron. Before you put me out of my misery, let me do something to try to make things right. I've already signaled for an emergency meeting with Kruchkov."

Tom looks nervously at Janicke. If he can't save himself, at least he can have the satisfaction of turning on his tormentors. "I sensed you'd come for me. Must be my damned new Vampire instincts! Might've been nice to develop them if I was on the right team. I'm not with the good guys any more. It's not my fault, Aaron. It's not my fault."

Tom stammers, trying to provoke a reaction. Any reaction. "Aaron, you'll appreciate this. I'm sure the Russians handle spies just like we do—sticks and bricks. Take this map. X marks the spot where we plan to meet. Prearranged meeting location. You'll find Kruchkov there. Go to Buftea. It's a village on the northwest outskirts of Bucharest. The meeting's set for 2200 hours. One hour variant. Our meeting site is in front of an old kiosk near the bridge over the river. I told him it was a lame site. He just grunted. What an asshole! From there, we're supposed to go to a safe house apartment across the street. You can see the meeting site from the window of the lobby of the apartment building."

Vampire 2 scanned the ops note written by the Vampire Kruchkov addressed to his spy, Maykov. The Cyrillic print is easy to read despite Kruchkov's crappy handwriting.

"Already have a Russian code name, Tom? That was fast. You've become one of them, I see. To me, you're not my colleague Tom Burns. You're fuckin' *Maykov!*"

Tom closes his eyes for the last time. A light snow continues to fall outside, glistening on the pavement against the glow of the streetlights. Just another quiet, snowy, winter night in Bucharest. From the street below, all is normal save for a bright flash of light seen briefly through the sliver of space between the curtains of Tom's apartment window.

Back in the apartment, the only vestige of Burns's existence is a singe mark on the floor and some minute traces of blood and ash. Vampire 2 carefully wipes the remains from the wooden floor with one of Tom's shirts, which he tosses into a dumpster on his way out of the area.

On the outskirts of the village of Buftea, Kruchkov waits near a small, dilapidated, empty kiosk, located near a narrow bridge that spans a small river—the scene is desolate, cold, and dimly lit by only one functioning streetlight. Snow has stopped falling and the night sky is dark and full of stars.

Aaron intently watches the Russian from the lobby of the apartment building located across the street from the kiosk. Casually he crosses his legs and leans back in a well-worn brown leather armchair, as if patiently waiting for a specific resident to emerge. The prop of a local newspaper masks his true intentions. It's the first time Aaron has gotten a good look at Kruchkov. He'll have only one opportunity to make a positive ID. Can't risk killing a human, an innocent, casual lookalike. He carefully reviews the available assessment information: size, gait, mannerisms, habits, etc. In an inner monologue, he curiously refers to himself as Vampire 2 and not as Aaron. A Vampire psychologist, if there was such a person, might say Aaron is trying to distance himself from what he has become and what he has to do.

Vampire 2 has already cut his teeth on Tom and is anxious to end this affair with Kruchkov. The unfortunate CIA officer Tom Burns became the first known case of a Vampire terminated by another Vampire. Since there is no historical record about how to kill a KGB Vampire, Aaron has to rely on his instincts and improvise as necessary. He was able to finish off Burns with surprising ease—a single, deep bite did the trick. But Tom hadn't been a Vampire for long. He lacked the will to fight, the will to live. Kruchkov will surely present a true test of his adversary's prowess.

Precisely at the appointed hour, the Russian is there, standing alone in front of the kiosk, directly under the streetlight. His dress and mannerisms blend nicely with the local environment, cheap and bland like something out of central casting. Kruchkov glances repeatedly at his watch. If Aaron's calculations are correct, his target will wait the usual ten minutes for his spy to arrive. When Tom doesn't show, the Russian will depart the area, return to the safe house, and revisit the meeting site one hour later.

Sure enough, after exactly ten minutes Kruchkov casually crosses the street to the apartment, unaware of Aaron's presence. Vampire 2 chuckles at his target's predictable tradecraft. It takes a case officer to catch a case officer.

As Kruchkov makes his way to the apartment building, Aaron rises from his chair and walks over to the single elevator at the other end of the lobby. He pushes the call button and stands with his back to the lobby. The yellow "L" light illuminates while loud, metallic groans emanate from within the elevator shaft. The old building is equipped with an ancient iron elevator, complete with a retractable metal cage door. The apparatus is drawn by visible cables and pulleys. It's likely been years since the old contraption has seen any maintenance. The elevator compartment itself is small and tight. Any more than two occupants makes for an uncomfortable ride. That's precisely what Aaron is counting on.

As Aaron steps into the elevator, he hears a deep, gruff, Russian-accented voice behind him say (in Romanian), "Hold the elevator."

Aaron holds the retractable door open for Kruchkov, who quickly enters the cage. The Russian's face is lowered. Such thick, furry eyebrows! His oversized hands are pulled up into the sleeve of a ponderous wool overcoat. Good. It'll restrict his movements. Kruchkov avoids eye contact and doesn't notice Aaron is dressed in only an Adidas gray sweat jacket and pants juxtaposed to the bitter cold outside.

The door emits a loud, metallic noise as it's pulled almost shut. Its scissor-type metal expansion mechanism stops to expose about one-quarter of an inch of gap between the door and the frame of elevator cage. The Russian Vampire pushes the button for the tenth floor; Aaron selects the seventh. Kruchkov's senses come alive as he sniffs inconspicuously, drawing in a pungent unknown scent.

The American Vampire has counted on the element of surprise. He has to make the most of a lethal first strike. Aaron's eyes glow bright amber. The tips of his fangs are barely visible below the bottom of his upper lip. In a flash,

Aaron pounces directly on the back of his target's neck, practically decapitating him with his first bite. The Russian Vampire screams in agony. Aaron watches in disbelief as his victim's gaping neck wound slowly closes up. The brief pause gives Kruchkov enough time to pin Aaron to the side of the elevator cage. The Russian Vampire tries to suffocate his assailant. He rips off his scarf, coat, and gloves. He's been grievously wounded by the fury of Aaron's assault, but slowly regains his strength.

Time to implement plan B. Earlier, Aaron loosened the retaining bolts to the top of the elevator cage. He reaches deep within himself in an effort to summon some sort of Vampire super-strength. He has to free himself from Kruchkov's vise. Seconds later, he's able to hoist the squirming target up over his head. With all his might, he hurls Kruchkov upward through the metal latticework and onto the top of the enclosure. Loosened bolts break free and ricochet throughout the elevator shaft like bullets. Kruchkov lands horizontally across two metal frame rail reinforcements to the cage's upper portion.

Aaron leaps upward and lands on top of the stunned Russian Vampire. The elevator stops for a few seconds before lurching slowly upward. Aaron grabs a slack portion of steel cable and lashes it around Kruchkov's neck and upper torso. But Kruchkov is far from done. He flails about wildly with amazing brute strength. This causes the elevator to screech to a halt somewhere between the seventh and tenth floors. The steel framework of the elevator shaft is twisted, as if placed under the extreme stress of an earthquake.

Kruchkov's feat of strength has come at a cost. He's thoroughly entangled in the cable. The steel cord is slowly tightening like a strait jacket around his neck and body as he attempts to twist and turn his way out. The warp of the elevator shaft has caused the retractable metal door to break free and rise upward, trapping his dangling legs in a slow crushing vise. The Russian is sprawled flat on his back on top of the elevator compartment, heaving mightily and shouting a string of obscenities.

The American Vampire stands over him. He uses his right hand to draw a thick steel shaft from inside the left breast pocket of his coat. He's not sure why, but he gives the Russian a nod of respect. Now silent, Kruchkov looks directly into his attacker's eyes and returns the nod. Red glow meets amber glow. His body relaxes in anticipation of a mortal blow. With both hands, Janicke takes careful aim at the Russian's chest, and then plunges the shaft deep into his heart.

The dying Vampire lets loose an otherworldly scream. His eyes throb fiery red in rhythm with his rapidly ebbing life force. He's left with only a bewildered expression and one last defiant grunt.

Kruchkov is dead. His eyes are deep black. After several seconds of sporadic flashes of brilliant light, he vanishes completely.

On his way out of the building, Aaron looks back at the scene of this epic battle. No casuals in the area. Residents are no doubt in hiding. See no evil. Hear no evil. This is Eastern Europe, after all. One thing strikes him as extremely odd. The apartment building is only four stories high. Why did the elevator have buttons for ten floors? Something to discuss later with the Chief.

Safely back in his apartment shortly before sunrise, Aaron is spent. He feels a jarring mixture of contentment, unease, and exhilaration. His operation was successful. But at what cost? He was damn lucky. The blows Kruchkov rained on him would have killed a hundred men. And yet his wounds heal rapidly and he feels no real pain. His powers increase with every bite. Thrilling!

CHAPTER 7
VAMPIRE 3

VIKTOR MARLOWE IS DESIGNATED TO BECOME TRUST VAMPIRE 3. His profile: counter proliferation (CP) expert. A Civil War buff (he bears a striking resemblance to Union general George Tecumseh Sherman). Long-distance runner. Wine connoisseur. Most important qualification: top-notch case officer.

Marlowe was promoted into the Senior Intelligence Service (SIS) as an operational specialist, which is exceedingly rare in the clandestine service. The usual criteria for advancement into the SIS ranks weigh more heavily on promotion-worthy qualities such as "savviness" and "corporateness." In Marlowe's case, those qualities were not considered, not even close. It seems Marlowe has become somewhat of a rarity in the DO, an ace recruiter of spies. As such, he has a track record of providing our president with a clear decision advantage over our adversaries during times of national crisis. In other words, he's a master at the theft of our enemies' deepest, darkest secrets. For Marlow, career progression comes a distant second to his love of the job.

There's a saying in the DO that 15 percent of the Agency's case officers produce 85 percent of its success. In the post–Cold War era of heightened political correctness and institutional risk aversion, elitism became a dirty word. Management would rather evenly distribute the spoils of success throughout the ranks to keep everyone happy rather than adhere to a meritocracy for career advancement. Promote museum keepers who forget the talented artists who paint the masterpieces they proudly display.

The fact that any officer like Marlowe would be considered an outlier for promotion into the SIS ranks is disconcerting to Wolf. After all, the only unique value-added CIA contributes to national security is its ability to recruit and handle spies and produce the intelligence information that can't be obtained by any other means. This is the essential, tangible product of the artisans of espionage.

Given his talents, Viktor Marlowe is expected to contribute greatly to the hopeful success of the Trust's mission, especially when granted full license to practice his *sui generis* style of operational black arts based in Bucharest and independent of Headquarters interference. Wolf's top cover combined with the unique position created specifically for Marlowe are the only reasons this SIS ranked officer can work unencumbered within a CIA Station where he outranks the COS.

Viktor invites Aaron to dinner. He wants to talk about something weighing heavily on his mind. The two meet at Le Bistrot Francais, one of Bucharest's finest dining establishments and one of the few places in town where the food and wine are up to Marlowe's discerning palate, and within a discreet venue of relative privacy. Viktor strongly suspects foul play was involved in Burns's disappearance. Rumors their Station colleague was murdered continue to circulate. Forensic examiners found faint bloodstains of an unknown type on the floor of his apartment, but no body. Only a few grams of ash within a circular heat singe pattern on the carpet.

Over his foie gras, Marlowe outlines his theory: the Russians must have murdered Tom Burns, but to what end? "It's not the Russian MO to assassinate CIA officers. Why the change?"

One of Viktor's many attributes is his soft, soothing voice. His recruitment target's grasp of Marlowe's empathy is aided by his delivery and penetrating eyes. Those qualities have served him well professionally. Marlowe's stable of personally recruited spies could fill a large brothel, or so the legend goes. Aaron listens warily while his colleague outlines his concerns.

Viktor picks at his salad. He's searching for some viable pretext to steer the conversation to the issue of Tom Burns. His subtle probes at insight from Aaron go unanswered. It's dangerous to "case officer a case officer" (attempt to manipulate a colleague). Such attempts are considered cheesy and quickly unmasked. To put it into civilian parlance, "Don't bullshit a bullshitter!" Better to just come clean right up front. For his part, Vampire 2's been mum about his recent Headquarters TDY to meet C/CE. This despite his usual enjoyment at sharing those details along with whatever tidbits of juicy gossip he's managed to pick up along the way.

Marlowe puts down his fork and reaches for his wine glass. He gives it a good swirl, then enjoys a long inhale of the rich bouquet before taking a sip. "Nice, but should have laid down for a couple more years. Now back to the subject at hand."

"You know, we might play a little spy vs. spy, but we don't go around killing each other! Isn't that strictly *verboten*?"

Aaron can smell Marlowe's suspicion he was somehow involved in Burns's disappearance. Intense suspicion smells something like burnt popcorn to Vampires.

Marlowe strokes his beard contemplatively. His soft Texas drawl underscores the seriousness of the subject he intends to broach.

"What came of this fellow Kruchkov? There's something suspicious about this walk-in. Personally, I think it was a provocation. After their meeting, Tom wasn't himself. You read his cable. Total crap! What do you think, Aaron? You saw the meeting go down. Well, what did you see?"

Viktor is leading the witness. He graduated near the top of his class from the University of Texas Law School only to discover he had no interest in practicing law. He joined the CIA quite by accident. An astute CIA recruiter recognized Marlowe's potential and sold him on a life of adventure. As Viktor likes to tell the story, his recruiter didn't lie, he just didn't tell the whole truth. According to Victor, he's never had to work a day since he signed on with the Agency.

Marlowe glances carefully around the room. Once satisfied no one can eavesdrop on them, he edges closer to Janicke. In response, Aaron nervously rubs his hair.

"Aaron, here's the way I see it. Kruchkov targeted Burns. I'm convinced deep in my gut the Russians are responsible for his disappearance. But why kill Burnsie? Our class clown! I mean, he's nothing special. Just an ordinary C/O. Why take such a huge risk for no gain? Right? Well, right?"

"Yeah. I agree. There's probably a more innocent explanation."

"Well, I don't believe in coincidences, Aaron. You read the local papers?" Marlowe is worked up. Like a dog with a bone, he won't let go.

"Okay, there was this strange incident in some piece of shit dilapidated apartment building in Buftea just the other day. Witnesses reported hearing a huge commotion. Of course, no one saw anything—probably scared shitless. Apparently the elevator was trashed. Blood splattered everywhere. They're calling it 'vandalism, teenagers.' I'm not buyin' it. Total bullshit!"

Aaron knows he can't bullshit Marlowe. No alternative: he'll have to strike after dinner. Too risky to put this off another day, especially in light of Marlowe's growing and unfortunately accurate suspicions.

"Viktor, I agree it sounds a bit strange. Teenage vandalism does seem a bit of a reach, even for the local cops, but you sayin' something like perhaps a drunken brawl in some random apartment building outside of town has some sort of connection to Tom's disappearance? Quite a stretch, even for a couple of dumbass paranoid case officers like us."

Viktor stares intently into the eyes of his dinner partner. Why doesn't Janicke show any interest in Burns's fate? And why hasn't Aaron seized on this bizarre news story?

Vampire 2 shifts gears in an attempt to distract Viktor from the true purpose of their meeting.

"COS is a complete ignoramus. Reminds me of King Lear. Guess that makes me the fool."

This odd non sequitur leaves Marlowe puzzled. Basically a twist on the old change-the-subject ploy. Aaron uses the momentary moment of confusion to reconsider his options.

"Viktor, I could really go for one of those expensive bottles of wine you've been hoarding. I can still taste that delicious, and I hope ridiculously expensive, Cabernet you picked last week."

Marlowe doesn't respond with his usual enthusiasm for oenology, a subject in which he's exceptionally well versed. Instead, he mechanically provides Aaron a critique of the restaurant's surprisingly extensive wine list. Even an operational artist and way-out-of-the-box thinker like Viktor can't imagine no human explanation exists for these anomalies. Being caught off guard by their target is every C/O's worst nightmare. Marlowe couldn't possibly be prepared to meet a Vampire. Vampires don't exist, do they?

"Aaron, let's split a bottle of wine at my apartment. Prices here are a bit steep. And I've got better stuff."

"Sounds good. Let's go!"

As they depart the restaurant, Aaron makes a quick mental note. He'll ask Viktor when they meet in the second life how the taste of wine compares between his new Vampire and former human self.

The two make themselves comfortable in the living room of Marlowe's nicely appointed apartment. Outside a heavy snow falls, nicely visible through the large, living room picture window. Marlowe is seated in a tall-backed Victorian-style chair trimmed in heavy blue material. Aaron is half sprawled on the matching couch seated at the end nearest to his colleague. An open bottle of Viktor's favorite French Bordeaux, retrieved from his private stash, along with two empty wine glasses appropriately placed on coasters, rest before them on the coffee table. The current edition of *Wine Connoisseur* magazine sits purposefully at the other end.

Marlowe reaches over to the bottle to refill their glasses. He stops, still stooped over at the waist with the bottle in his right hand, and rubs his eyes in disbelief.

"What the hell?! This isn't what I poured. It's a bottle of 1982 Mouton Rothschild. This is one of the most expensive bottles of wine in the world. Costs a fuckin' fortune!"

He recalls a confession made long ago to some of his wine club friends about his desire to one day acquire a bottle, exactly on the day after he no longer needed money.

Marlowe looks around, suddenly startled.

"Who put it here?"

With a shrug, he turns back to the wine.

"Aaron, I have no idea what's going on, but you have to taste this." He pours some into each glass and takes a long, admiring sniff, then swirls his glass before he lovingly takes a sip.

"Marvelous. Perfecto! Best wine I've ever experienced. Doesn't always age this well—and at this price! What are you waiting for, Aaron? Take a sip. Savor it. I don't know to what or whom we owe this, but I'm not going to pass it up."

Aaron also has no idea what's happening. How did this bottle just appear on the table?!

"What are you waiting for, Son? I'll give a toast drawing a comment from my favorite wine review. Lemme see. 'First, I cannot be. Second, I do not deign to be. Mouton I am.' Unlike Mouton, Viktor Marlowe does change!"

Viktor laughs at his own wine joke.

Aaron picks up his glass obligingly and drinks from it. He doesn't have the heart to tell Viktor he can't tell the difference between a wine that costs thousands of dollars and a cheap supermarket selection. He leans forward, serious.

"Viktor, this evening will change your life."

Marlowe strokes his wiry, graying beard. Has his destiny arrived so soon? At least his instincts were right. The ace recruiter long ago reconciled he would embrace his fate, good or bad, whenever it came calling. Time to answer the call.

Viktor stiffens in his chair and waits, expectantly, patiently.

Aaron moves in. He's but a few inches away from his target's face.

The ornery Texan side of Marlowe comes out. He stays Aaron with a raised right hand, palm out.

"Wait… wait one second."

He gulps down the remainder of wine from his glass.

"Now, do it, asshole. Whatever it is, just do it, but remember you hold nothing over me. I was a free man 'til the end. I'll see you in hell, you bastard!"

CHAPTER 8
CRISIS OF CONSCIENCE

It's 1:58 a.m. Aaron's in bed and has been tossing around restlessly in a struggle with his conscience. He killed Burns. He killed Kruchkov. There's no going back. In a repetitive nightmare, Janicke sees those bright flashes of light illuminated by his victims as they vanished from the face of the earth.

Then there's Viktor Marlowe. Aaron realized part of the excitement he felt after biting his friend was simply due to loneliness. He needs company! Doesn't misery love company? Until Viktor joined the ranks, Aaron was the only Vampire in town. This was way different than the exhilaration he felt with Burns and Kruchkov. Those feelings of guilt-filled remorse should be long gone by now. His psychological transformation seems to be lagging behind his physical transformation, both of which are still incomplete. He remembered Wolf's warning about the uncertain process he'd have to endure, a process in which his two natures—man and Vampire—tug violently at one another for control.

"Dammit Wolf, just how long does this shit take?"

His internal instability is worrisome—something he never felt back when he was human. Will his new existence extinguish all that made him human? What about conscience, guilt, remorse? Are they all gone as well? Has he lost the most unique of human qualities, the possession of free will? Despite their blood bonds of obedience and sense of collective destiny, even Vampires crave freedom, those uniquely wonderful human qualities he took for granted in his prior life. Oh well, too late for regrets now. Keep moving forward.

Vampire 2 needs to clear his head. Shortly after 7:00 a.m. he grabs his keys, leaves his apartment and goes for a walk. Absorbed in thought, he's been walking on autopilot for about thirty minutes when he notices strange looks from passersby. Some even point and stare. An old man dressed in a huge overcoat, fur hat, and heavy winter boots asks him (in Romanian) if he needs help. Aaron suddenly realizes he's out in a heavy snowstorm barefoot and dressed in only a pair of jeans and a T-shirt. Slightly embarrassed, he replies he's okay and rushes back to his apartment.

Later that night, he takes a long walk in the deep black of the Romanian forest. He needs to explore this surge of power in the raw conditions of the outdoors. The night is cold, crisp, and cloudless. The many tall hardwood trees are blanketed in snow. A full moon's light causes a dull shadow to cast on the fresh snow now coating a long pathway into darkness. As he walks, Aaron instinctively takes off his coat and lets it drop to the ground. His pace quickens and he removes his T-shirt. Without breaking stride, he walks out of his remaining clothes and begins to run, stark naked.

His head is clear. He's content in being the creature of his evolution. There's a limitless new world to explore. He's among the very few who will ever dwell in two worlds. And with one hell of a mission to boot!

Now euphoric, Aaron easily chases down a rabbit, breaks its neck, and feasts on its blood. Excitement surges throughout his body. The throbbing thrill of the hunt and the accompanying feelings of immortality combine to create a potion of pure ecstasy such as he's never experienced. When he hunts, his limbs tingle with raw energy. He's invulnerable, impervious to the cares and concerns of mere mortals. Aaron looks up to the sky, arms outstretched, standing before all nature. His fangs drip with fresh blood. His eyes pulsate bright amber.

CHAPTER 9
VAMPIRES 4 AND 5

THE LONG ROMANIAN WINTER HAS FINALLY GIVEN WAY TO SPRING. The days are gradually warmer and snow is still visible on the high peaks. Most of the picturesque countryside is accessible once more. Aaron has accepted an invitation to accompany two of his station colleagues on a long weekend hiking trip. Fortuitously, the Chief has designated these two to become Trust Vampires 4 and 5. Was this circumstance arranged by pure dumb luck? And just how did that expensive bottle of wine appear at Marlowe's the other night?

Any concerns Aaron may have harbored about Viktor Marlowe's (Vampire 3) transition have proven unfounded. Fortunately for Aaron, Viktor is a natural Vampire. Perhaps he was more endowed with Vampire-like qualities as a human being. As a runner and an outdoorsman, he is imbued with a deep appreciation of the raw forces of nature, the very same forces from which Vampires draw so much of their strength. Aaron recalls a comment Viktor recently made, some babble about his special fondness for all forms of life as they struggle to emerge, blah, blah, blah. A little too much for Aaron's taste.

Marlowe the human was a fanatical long-distance runner with an average tally of around fifty miles per week. His human long-distance records have now been completely shattered by his new Vampire endurance. He also hasn't lost his sense of humor. The new joke is how he'll have to devote as much income to running shoes as he does to collecting wine. And, fortunately for him, Marlowe has not lost his taste for fine wines best served with gourmet food.

Hopefully, the process with Vampires 4 through 7 will be as smooth as it was with Marlowe, fingers crossed. With Vampire 1 firmly ensconced in Langley, Vampire 2 has no backup should he encounter any snags. Vampire 3 (Marlowe) is not yet prepared for action. Wolf made clear he'll advise Aaron when the time comes to make Trust Vampires aware of one another. Aaron's plan is to recruit his next two targets during their weekend hiking retreat. There's a conflicting mix of morbidity and excitement at the prospect of adding two new, highly capable members to their team. After a long day's hike, Aaron and colleagues arrive at their cabin deep in the Romanian wilderness north of the village of Petrila, located high in the Transylvanian Alps. Liam Masterson and Wilfred (Will) Edison Lowell are an inseparable team credited with a number of highly successful operations logged over many years of service. Liam is the station science and technology (S&T) officer. He's referred to simply as "the Professor" for his patient, mentor-like people skills. Older than most of his colleagues, the balding Masterson is a PhD physicist who prefers the exciting overseas life of a CIA officer to the daily grind of the lab or teaching at his alma mater. Extrovert, outlier, and people person, Liam has the rare ability to break complex science down into terms even a case officer can understand. The gaunt Professor's love of the natural sciences is only rivaled by his keen interest in the cosmos. Always accompanied by his journal, he meticulously logs the scientific nomenclature of animal species, flora, and other detailed observations of nature. He's a passionate amateur ornithologist (bird watcher).

The erudite Wilfred is unrivaled in C/O ranks for his success in recruiting scientists, which is probably why he and Liam get on so well. Due to his vast experience in all things weapons of mass destruction (WMD), Will's current target is a secret Russian biological warfare (BW) program. Part artist, part philosopher, he's more of an introvert and has to work at being comfortable in social situations. Friends affectionately call him Teddy for his resemblance to former US president Teddy Roosevelt. President Teddy and Case Officer Teddy share more than just a physical resemblance. Wilfred's a true renaissance man, a throwback to a bygone era.

Teddy is intensely preoccupied with a survey of unique rock formations found primarily in this part of the world. Uncharacteristically, he left his camera behind and has enlisted Masterson's assistance to produce a photo journal of select geological examples. Teddy and the Professor share the same interests: intellectuals, loners, love of science and nature. They also share a mutual curiosity as to why C/CE chose to assign them to this relatively obscure, off-the-grid CIA Station. While their operational portfolios cover the entire region, the choice of Bucharest as their base of operations seems disturbingly random to these systematic thinkers. Speculations are endless as to what's behind C/CE Wolf's reasoning. C/CE doesn't make random decisions. They're about to find out just how right they really are.

As the three hikers walk along the densely wooded trail, Vampire 2 can't help but marvel at the attributes his two colleagues will bring to the team. Unique science and case officer skill set. Uncommon track record of success. Worthy additions to the Trust.

After an early morning start on their second day out, the group is now about seven miles deep into the mountain wilderness from their basecamp cabin. The cool morning air has had an energizing effect on the hikers.

Now down to business. It's time! Aaron knows he can't make the mistake of underestimating either of them. They're dangerously observant. Plus they do damn near everything as a pair. They'll be hard to separate.

The trail has become steep and difficult to climb. A light dusting of fresh snow has made the effort even more challenging. They're alone as a group. Hours have passed since they waved at the last passersby. The temperature drops quickly. Aaron mulls over how to orchestrate the best circumstances for his attacks. Per Vampire 1's instructions, first Teddy, then the Professor, in that order.

"After this… only two to go. Thank God!"

Aaron doesn't realize his thoughts were expressed audibly. Teddy is a few steps ahead on the trail and heard his whispered epithet.

"Thank God, what?" he asks playfully. He's used to hearing Janicke talk to himself. Liam is several steps behind Aaron, carefully cataloging wildlife in his journal.

Teddy's innocent question startles Aaron. He's jolted uncomfortably back to reality. Vampire 2 feels a surge like an electric shock shoot hot through his veins. The returned thrill of the hunt overwhelms the objections of his conscience. His internal monologue becomes a pep talk. He must strike! As Vampires these two will immeasurably boost the Trust. The Chief has chosen well. Without these two, it'll be well nigh impossible to challenge the System. Fangs start to appear with the tips slightly visible below Aarons upper lip. His eyes begin to pulsate a bright amber glow.

The Professor and Teddy have found a prime spot to hunt for mushrooms. They saunter slowly off the trail in search of their prizes, which they collect in an old and worn two-liter green plastic bucket with a bright yellow handle.

The Professor emerges from the woods after some time, excitedly waving his camera. Teddy and Aaron wait for him back on the trail.

"Liam, where the hell have you been? We thought you got lost."

"Teddy, I can't believe it, I can't believe my luck. I just got a photo of a slender-billed curlew."

"That's impossible, Liam. You can't find them here."

Teddy cranes over his shoulder to study the photo. Sure enough, it's a slender-billed curlew, one of the rarest bird species in the world.

"This doesn't make sense, Liam." The Professor points into the woods absentmindedly. Still in disbelief, he presses into the digital screen of his camera with the thumb and forefinger of his right hand to enlarge the photo.

"Exactly where'd you see it, Liam? I gotta see it with my own eyes. It's impossible, impossible. There're only about fifty of these birds left in the world—and they don't live here! I'll be right back."

Teddy strides off alone into the woods.

Aaron trails a few steps behind. First Lowell, then Masterson. Perfect. They've split up and are finally out of sight from one another. Teddy turns back around to the sound of footsteps.

"Teddy, please forgive me!"

CHAPTER 10
AGENT NUL

R**AINER WOLF CATCHES A BREAK.** While Vampire 2 takes care of business in Romania, Wolf is TDY (work travel) in Europe. While on a night train from Vienna to Geneva, he's approached by a volunteer. The volunteer purposely bumps into Wolf timed precisely as they pass between train cars. The male, dressed in a gray trench coat, black fedora, and dark glasses, keeps his head down to conceal his face as he thrusts a large manila envelope into Wolf's hands. Without breaking stride, the stranger offers a curt "*Izvinite*" ("Excuse me" in Russian) and calmly continues in the opposite direction. A couple of seconds is all it takes to complete the "brush pass," as it's known in intelligence jargon.

The smooth execution of the volunteer's approach is impressive. The guy's obviously been well trained. Wolf returns to his seat as if nothing happened. Although the rest of the trip is, thankfully, uneventful, he's pensive and alert. An hour later the train pulls into Geneva Cornavin Station, located in the heart of the city. Given what happened on the train, Rainer devotes more time than usual to ensure he's not under surveillance. Several hours later, after he's safely back in his hotel room, he carefully folds back the unsealed flaps of the manila envelope and pulls out the contents. Unbelievable! He can scarcely believe his eyes. He's holding a handwritten dossier that appears to be drawn from a top secret KGB file. It's explosive. Wolf activates his covcom and creates a Soft File. Wolf assigns the volunteer the agent code name Nul.

He chuckles. Nul sounds right. The word can have any one of eleven meanings in Russian. Is this guy a bona fide source? Alternately, this could well be a double agent operation mounted by the System. If so, against whom—Aaron, the Agency, the Trust? Is the System even aware the Trust exists? Is this a provocation, a probe of our defenses? Still too early to tell. Experience tells Wolf one thing: good or bad, this volunteer is a game changer. He studies the note carefully and memorizes the key details for vetting purposes.

Your Eyes Only!

Dear Rainer,

You may find this information useful as you prepare for combat.

Your Friend.

DOSSIER OF SYSTEM VAMPIRES

VAMPIRE ZERO: Vladimir Putin

Also known as "Vlad the Impaler" for his ruthless decision-making style. Feared as a modern Vampire reincarnation of the Romanian count made infamous for impaling his enemies and rivals on long, tree-like sharpened stakes secured into the earth. Wields absolute, uncontested power. Brooks no challenges to his authority. Usually imperturbable. However, when confronted with bad news, he is prone to unpredictable fits of rage. A master at manipulating his fellow Vampires against one another in order to ensure none becomes his rival.

Suffers from a mysterious process of physical degeneration that exacerbates violent mood swings. The experimental serum used to transform him into a Vampire is causing painful tissue and organ failure. As his condition progresses, his body is deteriorating. Gradually, these physical abnormalities also affect his mind, a condition he keenly senses. Unless a cure is found, the long-term prognosis is poor.

Harbors a personal secret he has not shared with anyone.

VAMPIRE 1: Iron Feliks

Assumed his Vampire code name to honor the creator of the predecessor organization to the KGB. There are whispers Iron Feliks appeared on the scene after the Bolshevik Revolution in 1917 and never died.

Vampire Zero's deputy and only System member who Putin fully trusts. First to stand up to endorse Kruchkov's plan to create the *Systema*. Putin seeks Iron Feliks's counsel on all matters, especially in a crisis. Elder statesman of the group. Hasn't displayed any of the physical and emotional instabilities that affect other System Vampires. Has never displayed a moment of doubt about their cause. Is prone to quote long passages from Bolshevik speeches.

Believes Vampires rank higher on the evolutionary ladder than human beings. Promotes Chekism as basis for the System's Vampire's values. Looks and acts the part of the distinguished fatherly figure with receding, slicked-back hair and closely groomed white goatee. Avid collector of KGB medals and Soviet pins called *znachki*.

VAMPIRE 2: Klemko

Assumed his Vampire code name of Klemko in order to honor the leadership of the KGB Second Chief Directorate who was responsible for running operations against the CIA in Moscow.

Formerly a general in charge of the Second Chief Directorate of the KGB (counterintelligence). Planned operations as head of the American Department of the Second Chief Directorate. Currently chief of liaison with foreign intelligence services for the FSB in Moscow.

Valued for his ability to settle disputes among System Vampires. Pragmatist. Cunning. Prone to occasional mood swings that can be attributed to chemical imbalances in his body. Deferential and respectful of Iron Feliks, although he considers himself the better Vampire. Makes all operational decisions in consultation with Putin.

Middle-aged with a full head of dark hair. Medium height and build. Dark blue, piercing eyes. Lives life with gusto, can be theatrical. Undeniable charisma.

Vampire 3: Kruchkov

Assumed his code name of Kruchkov in honor of legendary KGB chairman Vladimir Kruchkov. KGB general who led the First Chief Directorate of the KGB, now called the SVRR (Russian External Intelligence). Legendary recruiter. Was assigned to eleven countries over the course of an illustrious career. Heavy drinker, but handles it well. Sent to Bucharest to recruit a replacement mole inside the CIA for penetration that recently passed away, code name Abel.

Vampire 4: Rubik

Assumed Vampire code name in honor of a legendary KGB First Chief Directorate general who was widely respected in the service.

Close associate of Kruchkov. Served as KGB *Rezident* (chief), in India, Pakistan, and Saudi Arabia. Natural leader, nationalist, blunt, outspoken. Argues for taking the offensive against the Americans while the System has the advantage. Is a master of influence and propaganda operations. Active mind, never rests. Never lets his guard down, even among colleagues. Six feet tall, powerful frame. Piercing gray eyes. Thick gray hair streaked with lines of black. Clean-shaven. Athlete in his younger days. Well-disciplined. Highly competitive.

Vampire 5: Badanov

Assumed Vampire code name to honor a famed KGB spymaster who made his career by recruiting and handling moles and catching spies. Referred to respectfully as "the Chess Master." Earned this moniker for his skill at manipulation and deception. Cunning, cultured, devious. Soft-spoken loner who advocates scheming and treachery over a direct assault on enemies. Close ally of Klemko. Both see themselves as KGB officers first and Vampires second.

Laments physical changes making him less able to control his impulses and emotions because they cloud his analytical CI mind. Badanov's only rival in his ability to smell danger and human weakness is Klemko. Explores Vampire special senses and unique attributes to explore new ways to control and manipulate human targets. Disgusted by his physical craving for human blood. Architect of the plan to install Remington Philbin, code named Abel, as a Russian mole in CIA. Planned operation to recruit a replacement for Abel after his death. Philbin's recruiting and handling officer. Meets alone with Vampire Zero to discuss strategies to defeat the CIA. Vampire Zero admires Badanov's unrivaled paranoia.

The Gentleman Vampire. Fastidious with a pale complexion. Devotes attention to his dress and appearance. Tall, rail-thin, and a chain smoker. Long fingers, pale complexion. Balding. Wears glasses. Spends hours daily playing chess by himself against the strategies of legendary chess masters. Can sometimes be heard shouting, "Bring on Garry Kasparov."

Vampire 6: Volkov

Brilliant biological weapons researcher. Introverted personality. Continuously berated and humiliated by Putin and the other System Vampires. Responsible for the development of a cure for Vampire Zero's disease.

Medium height. Medium Build. Clean shaven. Unkempt, stringy brown hair. Wears large, round glasses in colorful frames. A bit eccentric. Exhibits nervous ticks. Suffers from severe depression, feelings of helplessness.

Vampire 7: Boris Smertsov

Only System Vampire who assumed the same Vampire code name as his human name. When asked why he kept his name, he said it was because he didn't want this tangible expression of his human life to die when he became a Vampire.

Putin respects his discipline and his ability to control Vampire bloodlust. Clear thinking, rational. The System respects his ability to apply human logic and reason to Vampire deliberations. Speaks quietly. Doesn't speak unless called upon. Displays little emotion. Hates Americans. Questions efficacy of "inelegant" wet operations.

Called Myshkin for his (un-Vampire-like) innocence and lack of killer instinct. Reasons that Vampires should not kill humans for their blood. Vampire Zero accepted Boris's rationale to rein in System Vampires' natural urge to kill humans without sanction. The System now approves killing of all humans except in cases of self-defense and in extreme circumstances when approval cannot reasonably be obtained beforehand. Vampire laws were adopted not out of any concern for mercy and compassion for human lives, but as a practical necessity to ensure the existence of the System is not compromised. Although rumors of the System's existence have leaked into the Russian special services, no Russian would dare speak openly of it on penalty of death.

Height 5'9. Medium build. Dirty brown hair. Unremarkable appearance. Regularly attends Bolshoi Theater. Suspected by some of having a secret sexual relationship with a Bolshoi Opera ballerina who he has acknowledged as being a close friend.

Vampire 8: Mercader, aka "The Assassin"

Assumed Vampire code name to honor the Cheka assassin Ramon Mercader, who killed Leon Trotsky with an icepick in Mexico City in 1940.

Indefatigable, axe-wielding bloodlust, hard-drinking, womanizing Vampire. Carries out his brutal missions with great zeal, but gets a rush out of hanging on the precipice of disaster. Putin admires Mercado's ruthless, efficient style—he gets the job done. The Assassin has never failed to eliminate his target.

Brings a signature "Vampire panache" to executions. Intimidation factor of his operations is highly effective; no one crosses Mercader.

Tall, well-built, strikingly handsome, black eyes, olive complexion, long, wavy, raven hair. Bodybuilder. Big fan of Arnold Schwarzenegger. Collector of American action movies from the 1960s–1990s. Favorite film is *Predator*.

Vampire 9: Terrible Ivan

Hulking, brooding presence. Unemotional, nonreactive to his surroundings, even to physical pain. Rarely speaks. Can be underestimated. Smarter than he looks. In charge of tracking and eliminating Putin's domestic enemies. Not consulted on decision-making, but very reliable in carrying out plans. Acts as Putin's personal bodyguard and henchman. Terrible Ivan's presence reminds others to maintain a healthy respect for and distance from Vampire Zero.

Wears long hair and a long beard. Putin allows this privilege as an exception to the System's no facial hair policy because of the intimidation factor. Tall, large frame, long black hair. Incredible strength. Has large scar running down right side of his face. Avid mountain climber, rock climber. Has conquered Everest.

Vampire 10: Beria

Assumed his Vampire code name to honor Lavrentiy Beria, Josef Stalin's interior minister who was responsible for the deaths of countless Russians during Soviet purges.

Referred to as the Sadist when not in earshot. Newest System Vampire and last in line in the hierarchy. Joined the collective following the passing of Abel. Young, fast riser, vicious and cruel. Imaginative thinker, but hit-and-miss operational planner. Questionable judgment.

Would turn on his mother if it would curry favor, especially with Putin. A master of torture techniques. Yes man. Obsequious mannerisms, tirelessly strives to please Putin. Has a Napoleon complex.

Short with a slight build. Completely bald. Has a nervous habit of constantly pressing his wire-rim, round European-style glasses up the bridge of his long, thin, beak of a nose. Has a shrill voice like nails on a chalkboard. Hobby: collecting medieval torture devices.

SOVERSHENO SEKRETNO **(TOP SECRET)**

CHAPTER 11
IN THE BELLY OF THE BEAST

V LADIMIR PUTIN HAS CONVENED AN UNSCHEDULED MEETING OF THE System Vampires in an underground command center in the Kremlin. The bunker is a legacy of the Cold War. A secret facility constructed to survive a US nuclear strike.

The meeting protocol is formal, as is custom in the KGB. First, all ten System Vampires stand until acknowledged by Putin, one by one, in counter-clockwise order at their assigned seats around a highly polished, oversized oak table. Seats are arranged in hierarchical sequence, from one to ten. The meeting convenes with each Vampire's report on recent activities. They speak in order of seniority. Putin is always the first and last to speak.

Vampire Zero is seated in the large, high-backed executive leather chair at the head of the table. After opening remarks and reports rendered by Vampires 1 through 10, Putin nods to Terrible Ivan, who briefs the group on recent actions taken to crush internal dissent. The Vampire reviews priority targets: political opponents, media whistleblowers, rogue oligarchs, and punk rockers. Especially punk rockers. Putin has a particular disdain for uncouth, rebellious youth.

Putin interrupts Terrible Ivan. "And the puppeteer. Is he gone yet? He has to go!"

"Yes, Sir! Consider it done!"

The gall to use puppets to mock Vampire Zero. Mercader follows with a quick review of the status of overseas wet operations. Putin is pleased with the Assassin's report that two ex-FSB traitors were recently found and liquidated.

"Did they suffer?"

"Well, of course. They will be screaming even in the afterlife."

Vlad the Impaler smiles. Vampire Zero asks if anyone has anything else to raise "except the dead." He snorts in admiration of his clever quip. Klemko expresses what all are thinking. "Vampire Zero, Sir, I must share with you my sense that *Tovarish* Kruchkov has been eliminated. I do not feel his presence in our midst. Do any of you disagree?"

"When Abel died, we moved to replace him." Klemko surveys the table to ensure he has the assent of his comrades to continue. "Kruchkov was sent to recruit a CIA officer in Romania. He hasn't returned. He's failed to communicate with us. That is not like him. I say for too long we have operated with impunity. We have become arrogant in our powers, secure that mortals are no match for us. It is clear Kruchkov should not have been sent without backup. We must learn from this before we make our next move against the CIA."

Vampire Zero's eyes flash bright red. He scowls. "This is precisely the reason I have convened this meeting, Klemko. I share your concerns. We must determine what happened to our brother. Do whatever must be done to get to the truth. There is no time to lose."

Putin makes eye contact with each participant in succession. It's a process that takes several minutes; a teaching moment. "*Vampiriy*, I sense a new rival has been born and is already in our midst. This beast aspires to be worthy, but looks can be deceiving. The Americans cannot control their incessant meddling in world affairs. Well, we can respect that. But their impudence to meddle in our affairs… That is intolerable! If we let the Americans take a finger, they will take an arm. Do any of you harbor any doubts concerning the problem that has brought us to this day?"

Vampire Zero is on a roll. "Let me refresh your memories of the cause that brought us into this world. We see how many of the Euro-Atlantic countries are actually rejecting their roots, including the Christian values that constitute the basis of Western civilization. They deny moral principles and all traditional identities: national, cultural, religious, and even sexual. They implement policies that equate large families with same-sex partnerships, belief in God with the belief in Satan. The excesses of political correctness have reached the point where people are seriously talking about registering political parties whose aim is to promote pedophilia. People in many European countries are embarrassed or afraid to talk about their religious affiliations. Holidays are abolished or called something different. Their essence is hidden away, as is their moral foundation. People aggressively try to export this model all over the world. This opens a direct path to degradation and primitivism, resulting in a profound demographic and moral crisis. If we do not defend our values, then who will?"

It's a verbatim reprise of one of Vladimir Putin's own memorized speeches. Vampire Zero abruptly calls the meeting to a close. In unison, they rise. "Vampires rule!"

As the Vampires file out of the room. Putin asks Badanov and Klemko to stay behind. The leader directs his remarks at Badanov. "This affair began when you, 'Chess Master,' suggested I dispatch Boris to liquidate Sergey Deniken in Bucharest three years ago. I recall your words: 'What better loyalty test than to require Boris to kill a friend who had had done nothing wrong?' Boris reported he accomplished his mission. I told you then I wanted proof. So you proposed I send Kruchkov to Bucharest to investigate the matter. 'Kill two birds with one stone,' you said. Kruchkov could take advantage of his presence in Romania to recruit a replacement for Abel. Only you and I know all this. Not Iron Feliks, not Klemko. We have a serious problem, Chess Master! There is a leak in the System. How do you propose we find the source of this leak?"

"Vampire Zero, I agree. There is opportunity hidden in this compromise of our operational security."

The Chess Master enjoys the prospect of unmasking a rival in his own game of deception and treachery. "With your approval, I will entrust Rubik with this operation. He will establish whether Americans have eliminated Kruchkov.

It's implausible. But if so, we will determine how these pitifully weak CIA officers got the upper hand over him. And I swear to you: we will bring back the head of the traitor Sergey Deniken and the body of our dear Kruchkov. I stake my life on it!"

Putin slaps his thigh enthusiastically. "That's more like it! That stake reference is clever, Chess Master. Inform Rubik. Tell him to see me before he departs on his mission."

Later the same day, on the heels of a televised patriotic address before the Russian Parliament, Putin meets with Feliks and Klemko in his Kremlin office—unbeknownst to Badanov—and informs them about Rubik's upcoming mission to Romania. He orders the two Vampires to mount an internal investigation to determine how Kruchkov was compromised.

"I smell treachery. We have been done in from within. Investigate the FSB and the SVR for the presence of CIA spies. It is our sworn duty to not abandon Kruchkov. The System must account for him and avenge his death. Bring him home. *Eto lichnoe delo!*"

Iron Feliks and Klemko stand as one and raise their fists in salute. "Vampires rule!"

CHAPTER 12
VAMPIRE 6

A ARON JANICKE HAD ANOTHER NIGHTMARE ABOUT A MISSED "BITE." Probably stress induced, but they seem so real. In his dream, Joe Leonardi, who's been designated to become Vampire 6, narrowly escaped his fate because his survival instincts were superior to Aaron's own skills. Vampire 2 sits up in his bead, drenched in sweat.

"Damn, he's good! Really not looking forward to this one."

Aaron suddenly feels ill. He's been deep in thought for so long he's forgotten to recharge. He needs to sink his teeth into a nice piece of raw meat fast, but he can't ignore his dream. Joe is something of an anomaly. His natural instincts are damn near as sharp as any Vampire's unnatural powers. Aside from his uncanny sixth sense, the youthful-looking, dark-haired, handsome Italian American is formidable physically, standing a sturdily built six-foot-five inches tall with an intimidating, athletic frame. With his direct and no-bullshit recruiting style, Joe exudes charisma. His agents love him. Aaron's greatest challenge thus far is soon to commence.

The only way to ensure success is to get the jump on Leonardi. Once more surprise is absolutely essential. A one-on-one encounter in a private place won't work. What about hypnotizing Joe? No luck there, either. Vampire 2 is certain his highly pragmatic, feet-on-the-ground target will be much less susceptible to a hypnotic approach than normal humans.

Janicke decides the best approach is to go old school. He'll confront his target the old-fashioned way, *mano a mano*. As one tough son-of-a-bitch, Leonardi deserves no less respect. Toe to toe it is! "Shit, here we go!"

After dinner the next evening, the two case officers find themselves in downtown Bucharest, alone in the back room of an old used bookstore located on the extreme southern edge of town. This is no coincidental encounter. To distract Joe, Vampire 2 plans to exploit his love of rare old books. The walls in the store are filled floor to ceiling with shelves containing old works from authors represented by almost every corner and language of Eastern Europe.

A tall wooden cabinet of map drawers in the middle of the back room contains a variety of material about how the region's geography has changed over time. As an avid collector of semi-rare first- and second-edition manuscripts, Joe's in his element. His passion for history also extends to a number of rare and unique artifacts: pistols, flint muskets, daggers, swords, etc. Aaron takes solace in the thought Joe will be still be able to pursue his hobby passion as a Vampire. Perhaps he'll even get to use some of those antique weapons on Russian Vampires.

The store is empty save for the owner's son, a completely distracted and heavily tattooed twenty-year-old seated behind the checkout counter. His headphones are turned up full blast and his face is buried deep inside a colorful magazine dedicated to tattoo art. His head bobs up and down to the sound of punk rock music blasting at very high volume directly into his ears. The head bob action draws attention to the bright, chrome metal piercing that protrudes obtrusively through the base of his nose, capped by large, circular, bright chrome studs at each end. A dingy smell of dust and mildew permeates everything. The heavily worn wood plank floor looks as if it hasn't been swept since the store opened many years ago.

Aaron and Joe saunter to the rear of the store, passing between arrays of tall, creaky, old wooden bookshelves.

"This store. It's a gold mine!"

Joe notices a thick, German-language catalog on, of all things, US cavalry memorabilia. He's taken a special interest in the mid- and late 1800s US Indian campaigns. To come across a foreign-language reference book on the US cavalry is quite a surprise. But there's an even bigger surprise. Included is historical commentary that portrays a completely different versions of events than anything he's ever read. And Joe's read everything he could get his hands on about the so-called Indian problem. It's as if the participants wrote the story of what really happened, for themselves. Joe browses excitedly through the pages of the large, dusty old book. His search for the author's name and the publisher's name is to no avail. Odd. Front cover. Back cover. Inside jacket. Nothing.

Perched behind Joe, Aaron prepares to strike while his unsuspecting colleague is engrossed in the contents of his treasured find.

"Hey, Aaron, I gotta buy this book. It's strange—this section starts off with 'The Real Story of Custer's Last Stand.' Who knew?"

Joe whirls around just when Vampire 2's fangs are about to bear down on his neck. "Hey, what are you doing, Aaron? Get the fuck off me, you pervert!"

Vampire 2 continues the assault, but big Joe will have none of it. He successfully parries his assailant's lunge. Aaron has a fleeting thought. Maybe he could appeal to Joe's sense of reason. Worth a try? As he backs away from Janicke, Leonardi knocks over a bookshelf, a mere speed bump to Vampire 2's relentless charge. A cloud of thick dust fills the air. So much for reason.

In the blink of an eye, Joe turns and runs out of the bookstore and down several blocks before quickly disappearing into the nearby woods. The dark forest provides only a brief refuge from the creature who stole the bodies of his friends and colleagues. In the meantime, the kid manning the store remains oblivious, his attention completely captured by punk music and tattoo art.

With the benefit of his tracking skills, its child's play for Vampire 2 to track Leonardi's trailing scent. A short while later, Joe has escaped the woods and made his way toward bright city lights and the safety of the crowd. Janicke knows his colleague all too well. The only question is which downtown bar will Joe choose?

As Vampire 2 enters the pub district, he picks up a faint scent hanging low in the air. Joe's definitely been here! He can now narrow his search down to several haunts his friend is known to frequent. Joe's favorite nightclub is the perfect place to seek hasty refuge from a lunatic. Basically a straight shot through the Cismigiu Gardens in central Bucharest. Vampire 2 has reacquired his target's scent, now strong and lingering on the park trail.

Fortunately, the nightclub is dark except for strobe lights throbbing to the beat of thumping, trance dance music. Vampire 2 catches a glimpse of Joe on the far side of the club, across the packed dance floor. He's stiff and straight with his back propped up against the rear wall. People are scattered in small groups before him. He's in an excellent position to observe anyone approach.

"Damn, Joe's damn good!"

Leonardi is clutching an open bottle of Budvar beer in his left hand. Under the circumstances, it looks more like a prop used to help blend into the crowd than a chosen libation. Alert to his surroundings, his eyes scan for trouble while his right hand rests inside his right front pants pocket, probably to keep the pocket knife he prefers to carry at the ready. In spite of being in shock, it's impressive how Joe has managed to maintain a cool, ready-to-take-all-comers demeanor. No wonder Rainer chose him. He might just become the most formidable Vampire in the Trust.

Vampire 2 calculates Joe will mount a final stand at the next strike. He also senses Joe has drawn inspiration from the pages of the US cavalry book he was perusing in the bookstore. He's chosen high ground to make his stand.

"Okay, I'm impressed, Janicke. Crazy Horse got nothin' on you. But there'll be no Custer's last stand here today. Back off!"

Janicke knows he can't approach Joe head on—too many witnesses, too much collateral damage. Instead, he comes up with a misdirection ploy. He disappears into the crowd and provokes an altercation between two patrons. The intoxicated revelers begin pushing and shoving one another, yelling insults. Their fight spills over onto the dance floor and more of the crowd is drawn in. Blows are exchanged. Someone hurls a chair. Bottles fly. Seems wanton bloodlust isn't the sole domain of Vampires!

Aaron moves unnoticed while the crowd is distracted by the brawl now spinning out of control. His quick-twitch physicality surprises him. The killer instinct reemerges with the bright amber blow in his eyes. His angle of attack is carefully selected.

Joe frantically looks around in all directions in a vain attempt to anticipate the direction of Janicke's attack. Vampire 2 pounces! It's over in the blink of an eye. Leonardi doesn't know what hit him. He staggers forward before collapsing into a comfy chair. The pole-axed case officer wipes away a spot of blood from the back of his neck, perplexed about what has just happened. Vampire 2 picks up the groggy Leonardi and drags him through the kitchen to the rear entrance of the nightclub, leading to a narrow alleyway.

"Gotta get him home," Janicke explains in response to the cook's inquiring look as he spirits Leonardi out the door. "Too many shots of Jaegermeister."

The cook nods sympathetically.

Within a block Joe passes out. Aaron hoists him over his shoulder in a fireman's carry and moves quickly through unlit alleyways to the outskirts of the city. Just before they enter the dark forest, Leonardi's eyes emit their first bright amber glow. Vampire 6 is born.

CHAPTER 13

VAMPIRE 7

Several hours later Vampire 2 is alerted about the receipt of another COVCOM message from Rainer Wolf. The lights are off and it's pitch black in his tiny apartment. He rubs his eyes as he reads the instructions. "Oh, man, this one's gonna be a challenge. Almost over. This shit's gettin' old."

The message contains the identity of Trust Vampire 7—a female case officer. Aaron's been ordered to recruit his colleague Elena Constantin. Her profile: early thirties, intelligent, sharp-witted, auto enthusiast, full of energy, superb writer, speaks her mind, and a very capable C/O. Within the male-dominated culture of the DO, Elena is one of the guys.

Elena grew up in a house with several older, athletic brothers. She's tough. Takes absolutely no crap from her male colleagues, to whom she humorously refers as "her cavemen." The attractive blond has heard all their dumb blond jokes several times over, which she generally follows by telling her cavemen: "Learn how to read. Get some new material. Reading really is fundamental, especially for clueless idiots."

Aaron just assumed all Vampires were males—they had to be males. Was there a female species? The Russians spawned the lineage of Vampire intelligence officers from which Vampires of both the System and the Trust were derived. Wolf showed Janicke the dossier provided by agent volunteer Nul. All eleven System Vampires are male, probably because there are so few female intelligence officers within the ranks of the Russian special services. It seemed logical their American counterparts would be the same, given the CIA's historical lack of diversity. To think about it, this seems awfully sexist, especially in this day and age.

After rereading the message closely to make sure he hasn't fallen prey to some sort of Vampire prank, Janicke reverts to a habit of talking out loud to himself. "Must be Wolf's show of commitment to the Agency's diversity program? Okay, seriously. Any C/O worth their salt should feel honored to be selected to join the Trust. Anyway, she's damn qualified, no doubt about it. Hell, yeah! Let's do this! Elena'll make a great addition to the team! The ying to Joe's yang!"

Aaron knows her well. Elena Constantin will bring a different set of skills into the mix. She's worked different target sets, all with success. A superb agent handler. Her people instincts are uncanny. She has an innate ability to sense deep vulnerabilities in her targets, which she's turned into successful recruitment scenarios many times over.

In an ensuing series of COVCOM messages from Rainer Wolf, one message in particular catches Aaron's eye:

"We're the underdogs. The Trust has seven. The System has ten. They have Vampire Zero, the extent of whose powers have yet to be tested. We need an edge. No females among the Russians. An American female Vampire will give us the element of surprise. The Russians won't see this coming. They're dismissive of women. To the Russians, Constantin will be unpredictable, a wild card. We need to trust our own experience. Women were dismissed in the CIA for too long, only to prove themselves many times over, and now they'll excel as Vampires. We're making history!

"In Trust. The Chief"

The Trust is almost staffed. Once Constantin's on board, it'll be time to bring the team together and combine individual skills. A quick skills inventory overview: Wolf, Janicke, Marlowe, and Leonardi made their bones on hard target recruitments and core espionage skills. Teddy and the Professor specialized in teamwork recruitments of S&T sources. Constantin mastered the full agent developmental cycle: spot, assess, develop, recruit, handle, and terminate agents. Her special gift is, however, her unique ability to apply soft skills rooted in human psychology. Her counterintelligence skills are savant-like. She's the absolute best at ferreting out double agents or to know when a case has gone bad.

A few days later, Aaron sets his plan into motion. Fortuitously for him, Elena's established a pattern of drafting her intelligence reports late at night after the other officers have left for the day. She prefers the privacy of an empty office where she can work undisturbed. As DCOS, Janicke can naturally work late as well.

It's Friday evening and the entire Station staff is out the door a bit earlier than usual. COS George is first to depart. Par for the course. As is his habit, George stops by Aaron's desk to half-heartedly request Aaron take care of something George himself should have done earlier in the week.

About an hour later, Aaron has secured his classified material in his safe and is working his way through the Station end-of-day security checklist. This happens to be Aaron's turn on the rotating weekly security duty roster. In sequence, he checks off the various requirements. All desks clear of classified material, check. All safes locked, check. Alarms in working order, check. On this particular evening, however, he double-checks to ensure Constantin is the last officer present.

Vampire 2 quietly moves to the area of the bullpen near Elena's desk. Elena is so absorbed in her work it takes several seconds for her to notice him standing next to the adjoining workspace. She senses his presence. Startled, she looks up at him from her rolling chair and laughs nervously. He doesn't respond. Elena's frightened by the grim expression on Vampire 2's face. His eyes narrow and seem to emit a faint amber glow. The expression on Elena's face shifts from fear to confusion.

"Aaron, hey, what are you doing here? Why are you staring at me like that? A little creepy, don't you think!?"

Confused, she attempts to disarm him. She knows Vampire 2's weird behavior isn't sexually motivated. He's not that kind of guy. But what then?

Vampire 2 hesitates momentarily, then moves in a couple of steps closer. He's kicking himself for not having made the leap while her guard was down. In spite of meticulous preparation, doubts persist. Yes, there's something different about biting a female colleague. It just doesn't feel right. *Maybe I am too much of a caveman. What the hell was Rainer thinking? I can't believe I'm doing this. Shit, here goes!*

Elena's instincts kick in. She takes full advantage of Aaron's momentary hesitation and damn near gets the jump on him. Her third degree black belt in Tae Kwon Do is evident in the speed and power with which she lands a roundhouse kick squarely to the front of Aaron's head. The blow, although perfectly delivered, has no effect on Aaron. Stunned, Elena assumes a defensive position. "Aaron, AARON! Have you lost your mind?!"

Vampire 2 has to end this before it gets out of hand. His advantage, as in previous "bites," is that Elena won't be able to fathom the reality that Aaron is a Vampire. Can he create an opening to momentarily disarm her? To come clean? To tell her what he has to do and why? He tries telepathy to connect with her, to reason with her.

"Look, Elena, I've been tasked to bring you into a team. An elite team. Our Agency depends on us. Our country needs us. And we need you."

His efforts at telepathic persuasion are apparently lost on his target. He tries to capture her eyes to use hypnosis, but to no avail. She keeps her eyes averted from his, relying on her peripheral vision.

Elena maintains her defensive stance, constantly adjusting her fighting position. Aaron moves in clockwise circles around her. He tries not to provoke an attack and looks for an opening to strike. *Impressive. She hasn't tried to run or call for help. She's intent on kicking my ass! Damn impressive!*

To Vampire 2's surprise, Elena can read his telepathic thoughts. In return, she sends her own signals. She understands what's transpiring isn't based on evil intent—exactly the opposite. It's futile to try to reason with Aaron. Whatever this is, it's bigger than the two of them.

Without warning, Elena relaxes her fighting position. Her fists unclench. Her arms drop to her sides. Now defenseless, she proposes a bargain, out loud.

"Aaron, wait. This doesn't have to end this way. You don't think I've seen the changes around here? I know I'm not the only one. There's something going on. I can help you, but not like this. Don't I at least deserve an explanation? Why are you doing this? Why me? Let's talk this out like adults."

It sounds desperate, but it's all she's got.

Vampire 2 drops his arms. He stands motionless and waits for Elena to finish.

"Okay, convince me right now. Convince me! I'm listening. Give me some reason to go along with this, convince me. Don't you owe me that much, you prick? I didn't know you were such an asshole, Aaron."

She's trying to agitate him, to create an opening for an attack. Vampire 2 assumes a fighting crouch, ready to spring. Elena holds up her right hand. "Wait! I'm seeing something. You're in Moscow. I'm in Paris. I see a Russian—not dating him. Not sure what he's doing there, or what I'm doing there. But he's one of us." She pauses momentarily to reflect. "What have we become, Aaron?"

Her clairvoyance stuns Aaron. He's temporarily frozen in place.

"Okay, Aaron. I can see now. There's no way to go but forward. I've seen my destiny. Your destiny. We're in this together—whatever it is. Bite me!"

Vampire 2 steps forward and hugs her. She grimaces slightly as she turns her head away. Elena Constantin has joined the Trust.

CHAPTER 14
AMERICAN VAMPIRES

I**N THE DARK AND SHADOWY SECRET WORLD OF RUSSIAN AND AMERICAN** Vampires, Bucharest has settled into a tense calm.

Aaron needs Rainer to assemble the Trust as soon as possible. He can't keep his colleagues apart much longer. They're still unaware of each other's Vampire existence and this house of cards is soon to come tumbling down. He wants them to know the truth—the justification of their sacrifice. As the power of his Vampire convictions increase, so does the depth of his commitment to his cause. His human attributes continue to fade. Vampires 1 and 2 aren't cognizant of how much they've changed, both physically and psychologically. They react with disdain to "foibles" of the human spirit such as meekness, modesty, compassion, mercy, and self-doubt. These human virtues smell like weakness to Vampires, vulnerabilities their enemies can exploit.

System Vampire Rubik arrived in Bucharest several days ago. He's been roaming the city in search of leads to his countryman Sergey Deniken and the fate of System Vampire Kruchkov. He's also making the rounds of Russian intelligence penetrations and has come upon a source within the Headquarters of the Romanian National Police. The source, a high-ranking deputy commissioner, passed photos and the investigative report of a rather curious disturbance that occurred in an apartment building in a small village outside Bucharest. According to the report, terrified occupants heard horrible screams but saw nothing. There were clear signs of a violent struggle. The building's lobby elevator was extensively damaged. Blood was splattered everywhere, but no body was found. Also, there were no fingerprints anywhere and, when the forensics unit tried to test samples of blood taken from the elevator shaft, the samples simply evaporated in the lab. Another SVR asset heard a rumor Sergey Deniken was still alive and in hiding, whereabouts unknown.

One late afternoon Rubik decides to take a brief respite from his investigation in a quiet downtown bar. A coincidence, perhaps, but Aaron and Teddy are locked in discussion at the opposite end of the long, white marble-topped bar. Coincidence, or did Rubik's senses lead him there? He's thirsty and indulges his preference for a tall glass of ice cold Russian vodka, served straight up. He downs it in one voracious gulp while perusing notes from his agent meetings, then orders another.

Teddy requested this meeting to calm his nerves. His mind continues to function in the refuge of a beautiful philosophical plane clashing violently with the reality of what he's categorized as a grotesque physical and mental transformation.

"Aaron, I tell you. I don't think I can handle the reality of myself as this vile, disgusting thing. I just can't. I don't even know what a Vampire is, but whatever it is, I don't want to be it. I'm repulsed by my own self. I mean, I dream about raw meat and blood. Sick. Disgusting. Please tell me this is reversible. Please, Aaron. There must be a way back."

Aaron inhales deeply and slowly exhales. He wants to say, "Get over it, Teddy," but restrains himself. He searches for something more nurturing. Nope. Nothing comes to mind. He's been at this too long and his tolerance for whiny Vampires is depleted. Teddy needs to suck it up and drive on. It's the Vampire in him talking.

"You think too much, Teddy. And no, it's not reversible. See, that was easy. Sorry, man."

Teddy catches his reflection in the mirror hanging on the dark red painted concrete wall behind them. He's shaking. "Well, thanks, Aaron. You've proven my point. All you've got left is this nihilistic sarcasm. You've lost your soul, can't you see? We've lost those qualities that made us human, worthy of living, worthy of life. We're living a big lie! I've got to find a way out, a way back. Better dead than unable to die. Whatever the hell is happening to us, it's tearing me up. I want out! Now!"

In his state of mind, who knows what Teddy might do? Aaron's demeanor shifts to compassion. His voice becomes more soothing. He orders another round of single malt scotch. "Make it peatier this time?"

Teddy shrugs listlessly. "Whatever."

"Teddy, you're right. There'd be something wrong if you didn't feel this way. You're still the same stubborn, iconoclastic bastard you always were. You won't lose those qualities. They're part of your nature. I tell you, there are many positive aspects to being a Vampire. Give it time. You'll see. It'll work out. This is all happening for a reason. Trust me, Teddy. Soon you'll meet the others. Then you'll understand why you were chosen and what we have to do."

Teddy pounces on the opening. "So there are others? Who, then? Why are we being brought together? For what purpose?"

"Calm down. Lower your voice, please."

"Aaron, look. You've always been up front and honest with me. I trusted you once, and I want to keep on trusting you. Dammit, Aaron, you haven't answered the most important question! Why? Why?"

"Look. I can't tell you why. I've already said too much. For now, you're going to have to accept my explanation for what it is. Answers will come soon. I promise."

Teddy leans forward, elbows on the bar with his head in his hands. Their silence is broken by a change of songs on the bar's music system. The painful sound emanating is from a Romanian rock band's rendition of an almost unrecognizable version of the Red Hot Chili Peppers song "Californication."

"Now listen," Janicke quips, "I really need to say this one thing. This music really sucks!"

"Yeah, sucks really bad." Teddy is morose.

Aaron defies Wolf's orders a second time. He simply can't allow his friend to continue to twist in the wind without so much as a hint that the pain he's going through is for a noble cause. Teddy needs motivation to go on. "You have to hang on, Teddy. Besides, we don't know how to kill a Vampire, even if we wanted to. Look, I'm only going to say this once. We're going to have to work together to eliminate a dominant force of Russian Vampires, and to do that, we need a counterforce. An elite squad. The best team the CIA has ever assembled."

Teddy sits upright and practically launches himself at Aaron to exploit this new opening. "Russian Vampires? What Russian Vampires? Who said anything about Russian Vampires? What do they have to do with this? Aaron, I don't want to kill anybody or anything, Russian or otherwise. I can't end my own life—or whatever you call this shit of an existence. But I can turn myself in. That I can do. The Agency will know how to deal with me."

Aaron puts a reassuring hand on his friend's shoulder. It feels more like a paw than a hand. "Teddy, look at me. Listen to yourself. Think you sound nuts, huh? You honestly think those Headquarters wonks will believe you? Your next assignment will be to a psyche ward. We need you, Teddy. YOU!"

Alone and unnoticed at the opposite end of the bar, Rubik's been watching the two Americans intently. Can this really be? He's overheard some words in American-accented English. He senses, smells, sees these two aren't ordinary humans. The Russian Vampire edges forward on his barstool, adjusts his winter cape slightly, then tilts his fedora forward in an attempt to obscure his glowing, red eyes.

Aaron and Teddy halt their conversation abruptly in mid-sentence. Their instincts are unexpectedly aroused. They're in the presence of something unnatural, otherworldly. Could it be another Vampire? Can't be! The two Americans go on an internal high alert. They peer across the near-empty bar in an effort to determine the source of their threat gag reflex.

The bar is occupied by only three people: the bartender, who's busy cleaning glasses and moving bottles of alcohol around, a rather distinguished person (Rubik) who looks out of place seated at the far end of the bar, and last, a disheveled drunk seated on a barstool positioned at an elevated drink counter affixed to the wall at the opposite side of the bar. The music volume is slowly cranked up to high.

The teetering drunk holds a whiskey glass in his left hand as he mumbles to an imaginary patron before him complete with animated gesticulations with his right hand, quite a humorous sight if not for the menacing presence of Rubik. The Russian Vampire is instinctively ready to dispatch any and all witnesses.

Still on his barstool, Aaron feels a surge of adrenaline as he readies himself for assault. For only the second time since he became a Vampire, Teddy's eyes pulsate a bright amber glow.

The two Americans rise from their barstools and take purposeful strides toward the man at the end of the bar. Aaron grabs Teddy's arm to ensure they stay in lockstep with one another. They stop just outside Rubik's reach. Aaron leans forward to stare down the Russian. The three stand frozen in a kind of Vampire Mexican standoff.

Rubik remains calm; he almost looks bored. He casually signals to the bartender for his tab. The Americans stare unblinking at their adversary. Rubik mumbles something in Russian to draw the bartender closer. As the bartender leans in, Rubik effortlessly kills the hapless man with one vicious slash across his neck. Blood flows freely from the open gash as the stunned victim disappears in a human accordion fold behind the bar. He's a witness—can't be helped. The Vampire's eyes glow red as he focuses his gaze on his American opponents.

With his bloodlust whetted, the Russian launches himself at the two Americans, who are now surprised by the fury of his attack. The Americans combine their strength to knock Rubik back several steps. He didn't expect the Americans to survive his initial strike. Time for plan B. Rubik has learned something important from this initial encounter. For the first time he'll actually need a plan of attack, a fight strategy. After all, like him, his opponents are not human.

All the while, the amused drunkard loudly cheers on the combatants. The inebriated man makes mock fight punches as his head moves in short, jerky motions from side to side. He becomes disoriented and falls off his stool. With great effort, he reseats himself and, with both hands, grabs onto the counter for balance.

The archfiends move with extreme speed and destructive power. The bar is quickly in shambles. Broken barstools and tables alike have been used as makeshift weapons. Neither can gain advantage. By himself, the Russian is stronger than either of his adversaries. But together, the two Americans match the strength of their rival.

As Aaron mounts another frontal engagement, Teddy searches desperately for something, anything he can use as a weapon. His eyes catch something mounted on the rear wall of the bar, just above the window with the blinking red neon sign. A large wooden crucifix—really! Will Lowell, our lovable Teddy, was not a religious man. He's certainly not religious now. The heavy cross is simply the best improvised weapon within his immediate grasp.

Rubik strikes a mighty blow that knocks Aaron to his knees. Teddy approaches Rubik from behind and calls him out. The Russian whirls around to realize Teddy has taken aim directly at his heart. Rubik glares defiantly at Teddy, daring him to take his best shot. Teddy glances over at Aaron, who's now back on his feet. Time seems to slow down as he hears Vampire 1's guidance enter his mind: this isn't the time to take on the System. Hesitantly, Aaron reaches out to stay Teddy's hand.

Rubik capitalizes on the Americans' hesitation. He strikes a blow that knocks Teddy halfway across the room, leaving him dazed. But the Russian Vampire has also come to the conclusion this is not to be his day of conquest. Now in retreat, Rubik stops at the front entrance, looks back at the Americans, and nods his head in a gesture of respect, which the Americans return. The red in Rubik's eyes slowly extinguishes as his form disappears into the cold night air, his cape swirling behind him.

The Americans exit quickly through the side door. On the way out, they survey the damage. Aaron looks over at Teddy and quips, "Isn't this a lot more fun than dealing with another 'F'in mealy-mouthed Headquarters cable?"

The bar is completely demolished. The only sign of life is the old drunkard who's barely able to remain upright. The front of his coat and pants are drenched by several spilled drinks. He's had a grand ole' time watching the combat from his slippery perch.

When the police arrive, the drunkard animatedly tells about the great battle between real Vampires. His heavily slurred explanation in colloquial Romanian is barely understandable: "Thar war three of 'em fightin'. Vampires... BIG fangs like this." The toothless lush places the index fingers of both hands pointed down at opposite ends of his mouth in an attempt to simulate fangs. "It was a helluva sight... they left jus' now b'for your eminens... ses a'rived."

The two Romanian cops interviewing the drunk look at each other and roll their eyes. A small crowd of curious onlookers has gathered on the sidewalk near the front entrance. The crowd is pushed several feet back by another police officer who's busy affixing crime scene tape across the entrance door frame.

In the background the covered body of the bartender is loaded into the back of a waiting ambulance. Once the rear doors are shut, the ambulance's emergency lights turn off and the vehicle moves slowly away. The poor drunk is hauled off in a paddy wagon, babbling incoherently about what he's just witnessed.

Later that evening, Janicke reports the details of their encounter with the Russian Vampire to C/CE in a COVCOM message. Wolf's response arrives minutes later. He'll travel to Bucharest immediately. It's high noon. Time to let the System know the Trust has arrived!

CHAPTER 15
THE TRUST

C IA Station—Bucharest, Romania. After a late night departure from Dulles International Airport, followed by a brief layover in the sprawling hub of Paris' Charles De Gaulle International Airport, C/CE's early arrival at Bucharest's Henri Coanda (Otopeni) International Airport is met by a clear blue sky and a very friendly, moderately attractive, buxomly female Romanian customs agent dressed in an impressively well-tailored uniform. The smiling, dark-haired, and mildly flirtatious agent surely has no idea the well-mannered gentleman standing before her is the Chief of the CIA's Central Eurasia Division. To her, he appears only as a well-dressed American of obvious importance.

Normally, Rainer Wolf would have been met by the head of the Romanian Intelligence Service, but this isn't a routine visit. His transit through customs was pleasantly capped off by an affectionate and lengthy two-handed handshake by the customs agent. During the encounter, she handed him a business card with her first name and cell number written on the back in pencil. Unfortunately, many intelligence officers have been bought that cheaply. Sex trap—oldest trick in the book.

Precisely one hour later, Rainer Wolf strides into Bucharest Station. He's arrived unannounced on a special visit. Six Station officers have been asked to attend a special briefing in the secure conference room.

C/CE is seated at the head of the table in a tall-backed, black leather office chair with his back turned to the Station officers now seated around the large, oval conference table, concentrated closer to the opposite end. The attendees are quietly curious as to why they've been assembled and why COS George isn't in the meeting. Their unspoken mutual assumption is that this has to be their supernatural coming-out party. At least they hope so.

Absent the usual pre-meeting banter, attendees sit erect, eyes focused on the back of the chair at the head of the table. Eye contact is avoided. In a bit of theatrics, the head chair turns around to reveal Rainer Wolf. He smiles, addressing each attendee with a welcoming nod. The Chief has been preparing for this moment for months. A bit of melodrama is to be expected. Tension mounts during the extended silent pause.

"I, on behalf of the CIA and our nation, have selected each of you because you possess certain unique qualifications. The foremost is your devotion to our country. Your sworn duty is to keep our country safe. You've demonstrated your willingness to set aside your own interests to serve this greater cause. That's why you've each been selected to join the Trust. You may have changed, but your loyalty to the United States has not changed one bit. Your mission, your purpose to safeguard our nation—by any and all means necessary—remains unrivaled. We are now confronted by a menace as grave as the threat of mutually assured destruction posed by nuclear weapons at the height of the Cold War. Today, we face MAD of a different kind.

"Russian president Vladimir Putin controls a powerful collective known as the System—*Systema*. His goal is not only to restore Russia to the status of a great power but also to crush the United States, its influence worldwide, and its ability to defend itself. It's a zero-sum game. As you may have surmised, Putin and the members of the System are Vampires like you."

The Chief pauses to give his words a chance to sink in. The room is silent.

"I simply can't apologize for making a decision each of you should have made for yourselves. Yes, I robbed you of your human life. I did not make this decision lightly. You see, there was no other way. We, the seven Vampires of the Trust, are the only thing standing between Vladimir Putin and world domination. Our one and only mission is to eliminate the Russian Vampires and restore the global balance of power."

Having sat in rapt silence long enough, the American Vampires jump all over their meeting host. Viktor Marlowe is first to speak. He's known Wolf longer than the others.

"Rainer, we've known each other since our Europe days. I'm not good with this. You should have asked me. You should have recruited me through persuasion, not tasked Aaron to bite me! It's a relief to finally know what's going on, but if you expect me to endorse your decision, I'm not ready for that."

Wolf is not surprised by Marlowe's complaint. He would surely feel the same if the bite were on the other neck.

"No, I didn't think you'd be fine with this, Viktor. You're too independent minded to accept what's happened. But think about it, Viktor. How liberating it'll be to operate with no restrictions, no one hovering over you, questioning your every move—your every bite! You'll be able to do whatever is necessary to accomplish the mission. We were made for this moment in history when the best among us stand tall. Humans or Vampires!"

Leonardi is plainspoken as always. "Sounds like you've convened an AA meeting, Rainer. Is this an 'intervention' where we're told we have a problem? I sure hope you know what the hell you're doing. What do you want me to say? That I'm happy to give up my good life and become a Vampire? Your errand boy, Aaron, bites me and here I am. I didn't have to become a flunky Vamp with Putin issues to beat those Ruskie bastards. I could have done it as a human case officer!"

Leonardi's comments are met by a round of applause from his colleagues.

"Joe, why do you think you're here? Consider what you've been able to accomplish as a C/O. Consider how much more you will be able to accomplish as a 'Vamp,' as you called yourself. You won't lose what you once had. You, all of you, will redefine the art of intelligence."

Leonardi shrugs, unconvinced. It's an intriguing thought, reluctant as he is to admit it.

Teddy is rocking back and forth in his chair and nearly falls over backward. His face is flush red. "Because we had no choice. That's why we're here. Because you gave us no choice. I find it hard to accept that anything good can come of something that began with a lie. I don't suppose you're up for a principled debate on this point, are you, Rainer?"

"No, Teddy, this isn't the time. Let's talk about your precious human principles. You want to know the truth? They aren't enough to deal with Russian Vampires. You'll come to see the moral stakes of our craft in a new light, with a clarity you've never experienced as a human. We're on our own. Alone. We must decide what is right and what is wrong for ourselves."

The Professor clears his throat. Color is drained from his face. He's analyzed the proceedings systematically. "I don't see any choice but to see where this leads. Rainer, if I understand you correctly, there is no turning back, am I right?"

"No, Liam, there is not."

"Well, then we should dispense with the intervention. To take up Joe's AA analogy, what are our ten steps to sobriety? Where do we go from here to redeem ourselves?"

Elena interrupts the Professor. "To follow up on Liam's question, what makes you think we seven can do something the whole CIA can't accomplish on its own—or the entire US government, for that matter? Isn't that the definition of hubris?"

"Boy, that's rough, Constantin."

Wolf's a bit shaken. This calls for candor.

"I don't have the answers, but I know something about our beloved agency. The CIA prematurely dismissed the Russians as a threat long ago and never looked back. What is the status of our *glavniy protivnik*? The Russians have never accepted the fact that they lost the Cold War when the USSR collapsed in 1991. Putin's System will never accept a US-dominated world. And why should they?

The Cold War ended in a stalemate. Each side still has thousands of nuclear weapons pointed at each other—weapons that can never be used.

"The System has enabled Putin to restore Russia's dignity plus regain the advantage by fielding a new, asymmetric super weapon—Vampires. They wield unimaginable power, a power much greater than anything the KGB could ever muster in Soviet times.

"Do you seriously think I could have approached the president, the director of the CIA, or anyone in the establishment about the existence of Russian Super-Vampires? Any recommendation for the US to respond in kind would have been made from the inside of my padded cell. My only option was to create a clandestine counterforce. Strictly off the books. Mutually assured Vampire destruction is the only way to restore strategic stability between the US and Russia."

"You'd trust us with that?"

Elena demands better answers from her ex-mentor. "Is this like mining the harbors of Nicaragua? Iran-Contra? Exploding cigars? How about mind control? Drug experiments—LSD! You know what happens when we get carried away."

"Hear, hear!" Teddy claps in agreement.

Rainer jumps in before he loses control of the group. "If the Trust is an ill-conceived quest and not a legitimate response to an existential threat, then nothing good will come of us. Consider Sun Tzu's words: know yourself and know your enemy and you will win a hundred battles. Who are we? Yes, the US is much more powerful than Russia, but our policy makers are doing a lousy job of defending our interests worldwide. Everything is politics. Short-term thinking. US policy on Russia is in shambles. By creating *Systema*, Vladimir Putin and his KGB Vampires have upped the ante. The KGB comeback plan they drew up after the collapse of the USSR unfolds in three stages. First: elimination of internal enemies. Second: elimination of external enemies. Third: restoration of Russia to great power status. All at the expense of the US."

Before anyone can raise further objections, Wolf presses on to complete the speech he's been drafting in his mind for months—years, actually. "Having consolidated power under *Systema*, Putin and his cabal of KGB allies moved to crush political dissent. The media was put *pod kontrolem* (under control). The special services, led by the FSB, were granted greater powers and more resources. The enemy within—dissidence, opposition—was silenced. The System is now aggressively turning its attention to the external enemy, the US."

"So why is this our business?" Teddy gives voice to what they're all thinking. "Let the Russian people settle their affairs among themselves. Decide their own future. Doesn't our existence only serve to legitimize Putin and the System?"

Marlowe unexpectedly rises to Wolf's defense. "Colleagues, the System changes everything. We're back to the dark days of the Cold War. Berlin Blockade. Cuban Missile Crisis. Invasion of Czechoslovakia and Hungary. A Vampire can't change its spots. Putin won't be content to merely create mischief within his own borders. Who can confront them if not us? If not American Vampires?"

Aaron is energized. "Viktor's right! Who can we depend on to do this? Not our beloved Agency. Not the feckless Europeans. Not the Chinese, who are more than happy to play us off one another. You'll be guided by a new morality, new instincts. Your eyes will see the world in light and darkness. You'll smell evil from a distance. Our senses give us an edge over humans. The System Vampires enjoy the same advantages. Just the other day, we got a whiff of how powerful they are in a bar right here in Bucharest. Right, Teddy?"

Teddy nods grudgingly.

All things considered, this "coming-out" party is going better than Wolf anticipated.

"We could go on all night, but it's best to get you all back into circulation, back into your routine. One more piece of business."

The Chief reads aloud a letter he plans to have Janicke deliver to Vladimir Putin during a liaison with Klemko in Moscow.

Dear Vladimir Putin,

The United States and the Russian Federation, formerly the Union of Soviet Socialist Republics, have been at adversarial ends of the global spectrum since we collaborated as allies to defeat Fascism during the Second World War. It was our finest hour.

Working together, we defeated the worst threat the world has ever witnessed, a Fascist evil set on a direct path of global destruction. Since this high point of our relations, however, our political and economic interests have drifted farther and farther apart.

We have since survived numerous flash points and have even come close to all-out nuclear war. A war between the two nuclear powers would have resulted in the destruction of the world. As history will attest, the best among us have always prevailed to reconcile our differences.

Alas, the best that resided among us are no longer with us.

It is thus with regret that I must inform you we again stand on the precipice of confrontation between our two countries. According to reliable information at our disposal, Russia has established a collective of Vampires, which you refer to as Systema. As the System's supreme authority, only you have the power to avert renewed geopolitical confrontation between Russia and the US. The System is antithetical not only to US interests but also to global stability. As such, we have formed the Trust to protect our interests and counter your every move, frustrate your every intention, and restore the strategic balance.

There is a way to avert needless confrontation and bloodshed. The System must be dismantled. In return, we will disband the Trust. There is no possibility of an accommodation between us. Compromise is not an option. I'm sure you will agree. We eagerly await your response to our most generous proposal.

ANDREAS JAWORSKI & ROLF MOWATT-LARSSEN

We wish you great tidings of comfort and joy during this special holiday season!

Wolf

CHAPTER 16
THE SYSTEM

VLADIMIR PUTIN HAS CALLED AN EMERGENCY MEETING OF THE System Vampires at his ornate dacha complex outside Moscow. A strong wind blows from the west and the sky is hidden by a heavy overcast of gray—gorgeous weather for the occasion. System Vampires sullenly file into the conference room to find Putin has just concluded a meeting with a special visitor, a monk named Volodya. The Russian Vampires have dubbed this monk Rasputin on account of the mystical influence he appears to wield over their leader. Father Volodya presents the sign of the cross to the assembled mass along with his salutations.

Vampire Zero is visibly moved by his private conversation with the monk. He allows Volodya to offer an invocation before taking his leave. "As you set about your sworn duties, always bear in mind that Russia's spiritual shield is as important as her nuclear shield. Stand firm, stand with your left hand, which goes from the heart, for Christ the Lord, for His undivided tunic, and, with your right hand, fight to the end for Orthodoxy and Orthodox Russia. This idea is more than a single man, more than a feat of one hero. This idea is as great as Russia, as sacred as her religion. This is the idea of the Orthodox sword."

After raising a hand in recognition of Volodya's blessing, Putin pulls a small gold cross out from under his shirt, kisses it ceremoniously, then returns it to its special place near his heart. He wears this cross to commemorate his baptism into the Russian Orthodox Church. Once Vampire Zero is seated, the System Vampires take their seats.

The religious overtones make the System Vampires squirm in their seats. Surely Vampire Zero must have a practical motivation for this display of piety. Perhaps he plans to wield the Orthodox sword as a weapon against the Trust. Despite whatever they believed as humans, Vampires have a natural aversion to religious symbols. Vampire values are generally the moral opposites of the virtues as taught by the Church. Jesus Christ defines humility. Vampires define hubris. They're self-centered and physically blood-bonded to their master. Christianity extols meekness and humility in response to injustice, whereas Vampires seek brutal conquest as a means to restore justice as defined by them.

Rubik has returned from his mission in Romania. He matter-of-factly renders a report about his coincidental encounter with Aaron and Teddy in the Bucharest bar. He also provides confirmation, obtained from trusted Russian spies, that their colleague Kruchkov is in fact dead.

Vampire Zero is sullen. "Rubik, did you bring back Kruchkov's body as I asked?"

"Sir, there is no body."

"What do you mean 'there is no body'? What did the Americans do with it?"

"I don't know, Sir. All I know is no body was recovered from the place where he died."

Rubik reports he was unable to acquire any confirmation on the fate of the traitor Sergey Deniken. KGB sources believe he is dead, but they have provided no concrete proof. The case remains open. All eyes shift to Klemko, who informs Putin about the details of his meeting with Aaron Janicke earlier in the day at FSB Headquarters.

"Yes, there are American Vampires. More than one. The American actually snarled about how he released Rubik from his clutches only so they would have the satisfaction of watching him return to Moscow with his tail tucked between his legs."

An enraged Rubik interrupts Klemko, pounding his fist on the table. "I'll return to Bucharest and kill that American Vampire with my own hands!"

Moving on quickly, Klemko hands Putin the letter from C/CE delivered by Aaron Janicke. Putin asks Klemko to read the letter out loud to the group. Klemko pauses briefly, clears his throat, then orates the entire letter, word for word, without interruption.

Klemko concludes his reading. The room remains deathly silent. All eyes are fixed on Putin. Vampire Zero is lost in a distant gaze. He looks down at the table and, as he reads the letter silently to himself, his eyes emit an intense red glow. Putin stands. The assembled group also rises. With a wry smile, he looks darkly at the group and wags the crooked index finger of his right hand. "If this is a declaration of war, so be it! Perhaps this test is exactly what we need to prove our superiority and establish our worthiness to inherit the earth. If we are unable to defeat these weak and corrupt Americans, then we are not worthy to rule our beloved Russia, much less the world!"

Rubik can't contain his emotions and flings his arms wildly in the air. "I told you so! We lost our chance to destroy the American resistance before it formed. We could have crushed them, but we waited too long!"

Putin pounds the table with his fist, startling the Vampires. The room again falls silent with all eyes locked on their leader. Without warning, Putin reaches over and unleashes a vicious slap across Rubik's face. "ENOUGH!"

Putin's command resonates like a clap of thunder. The faint smell of fear permeates the room. Fear smells something like ammonia to Vampires. Vampire Zero has never before struck one of his System Vampires. Klemko casts a glance at Iron Feliks, who tries hard to suppress a smile. Iron Feliks is keen to observe his colleagues' individual reactions. He's convinced their strength as a collective is derived from the juice of their raw emotions, squeezed and brought forth as an elixir to refresh their spirits. He's pleased at the prospect of war with the Americans. This existential enemy will serve to bring *Systema* closer together. Vampire Zero fumes in silence.

Finally, after what seems like an eternity, Beria pipes up. "*Tovarishiy*, there is nothing greater in life than a pitched battle against our greatest adversary," he offers, obsequiously currying Putin's favor. "Russia's enemies have become predictable—boring. Finally we have a chance to display our full powers against our reawakened *glavniy protivnik*."

Beria's words resonate with Putin. He walks over to Beria, who bows his head in deference. Putin places a hand on his shoulder. "*Tovarish* Beria. You have spoken well. We must never forget who we are, or the importance of our cause."

Putin turns to face the group. In unison with clenched fists and right arms raised bent at the elbows, they pronounce: "Vampires rule!"

CHAPTER 17
A DEAL WITH THE DEVIL

Rainer Wolf is emotionally drained on his return flight to Washington. Against Agency policy, he has upgraded himself to business class. It's so much harder to get things done since the new age bureaucrats imposed layers of draconian travel restrictions. How he misses the old days when support meant "just make it happen."

During their coming-out meeting in Bucharest Station, Rainer tried not to betray his own doubts about the future. The Trust members have the odds stacked firmly against them. Their enemy has the advantage in both numbers and experience handling the harsh realities of Vampire life. Russians are imbued with a sense of confidence derived from their defeat of every enemy throughout history who sought to conquer them. Historically, they refuse to quit no matter the cost in terms of human lives, or now, Vampire lives.

As he's floating in the friendly skies ever closer to the soul-robbing reality of the Washington Beltway, Rainer Wolf is in a moral quandary about what he's done. Maybe, just maybe, Abel was right. Perhaps he's blind to his ego. How could he be so damned arrogant as to believe he alone must save the world? As if he's some sort of chosen one with the fate of the entire world resting squarely on his shoulders. He's been an Agency officer for three decades and still thinks of himself as a CIA officer first, albeit now in a different form. This is one job the Agency could not possibly do. In today's Agency, if upper management actually knew the problem, they'd probably start a study group, bring in some outside experts, hire a think tank, form a steering committee, then decide not to decide on a course of action. They'd never sanction his CIA within the CIA. And they shouldn't.

He doesn't contest a feeling of quiet satisfaction and raises his glass for another sip of robust red wine punctuated by a silent toast to his colleagues, his comrades. He indulges in giving his new creation a label. A team? Too PC. Hopelessly bureaucratic. Not a syndicate like the Mafia, that's for sure. A collective, like their Russian counterparts? Too socialist. A colony? More in keeping with American Revolutionary tradition. Gotta give it more thought. Maybe he'll ask Janicke what he thinks.

The Chief returns to the inward-looking atmosphere of CIA Headquarters. At the time of his departure for Bucharest, Rainer was a shoe-in as the CIA's next deputy director of operations (DDO)—the senior officer in command of the Agency's worldwide network of spies. During his brief absence, rival Christopher (Chris) Kringle has managed to outmaneuver him for the prize. Wolf is upset. DDO-designate Kringle would be a wise choice, if he were a Vampire. His professional résumé, credentials and leadership qualities are impeccable. Widely respected. Noncontroversial. He's checked all the boxes. Done all the right things.

Recruiting spies and handling agents is not his forte. His operational accomplishments aren't what propelled Kringle to the top. He's more of a political insider. Policy makers sing his praises. The smooth operator has dedicated his career to pleasing the Washington power elite. His time in the field was purposely limited to ensure his name wasn't forgotten while he was away. He was once overheard exclaiming to a Headquarters colleague, "I don't know why anyone would want to be in out the field—the action's in Washington!"

The Trust's viability hinges on Wolf's assumption of the DDO position, a position from which he can expand organizational control over both DO assignments and operations in order to protect and deploy his Vampires. His intent is to place them into strategic locations overseas where they'll be best positioned for battle. He has to ensure the Agency can't get in the way, an impossibility if Kringle rises to the position. Chris Kringle has to go, simple as that. How to get rid of him? That's a problem.

Marlowe and Leonardi are in Langley on TDY. Wolf brought them back in case he needs additional muscle. These two were chosen because they've transitioned superbly and maintained their trademark attributes as case officers. Marlowe and Leonardi happen to be walking down the seventh-floor executive corridor when they pass the DDO-designate. Kringle is distracted by the details of a paper he's perusing and doesn't notice them standing five feet away.

Joe looks at Viktor and mumbles, "He never bit anyone!"

"Ha!" Marlowe chokes trying to suppress laughter.

Alas! The American Vampires can smell the faint sweet scent of the legendary ace case officers and spymasters lingering in the air even after all these years. It's a poignant reminder of the heroes who roamed these halls in decades past. The two C/Os briefly close their eyes in reverence to the operational history of the Agency's storied past. They stand in the middle of the hallway inhaling the fumes of operational excellence, deeply intoxicated, oblivious to the puzzled looks from passersby. Vampires have an unfortunate tendency to be blissfully unaware of how their behavior might be interpreted by casual observers.

For they know through their own experience and the Agency's best practices that leadership role models should be drawn from the best of America's war-hardened leaders, such as Generals George C. Patton or Ulysses S. Grant. Leaders who succeed by taking audacious risks to achieve uncommon success. Leaders willing to accept the occasional failure that comes with great success. Leaders who accept full responsibility for their successes, but, more important, for their failures. For any organization, it's easy to settle for comfortable leadership choices during peacetime. But the CIA is always at war.

Wolf invites Kringle to dinner at the Obelisk Restaurant located on Dupont Circle in Washington, DC. It's a gesture of respect between two friendly rivals. In contrast to Kringle's athletic, trim physique, his fit and healthy outward appearance, Rainer's keen Vampire senses alert him to some sort of serious physical defect. A pleasant, yet unpleasant surprise.

Until this moment, Wolf had no clue as to his innate ability to telepathically sense physical defects in humans. Is the peculiar scent he picked up from Kringle akin to an animal's ability to sense weakness in its prey? Is this newfound sensory capability limited to the detection of heart-related problems, or can he detect other human physical ailments as well?

Kringle, as it turns out, has a developing but potentially controllable heart valve disease. It's a secret he's managed to keep concealed from his Agency colleagues. He's afraid knowledge of his condition will cost him the promotion to DDO. The best-case scenario would be a delay until he receives treatment and is medically cleared. By then, he's likely to have been politically outmaneuvered by a rival. Kringle has, in fact, conspired against Wolf in a ploy to line up sufficient internal Agency support for his power move.

Over the course of a phony cordial dinner, Wolf searches for vulnerabilities in his colleague as he would in a target. To his surprise, he can hear his rival's heart beating! The sound is faint at first, but unmistakable. A little later, between appetizers and the main course, Kringle feels his chest tighten. The bewildered man orders more water and takes a sip. A small bead of sweat has formed at his right temple. Wolf carries on as if unaware, but he knows exactly what his (now) target is feeling.

If Chris Kringle could only imagine what his old colleague and dinner companion is doing behind that façade of collegial dinner conversation. Wolf is, with mixed degrees of pleasure and doubt, slowly and inexorably inducing a heart attack.

"Hmm. Can I turn his defective valve off—close it?" Telepathically, Wolf projects his mind's intentions directly into Kringle's heart. The effect is similar to placing a frog into a pot of water at room temperature and slowly turning the heat up. Kringle's heart ailment slowly worsens while his ability to fathom his condition has been disabled.

It happens suddenly, right there in the restaurant. The expression on Kringle's face shifts from confidence to confusion. His eyes grow wide as he's overwhelmed by the painful pounding in his chest. Wolf can hear the telltale heart pounding loudly, steadily increasing its rhythm unsustainably. The heart beats in uncontrolled acceleration, but only Rainer Wolf can hear it. Shortness of breath turns Kringle's face beet red as he gasps for air. He reaches for Rainer's arm and falls from his chair to the ground.

Restaurant patrons watch the unfolding heart attack morbidly, too shocked to intervene. The waitress uses her cellphone to dial 911. Her desperate, Russian-accented call to the emergency operator is truncated: "Heart attack. Restaurant Obelisk. Hurry, please hurry."

With both hands, the stricken man grabs his chest. He arches his back and rises slightly, then collapses onto the floor, his eyes open and fixed in disbelief on Rainer Wolf. Well, that certainly casts a pall on things!

Wolf responds as any person would under the circumstances. He is horrified. "What have I done?!" he mouths under his breath. Wolf responds instinctively, leaping into action to perform CPR on his colleague. At that very moment, he wants Kringle to survive, if only to exonerate himself. Killing the good guys is not supposed to be part of the deal.

Paramedics quickly arrive and take control. Life-saving equipment is spread out and attached to Kringle's limp body. Wolf gives them room to work. Caught in the throes of a life-and-death emergency, he watches the paramedics work on Kringle's lifeless body, hoping it will respond to resuscitation. The paramedics whisk Kringle off to the emergency room. He never regains consciousness. Later that night Wolf gets a phone call. DDO-designate Chris Kringle has passed away.

Did he kill his rival with his mind? Surely Vampires haven't been gifted with the power of life and death. He consoles himself with the self-serving delusion it was Kringle's time to die with or without his intervention.

Within days of this tragedy, Wolf is informed of his appointment as the next DDO. He's given the news while at the funeral of his friend, colleague, and rival. The new DDO-designate manages to wax philosophical to the large crowd gathered in the Washington Cathedral. The final sentences of his glowing remarks give praise. "No one can replace Christopher Kringle. He was a great man and a true patriot who gave his all for his country."

Well, that much he certainly did! Wolf is momentarily saddened by the thought no one who attends his funeral will ever call him a great man. But, like his eulogy for Kringle, people say many grandiose things they don't really mean.

After the funeral, Marlowe and Leonardi discreetly approach Wolf with a secret salutation meant to be shared only between Trust Vampires. They mumble it quietly after confirming no one is within earshot. "All Hail the Chief! Long live the Trust!"

CHAPTER 18
WIRING THE WORLD

R AINER WOLF'S FIRST OFFICIAL ACT AS THE DDO IS TO ORDER A WAVE of reassignments throughout the Directorate of Operations. He sends a message to all CIA overseas franchises. Wolf makes one point crystal clear: during his tenure as DDO the priority for advancement will be operational excellence. Every officer will be expected to recruit spies and produce FI (foreign intelligence) and CI (counterintelligence). Fieldwork will be rewarded. We will not stray from our core mission to pursue secondary objectives. The rest, as the Russians like to say, is *meloche*—loose change. These sweeping changes provide cover for the reassignment of Trust Vampires into strategically important positions overseas.

The new DDO is also motivated by a desire to jump-start the DO—to reset the mission and priorities of daily work. Wolf never lost hope the Agency will eventually find its way back to its operationally focused Office of Strategic Services (OSS) roots.

Former Bucharest DCOS Aaron Janicke is assigned to Moscow as chief of the Station. He's subsequently promoted into the Senior Intelligence Service, the CIA's equivalent of the military's general officer ranks.

The new DDO calls COS Bucharest on the secure line with the news it's time for him to retire. Wolf doesn't suffer fools gladly but makes a temporary exception for Des George. A brighter bulb would have recognized something was amiss in Bucharest and somehow interfered with the master plan. But fools can be useful when trying to assemble a secret group of Vampires. Des George, who wanted badly to serve as an executive assistant to any CIA senior, is so stunned by the news he takes the rest of the week off.

Viktor Marlowe is dispatched to Zurich, where he'll keep his eyes on the inner workings of global finance and commodities while worming his way into the Swiss banking enterprises. In addition to his ability to navigate the intricate maze of the global financial system, he's the Agency's ace at disrupting rogue states' efforts to acquire weapons of mass destruction.

Joe Leonardi is bound for Rome. Beyond a pursuit of the standard suite of operational targets, Leonardi has been secretly tasked to develop connections to the Vatican, itself one of the most powerful intelligence organizations in the world. Exactly how cooperation with the Vatican might prove useful is as of yet unclear. But given the unknown, it would be foolish to dismiss the power of the church in an inevitable battle between good and evil.

Leonardi, as it turns out, is a perfect fit for the Rome assignment. As an agnostic at best, he won't be awed by the scope of his task to cultivate sources within the Vatican. Joe's widely regarded as the DO's top headhunter. He's yet to meet a source he can't recruit and still complains about how he doesn't need to be a Vampire to convince people to become spies. He's still forlorn about his former "excellent life" as a hot-blooded Italian-American case officer. If only he could actually speak Italian, other than through exaggerated hand gestures and his love of pasta.

Teddy and the Professor are headed as a team to Istanbul, where they'll cover the east-west corridors used to ferret weapons of mass destruction to rogue states and terrorist groups. The tandem is tailor-made for this grim duty. The pursuit of nuclear proliferators and traffickers of biological weapons is a cat-and-mouse game that requires extensive targeting skills and arduous operational preparation. The two experts rarely miss a lead, especially since they've honed their savant-like technical instincts as Vampires. They've also been tasked to identify weaknesses within the System's DNA and, alternatively, to identify any hidden strengths and vulnerabilities potentially resident within Trust Vampires.

Elena Constantin is off to Paris to demonstrate her prowess in a city known for espionage intrigue. The City of Lights draws intelligence services from all over the world. The quality of the opposition will challenge Constantin. Her strategic placement within this European hub will increase the odds the Americans will be able to get a jump on their Russian counterparts. Elena has already developed a reputation for parlaying a combination of charm and brute force into the production of valuable intelligence. "Find secrets and steal them" is her motto.

Of course, there is some institutional discontent with Rainer Wolf's ascension to the crown of the clandestine service. The smiles and congratulatory handshakes belie the jealous rivalries that fester in the CIA's upper echelons. It's a ruthless business and the knives are always out—even among humans! In his lighter moments, Wolf jokes to himself about how saving mankind might be easier than fixing the DO.

Wolf has a clear advantage over his unsuspecting seniors. The Agency's top brass is distracted by its emphasis on servicing the president and senior administration decision makers. No request is too small to be satisfied ASAP, whether it's of national security interest or not. "Please the customer" has become the new mantra.

The Agency's current priorities suit the Chief, although he's saddened by the cultural changes realized since he joined the organization some thirty years ago. Wolf has to have complete command of the CIA's operational organizational chart if the Trust is to have any hope of success against Vladimir Putin's relentlessly focused System.

During the second of his weekly staff meetings, the new DDO introduces his newly appointed chief of the Counterintelligence Center, Alan Tourier, who's been charged with reinvigorating the now-stalled mole hunt. There is irony in his announcement about the relaunch of the mole hunt. Too many unresolved CI anomalies to ignore. The hunt must continue despite the fact that the actual mole has already been found and eliminated. Nonetheless, the show must go on. Only Wolf and his Vampires know the truth. Remington Philbin was the Russian mole.

Tall, scarecrow thin with an Einstein-like mop of salt-and-pepper-colored hair, the bespectacled, refined if somewhat effeminate Alan Tourier is determined to catch what he is convinced is a long-standing Russian penetration of the CIA. The detail-oriented spymaster is taking a fresh look at all the evidence. Tourier has instructed his CI analysts. "Give me everything. From all sources, reliable or not. Walk-ins and volunteers. Even crazies."

There's nothing wrong with zeal and determination as long as his forays into the past don't stumble across the fantastical story from an old Bucharest Station walk-in. The new CIC chief is absolutely convinced the Russians have a mole in the CIA. But Wolf is prepared, just in case. He knows the new CI chief has a secret: in his zeal to climb to the top, he deliberately created false leads and information on officers to taint them as suspected Russian spies and cast a cloud over them. He's not alone.

CHAPTER 19
ACCIDENTAL ENCOUNTER

Elena Constantin's transition to Paris is going quite well. She's been at Station for only two weeks, and as expected of all Paris-based officers, is attending the first in an endless string of diplomatic events. She welcomed the chance to network in a new environment and showcase her ops skills. Or so she thought!

The new XXXXXXX XXX is attending her first formal diplomatic reception held in the ballroom of the luxurious Champs-Elysées Plaza Hotel. Dressed elegantly in a dark blue ball gown and matching high heels, Elena has drawn much attention from the international pool of largely male diplomats. She sails effortlessly through the crowd and deftly parries the efforts of various hunters eager to draw her into private conversation.

As the clock strikes 10:00 p.m., her Vampire senses begin to tingle. Contrary to her calm and collected outward demeanor, her senses are aroused. She turns violently to meet the eyes of System Vampire Mercader, standing on the other side of the large reception hall. The dashing Russian is wearing a black tuxedo with a light blue bowtie and matching cummerbund. He hands his glass of champagne to a waitress, picks up a napkin and taps it lightly against his lips, then strides slowly but purposefully toward Elena. The dense crowd parts before him as he floats toward her. His eyes flash red. Her eyes return a bright amber glow, beckoning him. She aches to test her strength against the Russian Vampire!

The huge ballroom overflows with formally dressed guests nibbling on hors d'oeuvres and sipping champagne. Everything now moves in slow motion while Elena and Mercader size each other up. Neither can take their eyes off the other. The sounds of the crowd are muted by their fused power of concentration.

Elena hears the Assassin's footsteps moving closer. She counts to herself. 1, 2, 3, 4, 5, 6, 7, 8, 9. Mercader's eyes glow again before he disappears into the crowd. Suddenly he breaks contact. Elena can smell his scent lingering in the air. She's certain Mercader will reappear. But when and where? The Oracle, as the team affectionately calls Elena, has just met the Assassin.

Elena Constantin doesn't believe their meeting was a coincidence. It took restraint on both their parts not to attack one another right there in front of Paris's finest. Upset at being rebuffed by her mystery target, Elena knows they'll meet again before the night is through.

Later that night, Elena rounds a corner on a narrow, dimly lit, cobblestone side street and is stopped dead in her tracks by the scent of Mercader. He's casually standing less than a half block away. It's almost morning. The sky turns a shade lighter with each passing minute. The Vampires move tactically into the darker shadows where there is less risk of distraction from chance encounters with passersby. Elena slowly removes her high heels and places them carefully on the ground, never taking her eyes off her target. Mercader removes his bowtie and slides it delicately into the right side pocket of his tuxedo jacket. Red and amber eyes lock on one another.

Watching from the nearby roof ledge of an apartment building, a gargoyle smiles in approval. It's perched on the edge of a classical Parisian building, wings partially spread in anticipation of the unholy combat below. With a nod, the archfiends acknowledge one other as they assume fighting stances. They both lust for mortal combat.

The two Vampires stalk one another; their steps outline a lethal circle counterclockwise in direction. No words are spoken, no movement wasted, no vulnerability exposed. They're instinctively aware of one another's fighting styles. The Assassin is known for his sudden and overpoweringly violent blows—roughly the human mixed martial arts equivalent of a single punch knockout. Speed and power over technique. He senses Constantin was a human master of the martial arts. She employs a hybrid style drawn mostly from Kung-Fu, Tae-Kwon-Do, Jiu-Jitsu, and Kendo martial arts.

Without warning, both Vampires simultaneously stand up straight, nod respectfully to one another, and walk off in opposite directions. Elena reaches down and grabs the straps of her high heels before slowly walking barefoot back down the cobblestone street. She knows patience is perhaps the greatest virtue of an intelligence officer, but why is patience being imposed on her now? She's frustrated. The two Vampires acknowledge a decision made above their pay grade. This impulsive test of strength won't serve their collective interests. At least not today.

Despite irreconcilable animosities between the Trust and the System, they share a developing Vampire code of honor that places self-discipline, obedience, and loyalty above personal ambitions—albeit grounded in polar opposite values. Vampires may sneer at the folly of human salvation, but even Vampires seek to find sense in the chaos of the universe. Vampire rules will have to suffice.

CHAPTER 20

MOSCOW RULES

System Vampires are assembled in the Kremlin underground command bunker. It's shortly after 11:00 p.m. and Putin has just been briefed on the aborted confrontation between Mercader and Elena Constantin in Paris.

"I could have killed her!" Mercader is worked up. "Why was I forbidden to end the miserable existence of this female abomination, that American bitch who dwells among us? It's bad enough the Americans have Vampires. Now they insult us with a female!"

"Enough, Mercader!"

Vampire Zero appreciates the Assassin's warrior spirit, but blustering bravado isn't useful in this situation.

"So the Americans use a woman—very clever. How can you be so sure you can defeat this new creature, the one you know nothing—nothing—about?! Have I taught you nothing? Patience! We must study these American Vampires before we move in for the kill. A blind fighter wins no fights. What can you tell me about her powers? Describe everything you felt when you stood before this

Vampiress, before you were stopped from tearing her apart, limb from limb. Tell us, Mercader."

"Of course I studied the bitch. I would have to say that in most ways, there is little to distinguish her from us. Of course, she's a woman... weak... attractive. Very attractive."

Mercader is contrite. He is blushing. He flashes his bright white teeth flanked by huge, sharpened fangs.

"I would not underestimate her fighting ability. She has advanced training in unarmed combat. With knives, swords, and other weapons. Not that she could take any of us."

The Russian Vampires laugh dismissively. Of course not.

"But there is something else. She is different from the others, and it's not because she's a Vampiress. I cannot put my finger on it. More study is merited so we can orchestrate her demise at the time and place of our choosing. If I may be so bold, Vampire Zero—Sir, I request the honor of being her executioner when you feel the time is right."

Putin interprets the averted showdown in Paris as a good omen. "Mercader, you have done well in subordinating your desires for the greater purpose of defending *Systema*. This war will transpire according to our rules. Moscow rules! So the Americans introduce a woman into the game. Interesting. Iron Feliks, what is your advice in response to this challenge?"

Iron Feliks has been conspicuously jotting down notes. He draws on his encyclopedic recollection of KGB methods of intimidation as applied to dissidents and free spirits, all to maintain order and control for the Communist Party. The revolutionary legend clears his throat dramatically. He draws passages from his namesake's own speeches in Bolshevik times.

"We must bring terror to the Trust. We stand for organized terror—this should be frankly admitted. Terror is an absolute necessity during times of revolution. Our aim is to fight against the enemies of the Soviet government and of the new order, our order. We judge quickly. In most cases only a day passes between the apprehension of the criminal and his sentence. When confronted with evidence, criminals in almost every case confess, and what argument can carry greater weight than a criminal's own confession?"

Putin is not sure about the point of Iron Feliks's descent into the mindset of the Bolshevik revolution, but it sounds good to his ears. He issues new guidance.

"If the Trust is not willing to abide by the rules of a gentleman's game, then they have brought this onto themselves. Two can play this game. From this day forth, any restraint we have displayed toward the CIA is no longer required. You can blackmail them. Drug them. Harass them. Harm them. Use any methods that please you. I will not restrain you. We must not just defeat them, but crush their spirit!"

Beria is sputtering to get a word in edgewise. He isn't about to lose this golden opportunity to suck up to his master. He tries to one-up Iron Feliks by channeling his own namesake. "This so-called Trust doesn't understand the nature of war. They play checkers. We play chess. Ha! They don't know that a more effective—if somewhat longer—war can be fought with bread or, in our case, with bioscience and the wisdom of our art. Trust Vampires are still suckling their mothers' breasts. They still crawl on all fours, and a female challenges Mercader to a fight? The Americans have never won a war against Russia. And they never will!" Beria gives a fist pump for emphasis. The shrieks of his high-pitched voice are made even squeakier by his raging Vampire hormones.

They wait for Putin to render the last word. His demeanor is subdued after listening attentively to the revolutionary exhortation of his truest believers. He looks up and gazes deeply into the eyes of each Vampire, one after the other. They steel themselves for Vampire Zero's usual end-of-meeting speech. Iron Feliks and Beria have clearly inspired their leader who emulates by exhuming passages from his own past speeches in assessing the new threat posed by American Vampires.

"Behind the Chekist sword and shield lurks the Third Rome. We are a power greater than the declining United States in the West. We are a power greater than rising China in the East. We will unleash our fury on these weak Americans. We will annihilate them before they have a chance to consolidate their powers. They struggle with what they've become physically and psychologically. Being Vampires does not suit their character. We have an advantage over them because we have an unshakable vision of uncompromising faith and patriotism without sentimentality or weakness. These are the forces that animate Russia's Vampire warriors today."

Putin's voice trails off. He nods his head forward slightly, then clutches his forehead with both hands, in pain. System Vampires rise as one and recite. "Vampires rule!"

Meanwhile, in Langley, Virginia, Wolf has just read Aaron's report about Elena's encounter with Mercader. He's intrigued by the events in Paris and drafts a COVCOM message to Vampire 2. The DDO writes: "Who do you think would have prevailed if we had let Elena and Mercader fight to the death?"

A COVCOM reply is received almost immediately: "I don't know. Constantin felt confident. I would say she felt certain she could vanquish her male adversary."

Wolf: "Male adversary or System adversary? Which is it? Is there a difference between the two?"

Janicke: "Point taken. Only Elena knows for sure."

Exactly Wolf's point. The Trust needs to know more about the vulnerabilities of their enemy. It was not entirely clear who had the upper hand between Elena and the Assassin. It's not yet time to engage them.

CHAPTER 21
THE SERUM

ALTHOUGH THEY NEVER SPOKE OF IT ALOUD, SYSTEM VAMPIRES ARE individually deeply concerned about the symptoms Vampire Zero is no longer able to keep hidden. They see and feel his deterioration. Questions about his illness are raised only in hushed tones. As their leader's health declines, instability grows within the entire System.

Unfortunately, several System Vampires also experience physical abnormalities, albeit with milder symptoms. They intrinsically know their fate is inextricably blood-bound to his. A nervous anxiety prevails to be on the lookout for any signs of a cure. Anxiety smells like Limburger cheese to Vampires. With the exception of Iron Feliks and Volkov, they are unaware of the secret efforts underway to develop a cure for Vampire Zero.

At the conclusion of their regular meeting in Vladimir Putin's command bunker, Dr. Volkov and Iron Feliks are told to remain behind for consultations. Volkov provides an update brief to an obviously agitated boss on the progress of his work. The bioweapons scientist has been working nonstop in his private laboratory located within the Sergey Posad Russian Biological Warfare Research Facility just outside Moscow's city limits. Nervous and agitated, he reports his lack of substantial progress. The all-important cure continues to elude Volkov's tireless efforts. He's nervous to the point of uncontrollable twitches and facial tics. He avoids eye contact with Putin.

"Sir, I believe I am getting closer to a breakthrough. When my work is complete, I expect the cure to take the form of an injectable serum tailored to your blood specifications."

Not what Vladimir Putin wanted to hear. Volkov's progress timeline is vague, much too vague. He's stalling. Vampire Zero leans forward and buries his head in his hands; his head slowly comes to rest on the heavy oak table. He long ago experienced the uselessness of consulting with doctors. They stick around for a short spell, disappoint, then disappear. His last remaining hope is Volkov. As a Vampire himself, he's the only scientist with the potential to develop either a cure or an interim solution. Volkov's failure would seal Putin's fate.

Vampire Zero's physical deterioration, although much milder than Yuriy Andropov's immediate and severe reaction, is based on the original serum, with obviously ineffective modifications. To vent his frustration with Volkov's lack of progress, Putin has devoted countless hours to digesting the voluminous amount of laboratory analysis data of Andropov's blood serum. He's amassed an encyclopedic knowledge about the pathophysiology of blood disorders.

The harrowing account of the former Soviet leader's brief resurrection as a Vampire before he mercifully died and was buried for good is ever present in Putin's mind. For like Andropov in Soviet times, Putin regards himself as essential to ensuring Russia's future. In fact, Putin has taken to seeing himself as synonymous with Russia itself. It is the greatest delusion to which a man or Vampire can succumb. It is also as detrimental to Putin's health as it is to Russia's vitality as a great nation.

Despite the usual barrage of assurances from Volkov about an imminent breakthrough, Putin's facial expression clearly demonstrates grave doubts. He motions for Volkov to come closer as he describes his symptoms, the progressive signs of physical decay, in clear detail. He presents his symptoms clinically, as if discussing something as trivial as a sprained ankle. Stamina continues to decline, lack of appetite, depression, sudden mood swings. Headaches. Severe migraines. Volkov is twice told to repeat essential details that might present clues for a cure.

Volkov's second recap of the symptoms is interrupted by Vampire Zero's sudden mood swing. Without warning, Putin's mood turns pitch black. His piercing blue eyes are mixed with intermittent flashes of dark red. They lock in on the terrified bioscientist, who can't turn away from the intensity of Putin's stare. He speaks to Volkov in a low, hypnotic, monotone voice. Volkov experiences a dull throbbing pain growing incrementally worse. The pain seems to have originated deep in his extremities and is now spreading throughout his body. Vampire Zero has transferred the torturous pain of his own symptoms onto a new host. He wants Volkov to feel the full experience of his condition. The inescapable severity of the intense, stabbing pain is centered on the scientist's forehead, chest, and stomach. His left eye is hostage to an uncontrollable, violent twitch. His migraine is so intense that the colors of the room fade several shades lighter. Even the large fluorescent overhead lights can't escape the power of Putin's spell as they swing slowly back and forth. Lights flicker rapidly on and off. Several explode. Bursts of light stream sparks from ceiling to floor. With Volkov on his knees screaming in agony, Putin finally relents. This demonstration of power was intended to motivate.

Putin's only hope for a cure is crumbling under the weight of his inner demons. Volkov is suffering from inhuman mental and physical anguish. Although he's managed to keep the details of his own deterioration to himself, his dreams are vividly haunted by terrible, recurring visions. His inescapable visions depict graphic images of all-out nuclear war with the US. Initially traumatized by these scenes of mass destruction, he now feels pleasure at the prospect of their ultimate fulfillment. He welcomes sleep and a nightly return to the delight of those terrible dreams as his only respite from bone-soaking pain.

One night, Volkov's dream takes him into the launch center of a Russian nuclear missile silo. The extended index finger of his right hand hovers momentarily atop the launch button. He smiles as his fingertip makes contact and he slowly applies pressure, causing the red button to depress deep into the control panel. Thermonuclear war has been initiated. The power to release the ultimate destructive forces of nature unleashes within Volkov a physical climax of pent-up emotions. A flash of super bright light and the accompanying blast wave are his only companions before he awakens. His pain is gone. His destiny is clear.

In a final act of desperation, the bioscientist tries to excise the demons within him. He reflects on better times, reflections of an innocent past during the height of the Soviet Union when he was a young, ambitious scientist with a bright future. Relief is, however, short-lived. The black clouds of Armageddon soon return.

Volkov's tone is firm and confident. Now without fear, he looks Vladimir Putin directly in the eyes. In a desperate gamble, Dr. Volkov makes a promise.

"Sir, the serum will be ready in forty-eight hours."

CHAPTER 22
THE MARK OF CAIN

Half a world away, in McLean, Virginia, Rainer Wolf is also afflicted by near-crippling symptoms. Terrible migraine headaches, numbness in his fingers and toes, and sharp, shooting pains radiating up and down the length of his spine are his daily companions.

The physical ailments are accompanied by dreams in which he's floating aimlessly in an empty, zero-gravity void. In the blackness, he's unable to distinguish up from down. Confused and disoriented, he tries desperately to reach a faint light visible within a horizon beyond his grasp. Is this the way back? Human or Vampire? If he could still choose between the two, which would he choose?

Wolf understands he has to conquer his physical and mental anguish—otherwise he'll be unfit to lead the Trust. Should this progress to incapacitation, what then? Wolf isn't yet ready to share the details of his growing affliction with the Trust. He needs to talk, gain some perspective. One name springs to mind. An outsider, someone in whom he can confide, someone he trusts implicitly. The outsider is a retired colleague and one of his oldest friends, an irascible soul of first-generation Irish heritage named Flynn O'Donovan. They agree to meet the following Saturday morning for a walk in the woods of Rock Creek Park in Maryland.

O'Donovan approaches Wolf wearing a huge smile across his pale, Irish face. His bald scalp glistens in the sun. His dedication to fanatical physical workouts is still evident in his physique. Before he can escape, Rainer is wrapped up in a big bear hug. Rainer begins.

"How long's it been? Way too damn long since we've seen each another. It's great to see you, old friend. Hey, how's Jane?"

"Great, old man! You should see her garden—the roses! I tell ya', she's outdone James Jesus Angleton himself."

Rainer laughs at the reference to the Agency's former counterintelligence czar, who reigned from the 1950s to the 1970s. Among other things, he was an avid, meticulous horticulturist. In some ways, both good and bad, Wolf's styled himself after the legendary spymaster.

"And what the hell are you doing with your time, Flynn?"

"Stop by. Really do it this time, Rainer. You always say you're gonna stop by, and you never show. Hey, I wanna show you my latest acquisition. Came across this Saba phono super 8 in mint condition at an antique auction. Got it for a song. Sweet, huh? Oh, and you'll like this, I've upgraded my sound system—after all, a great opera singer like Maria Callas deserves only the best."

Rainer makes a mental note to stop by their house. Just the therapy he needs. He's always felt good—happy, actually—in their company: the smell of Jane's gourmet cooking, the soothing notes of soft classical music streaming in the background, and a nice glass of Cabernet in hand. Flynn notices his friend's preoccupation and comments about how pale and drawn Wolf looks.

"You work too much, old man. What's up? You look like shit. When you finally gonna hang up the cleats, or in your case the tutu? None of us are irreplaceable. Ya' know, there's a big world out there to explore. I don't know anyone who wished they'd have worked longer, but I do know a lot of people who wish they'd have retired sooner. Made more time to enjoy life."

Enjoy life. What a thought. Why hadn't he thought of that? Rainer shakes his head. "Flynn, I need to tell you something in strictest confidence. You can't breathe a word of what I'm about to say to anyone—including Jane. I know that's not fair, but do you agree?"

"Yeah. Okay. Of course."

"Brace yourself. This may be a bit hard to take. I'm just gonna say it. I'm a, a… Vampire!"

The Irishman bursts out laughing and covers his mouth with his left hand. "Great, and I'm a Zombie. Nice to know. Funny, you don't sound like what's his name, the famous Vampire actor. Blaaahh, blaaahh, blaahh."

Mildly amused, Rainer takes control. "No, really. I'm dead serious." Flynn's facial expression changes abruptly from humor to concern. "And the famous blaaahh, blaaah, blaaahh actor, as you put it, is Bela Lugosi—asshole. Look, forget everything you think you know about existence, nature, life on earth. Bear with me while I try to explain. If you still think I'm nuts, I won't bother you any more."

The two sit on an empty park bench well off the walking trail. Wolf leads his oldest Agency friend through the entire story, from the mole hunt through to the creation of the Trust. Flynn listens impassively, doesn't say a word. Wolf has no idea what he's thinking.

"Rainer, only you could paint yourself into a corner like this. I still haven't decided whether you're nuts or not, but what can I do for you? Hey, I know a good wooden stake provider—top-quality stuff."

"You SOB. Again with the humor. Only you could turn this into a lame-ass joke, very lame-ass. Wooden stake provider, really? What next, bulk orders at a discount? I hope they're US-made hardwood, not some Chinese knockoffs."

Levity has a positive effect on Wolf. He came to the right man. His secret is safe with Flynn O'Donovan.

"So do Vampires still appreciate a few sips of good Irish whiskey?"

More subdued laughter. Rainer can't remember the last time he laughed this much. "Listen. Flynn, I need you to do what you've always done—tell me when I'm full of shit whenever it needs to be said. But I need more than that—I need a trusted advisor. I just don't trust my judgment. What I haven't told you is, well, my condition, it seems to be unstable. I'm not so much worried about myself, but I won't put the others at risk. So it's time to bring in an outsider—kind of a human spiritual advisor."

"I'll try to help, Rainer. It's always been my distinct honor to tell you to go to hell."

"Thanks, old friend. Wooden stake provider—really?"

Flynn rubs his right hand across the top of his head, unsure where to begin. His brow is deeply furrowed in concentration. "So this battle of good versus evil has begun and it's for all the marbles—the future of the world, right. That's a lot to swallow. Vampires are silly fictional characters. Never gotten into the genre myself, to tell you the truth. And now I'm sitting on a park bench with a real, no-shit Vampire. Tell me, are you real or have you stolen the body of my friend? Who exactly am I talking to? Is Rainer Wolf still in there? I need to know, now. He was a dear friend. How do I know you're still my ole' friend?"

Wolf's nostrils flare. His eyes flicker flashes of amber. Flynn really should show more respect! Flynn accepts the glow in Rainer's eyes as proof of Wolf's Vampire bona fides. He's suddenly fearful for his life.

Flynn doesn't miss a beat. "See how you're staring at me? That's not Rainer Wolf. Now don't get mad. I'm just being honest."

Wolf has a strong urge to bite Flynn O'Donovan right there—to kill him with one violent penetration of his razor-sharp fangs. He struggles to bring forth the remaining vestiges of the man he once was. His inner voice screams a reminder the human sitting next to him was and still is his closest friend. The amber glow is his eyes softens until it is extinguished. He's all but resigned himself to the reality that the most precious gift of his human existence—his conscience—is lost.

"Now do you see why I called you? I need your help to come to terms with who I am. So what's your counsel, old friend?"

Flynn hesitates. He's reluctant to say anything that might offend Wolf. "Rainer, I think you should see a priest."

His voice trails off. Wolf should have anticipated his devout Roman Catholic friend would want to help save his soul. Flynn takes encouragement in Wolf's look of resignation.

"Look. I know you're not religious, but your suffering isn't limited to your mind and body. It sounds to me like you're searching for your lost soul."

Wolf subconsciously strokes his closely cropped silver beard. Since becoming a Vampire, his skin has turned tougher, leathery. The beard helps smooth out his face. "Look, I'm at my wit's end. At this point, I'll try just about anything. I assume you have someone in mind. Who's this priest? Where can I find him?"

The Irishman places a reassuring hand on Rainer's left shoulder. "His name is Father John. He's my parish priest in the Catholic Church in McLean."

"And you trust this Father John?"

"I'd trust him with my life. Look, there's one thing you need to know. Father John was one of us, a CIA case officer. Left the Agency after several war zone tours. Doesn't like to talk about it. He left, returned to the seminary, and became a priest."

"Well, I guess he knows how to handle sensitive information."

Wolf and Flynn embrace then head off in opposite directions.

The following Sunday, Rainer Wolf is seated in the back row of pews during morning mass. Although he'd much prefer to remain unnoticed, his presence draws whispers and quick glances from several Agency colleagues in attendance. After mass, Wolf remains seated until the last parishioner has departed. He approaches the young priest, who has just finished the last confessionals.

"It has been far too long since I've been to church, Father."

"Yes, I know. I'm glad you came. Flynn said you might stop by. You're welcome here anytime."

Even though he knows Wolf's not Catholic, Father John offers to hear his confession through the screened window of the confessional booth. He's not at all surprised with Wolf's request to give his confession face-to-face. The two find themselves seated aside one another in the last row of pews.

"I'm not sure how to begin, Father, so let me get straight to the point. In the world I live in, a battle is raging between good and evil, light and darkness. In my world, these are not metaphorical images. They're real. Our adversary is equally determined to emerge victorious. We must fight until we prevail or our existence is extinguished."

Father John perks up.

"Existence? Or do you mean to say life?"

"I mean to say existence. Human beings are not the only form of intelligent life in this world. Surely, Father, that doesn't surprise you."

"No, Rainer, it doesn't. Tell me, what do you expect from me in order to assist you in this struggle against evil?"

"I don't know, Father. If it's truly evil we're fighting, then surely we can summon the power of God to our side."

"Don't you think it's for the Lord to determine what's good and what's evil? Not for man to judge?"

"That'd be nice, if evil would only cooperate, Father. Don't you believe God wants us to do everything in our power to banish evil from the earth? Perhaps make his job a little easier?"

"I suppose that depends on how far you intend to go, Rainer. There's only so much we as mortal beings can do. We all bear the mark of Cain. Our blood is tainted by sin. Evil will exist as long as humans exist. I don't know your adversary, but I confront our main adversary every day. It's not metaphorical. It's real."

"Good point. Please forgive my hubris. Father John, may I see you from time to time? I'd like to continue our discussion, but please, with your utmost discretion."

"Of course, Rainer. I'm here for you. And God will hear you, wherever you find yourself. Of that you can be sure."

They stand and shake hands.

"Rainer, I'll pray for you. Will you also pray for me?"

The priest's request surprises Wolf.

"Yes, I will pray for you, Father John."

CHAPTER 23
MOSCOW LIAISON

Aaron and Klemko meet for the first time since Janicke hand delivered the Trust's letter to the System over the last Christmas holiday. The purpose of this regularly scheduled liaison is to ostensibly cover standard business between COS Moscow and the Russian chief of liaison. Both sides, however, sorely need time on target for assessment purposes.

Aaron is seated in Andropov's library in the old KGB Headquarters, a massive room decorated in dark wood paneling, heavy red velvet curtains, and two sets of wall-to-ceiling bookshelves. No amenities are offered, but an FSB officer, in full dress uniform, is posted at the exit nearest Aaron. Outside, Bolshevik revolutionary Feliks Dzerzhinsky's statue stands guard prominently in the center of the square named in his honor. Klemko deliberately arrives almost an hour late. Janicke is unperturbed by the snub.

"Ah, Aaron! It's so good to see you again. I hope you enjoyed the holidays! I wanted to give you some time to absorb the atmosphere of our former chairman's study. Did you notice our fine book collection? Many excellent classical works."

"Yes, doing fine, thank you. Nice books. And how were your holidays?"

"Fine, fine, but unusually busy. I did find time to do some hunting. Actually, I returned just for our meeting. Everyone needs a break once in a while to relax in the great outdoors or the senses tend to go dull. Don't you agree, Aaron?"

"Can't argue with that. I could use a day off myself. What do you like to hunt?"

"Small game. Rabbits. Birds."

"Sounds tasty."

Klemko smiles mischievously. He enjoys psychological sparring with his target. The Russian sheds his camouflage jacket and takes off his hat. He carries his coat in the crook of his left arm with the hat in his left hand. His spit-shined, knee-high brown leather boots give the impression he was on horseback. In a rather disingenuous show of mock concern, he puts his right arm on Aaron's shoulder.

"Aaron, I'm happy to learn you're a Vampire. Based on our video surveillance of your apartment, I was a bit worried about you. Thought you might ruin your eyes reading in the dark. And how do you like your apartment?"

Aaron doesn't skip a beat. "Hope you got some good photos for my file. Any cameras in the bathroom?"

"Of course, Aaron. Only the best for you. One day we must exchange our own files. Mine for yours, and yours for mine. We'll meet on the Glienicke Bridge in Potsdam to make the exchange. Ah... the bridge of spies. It's really a shame the Cold War is over, isn't it? The world is a much duller place, don't you agree? Let's go to my office so we can talk in private."

Their footsteps echo loudly on the white marble floors as they walk the short distance to Klemko's office. The building is eerily quiet and nearly empty.

Klemko ushers in his guest. Janicke strides purposefully through the massive, highly polished oak doors. A set of raised wood panels is featured on the inside center of each door. Into each panel is carved a revolutionary scene of peasants being led uphill into battle by a larger-than-life figure wearing a Soviet-style military uniform.

The vast room has high ceilings rounded at the edges where they're met by badly faded walls painted in light blue. The effect is embellished with oversized crown molding stamped with a repeating pattern of spear tips. The décor is czarist-era ornate, complete with large ceiling medallions at the base of two heavy, crystal chandeliers. A picture of Vladimir Putin hangs on the wall behind Klemko's enormous oak desk, set in a large, ornate gold frame, complete with icy blue-eyed stare.

Aaron is directed to a couch in the oversized sitting area. Bookshelves bearing Soviet- and KGB-era books line the walls. Two full-length windows are covered by a set of decorative white sheers and heavy, blue velvet curtains tied open by sections of gold rope with tasseled ends. The predominantly red pattern Oriental carpet looks as if it hasn't been aired out in a long time.

Klemko hangs his camouflage jacket and hat on a coatrack near the door and joins Aaron. The two Vampires perfunctorily review a list of agenda items. Inane items of protocol dominate their discussion and only reinforce the banality of CIA-FSB liaison cooperation. Despite the Groundhog Day protocol, the topics of which haven't changed since the fall of the Berlin Wall, this particular meeting isn't about finding ways to improve collaboration. Instead, they take ample time to size each other up, like two alpha wolves whose paths cross in the Siberian forest. Klemko smells a bit like vinegar to the American Vampire. Aaron catches his host occasionally sniff the air, smack his lips, and take mental note of his observations.

Based on their initial direct encounters, subtle differences in Vampire physiology are beginning to emerge. The Russians are more intensely physical. They have a keener sense of smell. The Americans' visual acuity seems sharper. Their ability to bend time is more developed. Other differences stem from variations in American and Russian languages, culture, society, and history.

Despite his persistent humorous jabs at his guest, Klemko is on his best behavior. An edict has been issued to the entire suite of Russian intelligence services to temporarily desist from any attempts to mount provocations against the CIA Station. Known is that the order came from Putin. Unknown is why.

There is, however, an ambitious FSB officer, Lieutenant Pokorny, who has unfortunately interpreted this as an opportunity to advance his career via a clever provocation executed while his colleagues are on the sidelines. Pokorny makes the fatal decision to pursue his personal glory. The poor, overly ambitious lieutenant isn't aware this operational stand-down came directly from Vladimir Putin himself.

On his own initiative, Pokorny secretly sent a walk-in into CIA's Moscow Station with bogus, fabricated information about the biological weapons facility at Sergey Posad. Unfortunately, the unwitting FSB lieutenant picked the wrong source of feed material for his ill-advised double agent. He was clueless about the sensitivity of Sergey Posad to the System—and to Putin personally.

COS Janicke watched the walk-in interview broadcast live to a TV screen in another Station office. He immediately sensed the provocation by the FSB. Janicke and the interviewing case officer, quickly came up with the details of a suitable location outside Moscow as well as a time to meet three days from now, which they issued to the walk-in.

Three days later FSB enforcers, under the command of Pokorny, lie in wait. They are well hidden in various position around the meeting site located at the edge of a semi-abandoned row of dilapidated warehouses. Several CIA officers are concurrently moving throughout Moscow to give the false impression that the Station took the bait.

Pokorny is absolutely delighted with the prospect of independently baiting, capturing, and publicly humiliating a CIA officer. The Russian media will hail his clever deed as Russian superiority. Of course his superiors will naturally recognize the talent of this underappreciated patriotic officer.

As Pokorny waits to spring his ambush, he imagines himself standing in the FSB chief's office, where the head of the service effusively praises his initiative, punctuated by a formal award presentation. Screw the order to stand down! He's winning a place for himself within the small circle of the FSB chief's favored young officers.

The FSB team waits all night and into the early morning hours. To their disappointment and to Pokorny's ire, no one shows. He's now even more resolved to entrap an American spy before the ban on provocations is lifted. Later that day, Pokorny reports to his superior what he did and why. His superior, Colonel Petrov, turns white.

Several hours later Pokorny finds himself in the basement of Lubyanka Prison. He's been led into a room with harsh lighting and dingy white-tiled walls. Several metal tables on casters are scattered haphazardly about, their contents hidden under large squares of white cloth. A heavily stained, gray concrete floor angles gently down toward a rusted circular steel grate, the cover to a drain located in the middle of the room. The smell lies somewhere on the spectrum between rotting flesh and industrial-strength antiseptic.

Pokorny is dressed only in his white service-issue underwear, and wide leather straps restrain his chest and limbs securely to a solid metal chair with armrests. Pokorny is frightened and sweating profusely. His eyes burn and what's left of his voice is little more than the scratch of a raspy whisper. A guard dressed in FSB desert camouflage uniform minus rank insignia and name tag enters the room. He avoids eye contact with the poor lieutenant and carefully places a chair in the center of the room, directly over the drain, faced in the direction of a closed door, the only entrance—and exit. The FSB guard leaves the room and after what seems an eternity, the light bulb hanging from the ceiling directly above his head starts to flicker as the gray metal door slowly opens.

Terrible Ivan enters the room alone. He looks directly at Pokorny and offers a particularly evil smile.

No one hears the condemned man's screams.

CHAPTER 24
FEEDING FRENZY

Like their human counterparts, Vampires struggle to identify and subdue their weaknesses. One of the most daunting aspects of being a Vampire is learning to control one's craving for human blood. If left unchecked, the bloodlust will take control, much the same as how humans can become addicted to drugs and alcohol.

In Zurich, Viktor Marlowe craves blood. Against his better judgment, he increasingly enjoys the excitement of the kill. Even the thought of being nicked by his own razor while shaving mildly excites him. He knows unconstrained bloodlust will negatively impact the mission. He simply can't allow his urges to get the better of him.

On this particular evening Viktor is dining with Swiss banker Herr Peter Brockmann, the CEO of a large international bank. They dine alone in the CEO's private suite located on the penthouse floor of the bank building. Brockmann looks the part of the stereotypical Swiss banker: impeccably dressed, multilingual, sophisticated, urbane. Unlike most Swiss banking magnates, Brockmann exhibits traits of Asperger's syndrome–driven obsessive-compulsive disorder.

Most people consider his unique complexity maddeningly distracting. These peculiarities have no effect on his case officer.

In previous meetings, Marlowe identified an exploitable vulnerability used effectively to recruit the Swiss banker as a source. It seems Brockmann has a healthy ego. Viktor has over time capitalized on the Swiss banker's eagerness to impress the American via demonstrations of his mastery of global commodities and financial markets. With Viktor the banker can talk to his heart's content. The man's a savant.

Viktor gently swirls his glass of robust red wine, enjoying its depth and sublime aroma. Nothing quite like his last Bordeaux as a human, but quite good. Becoming a Vampire hasn't changed his appreciation for fine wine. In fact, red wine usually suffices as a symbolic substitute for blood. The first Vampire wine snob, Marlowe finds his tastes are well satisfied, especially if red wine is accompanied with black and blue beef served very rare.

Tonight, however, the usual substitutes simply don't suffice. Viktor Marlowe is locked in an internal struggle to control his desire for human blood. It's been far too long since he's raised a glass of the good stuff. Tonight, the wolf is eying the lamb who has innocently wandered from the herd.

Control is regained through rationalization. With intense focus, Marlowe's able to temporarily banish the thought from his mind. Satisfying his cravings at the expense of losing his key Swiss International banking enterprise contact is totally out of the question. Brockmann's just too valuable a source. He's tracking the System's substantial fortune dispersed over a complicated spider web of front organizations worldwide.

On this night, Marlowe's faith in Brockmann is well placed. The banker rather smugly hands over a stack of banking transactions from several personal accounts tied to Vladimir Putin. An unexpected coup. In exchange, the banker is rewarded with an envelope containing a handsome bonus from his handler.

After dinner, the American Vampire departs in a mild daze headed toward the downtown bar district. He ducks into a narrow alley that extends upward along a steep, cobblestone-paved incline. To avoid people, the drooling Vampire meanders to a point just below the crest of the incline, where he spots a black mongrel dog tearing away at a large black garbage bag. The ragged-looking dog bares his teeth and growls in defense. In response, Viktor bares his fangs and growls back, causing the mongrel to cower into a nearby corner. Overwhelmed by compulsion, Marlowe moves in; his eyes glow bright amber.

About the time he's satisfied his bloodlust, the sight of a prostitute ambling up the alley catches him off guard. Completely distracted, the woman is taking a shortcut to save time on her way to meet one of her regular customers. This feeding frenzy has left Marlowe in such a state of euphoria he has completely discounted his defensive senses, now aroused—someone approaches!

He looks up to see an attractive, yet prematurely old-looking woman in her late twenties. Tall, slender, with dark hair and beautiful, olive skin. Could be ethnically North African or perhaps Iranian. She's provocatively dressed in stiletto heels, a very short skirt, and a blouse buttoned down to deliberately highlight her ample cleavage.

Standing face-to-face with the prostitute, Marlowe's tempted. Is HE really to blame if this lovely wench violated his privacy? No doubt, she'd make a fine dessert to cap off such a special evening. Lustful musings are interrupted by the loud inner voice of his conscience: "Discipline, Marlowe. Control yourself, dammit. Walk away!"

He's momentarily distracted by the glint of a small gold cross, illuminated by moonlight and suspended by a thin gold chain worn around the poor woman's neck. It rests at a point just below the indentation of her throat near the top of her chest, nicely highlighted against the woman's olive skin. The woman is left catatonic with fear. She clutches the cross tightly in the fist of her right hand while bracing it with her left.

Embarrassed by his lustful thoughts, Marlowe attempts to wipe the mongrel's blood from his mouth. He looks down at the unrecognizable pieces of flesh torn from the dog's body. Marlowe's beard, as well as the front of his sport coat and white shirt, are soiled with blood mixed with tiny bits of flesh.

The woman shrinks back in horror. Marlowe slowly moves to within a few inches of her face. He sniffs her aura as he studies the physiognomy of this unfortunate soul and momentarily considers taking her back to his apartment.

Again his inner voice erupts like a volcano to the surface. "You're not thinking clearly, Case Officer!"

Dazed and in shock, the woman succumbs to Marlow's powers of hypnotic suggestion. Her memory of this incident is mercifully erased. The fortunate prostitute continues her carefree stroll through the alley as if nothing out of the ordinary has occurred. She doesn't notice her small clutch purse still on the ground as testimony to her brush with death.

From this day forth, Viktor Marlowe is affectionately given a new Trust moniker—Mad Dog.

CHAPTER 25
MAD SCIENTIST

S INCE HIS LAST MEETING WITH VLADIMIR PUTIN, DR. VOLKOV has been working frantically on the cure. The degenerative disease he shares with Vampire Zero will ultimately consume him as well. He's haunted by his pledge to have the serum ready within forty-eight hours.

Volkov is in Sergey Posad working another all-nighter. He's shadowed by the specter of fear—the manifest fear of failure. Time is running out, not just for Vampire Zero, but for Volkov's own survival. His two principal human assistants, Aleksander and Grygor, timidly brief the scientist on the results of the latest round of serum experiments. They're unaware of the true purpose of their supervisor's strange, unorthodox science and know not to ask unnecessary questions that could only draw them deeper into this unnatural research. Between themselves they've adopted the motto "Hear no evil. See no evil. Speak no evil." They're convinced Volkov is mad.

Aleksander gives Volkov a progress report after completing the rounds at the animal enclosures. "Sir, I regret to inform you the experiments have all failed."

"What do you mean, failed? Have you used the latest serum?"

"Yes, Sir. They're all dead. Same symptoms—even more grotesque. Before they died, their bodies swelled up to twice their normal size. They were extremely agitated—violent convulsions. Full details for each test subject are annotated in the chart."

He hands Volkov the report.

"Leave me now."

Aleksander scurries off before Volkov changes his mind.

Volkov stares blankly at the stack of scientific papers. He pulls a slide from the top shelf of a refrigerator and places it under a large digital microscope. His touch on the magnification dial is well practiced from countless hours of studying blood samples. Same stuff, nothing new.

The scientist spins the dial to the combination lock of his personal one-drawer safe in order to recover an accordion file labeled "The Effects of Aging on Vampires." His attention is focused on the detailed test results of blood drawn as part of a dizzying number of previous animal experiments. Still unsatisfied, the doctor reaches well into the back of the safe drawer for a file labeled simply "Andropov." The two files are placed side by side on his desk.

Mumbling almost incoherently and convinced he's missed a simple, yet important detail, the scientist again reviews the essence of what he's learned. "Let's see… Vampire organs and tissues break down prematurely due to accelerated aging process. But why? Why is the physiology of a Vampire so unstable?"

Then it dawns on him. Of course—the body, the host, is not a living creature! Vampires are not truly alive or dead. They suffer from a condition of being "undead." The anomalies of Andropov's blood don't carry over to the animal experiments. The instability is not a normal biological process common to other animals. The solution was in front of his eyes all along. In clinical terms, Volkov believes Vampires inhabit a third world—a state of existence trapped between life and death. This condition cannot be replicated with any other animal species. It also explains Vampire attributes such as the ability to hypnotize humans and connect with one another's minds. This transient state of existence might explain the Vampire ability to perceive and navigate through folds in space-time with their minds.

Volkov is too experienced a scientist to ignore the fact that he has no experimental basis for such a dramatic conclusion. Peer review is out of the question. Besides, his mental state renders his scientific judgment suspect. Time has run out. Animal experiments are pointless. Only one option remains.

The scientist carefully mixes a batch of serum after making some precise recalculations to adjust for use in a nonhuman subject. He has just one chance to get it right. If his calculations are off—banish the thought! Two-thirds of the bright orange fluorescent contents of the test beaker are carefully pulled into a large seven-gauge syringe.

Volkov pushes up the left sleeve of his lab coat to expose his inner forearm. Hesitation. He takes a moment to collect his thoughts. For the first time in recent memory he's actually optimistic. Great science requires great risks. The doctor imagines the look of sheer delight on Vampire Zero's face when he's finally handed a cure. He'll offer himself as visible proof of success! With that fervent hope, Volkov injects the bright orange serum deep into the large vein in his arm. The biologist-Vampire attempts to record the effects as they occur in his personal notebook. Perched on a lab stool, he begins to note minute changes in his balance and motor skills.

"2100 hours: Injected 105 cl modified serum (See File: Andropov)."

"2105: Feel lightheaded. Probably nerves reacting to biological changes."

"2115: Tingling in the extremities. Fingers and toes going numb. Motor skills deteriorating. Note: Encouraging. In animal experiments, effects were immediate in all cases. Death occurred within minutes."

"2130: Still no serious adverse side effects. Note: Body adjusting?"

The effects accelerate. At 2135 hours Volkov falls uncontrollably off his stool. Dizzy and nauseated, he lies on his side clutching his pen and notebook, still determined to record data as long as he's physically able.

"2145: Eyesight blur. Hour hand clock stop?"

"Numbness trunk torso 50%. Loud hum sound both ear."

"See Only Loud Brite Lite nuklrMushrmKldItthksjnFuhimGet!!about ??8?!1it!10&7*"

A page of illegible entries follows. Then another page full of apparently random zeros and ones. Binary code?

At precisely 2200 hours, Volkov emits a long stream of extended terrible shrieks. The building shakes as if hit by an earthquake. The entire facility lies in shambles. Volkov's otherworldly screams have an immediate, frightening effect on Aleksander and Grygor, who run to the door of his laboratory. The door is locked from the inside. They peer cautiously through the small, heavy glass window of the thick metal door. Nothing but a lab in shambles. They look at one another in abject fear. They look again.

"This can't be real. We must be hallucinating!"

Volkov's body has swelled to grotesque disproportions. He's physically transformed into a hulking beast, badly deformed and hunched over. He—it—cannot stand erect. Its spine is remarkably curved by the protrusion of a large hump at the center of its back. Large bumps and welts, some the size of watermelons, cover much of its arms and legs. Long strings of thick, opaque green saliva secrete from its pores and mouth. Huge, stalactite-like fangs drip this awful ooze from the roof of its mouth. Its saucer-like eyes glow an intensely deep blood red. Volkov has become a Super-Vampire!

CHAPTER 26
FAREWELL TO GEORGE

FINALLY, A BRIGHT AND SUNNY DAY IN MOSCOW. Aaron has managed to avoid yesterday's bad weather by lounging in the dark living room of his apartment. The leisurely Sunday morning passes slowly and he's finished reading the local newspaper. On TV, an impeccably dressed news anchor announces the deployment of patriotic Russian troops to Belorussia, on the invitation of President Aleksander Lukashenko. The Russians are participating in joint military exercises in the Hrodna region along the border with Latvia and Lithuania. The news anchor concludes the show of force is necessary to counter NATO's intention to intimidate Russia through its allies. The Russian government interprets this provocation as a precursor to invasion. Aaron shakes his head and presses the button of the remote control to turn off the TV. Even in the digital age, propaganda is alive and well.

Time has given Aaron perspective to appreciate the many advantages a Vampire has over humans. Why do people live such unnecessarily complicated lives!? They willingly choose to live in small psychological boxes with blinders on. Their halfhearted search for the meaning of life denies them the chance to "stop and smell the roses." Always living in the past or for the future, but rarely for the moment. As a Vampire, Aaron is happiest during his long, mostly late night forays into the thick Russian forests outside Moscow. He's free to roam, to stalk and kill his prey. The gift of effortless movement in communion with a full array of wild animal species is a gratifying counterbalance to the Vampire's raw predator instincts.

Nature is a wonderful outlet. It's also a dangerous pursuit. If Aaron gets sloppy, he runs the risk of being observed by the locals. Aaron's grown to respect the skills of the FSB surveillance teams assigned to shadow his every move. It is, however, great amusement to play cat and mouse with them.

It's clear Rainer Wolf isn't as happy about being a creature of the night. His unsteady state of mind worries Aaron. He's always worried about tomorrow. Wolf's protégé has long sensed a loyalty conflict brewing within his boss. Despite Aaron's reluctance to express his concerns, he's resolved to do so at their next face-to-face encounter.

The Trust has a new spy. The long-discarded walk-in to Bucharest, former FSB officer Sergey Deniken, was finally located and recruited by Aaron. The Russian was hiding out in a small village in Transylvania. Every month, Janicke returns to Romania to clandestinely meet with Deniken; he is but one of a growing stable of spies the Trust keeps off the books from CIA Headquarters.

Deniken agreed to work with the Trust in exchange for CIA protection, and hopefully, resettlement in the US. Of course resettlement hasn't been promised and will never happen. Janicke promised to do all he could to protect the former FSB officer, but warned, given the circumstances, that Deniken is on his own.

The new spy also agreed to report on his friend Boris Smertsov. Janicke is determined to find out why Boris warned his friend in defiance of Putin's orders. Boris must know it's only a matter of time before Vampire Zero learns the truth. The Russian Vampire's vulnerability to compromise is leverage in a potential recruitment pitch to turn him to work for the Trust.

The day drags on and Aaron drifts off to fond memories of his last day in Bucharest. He's in Station bidding farewell to his Trust colleagues, all of whom are present. Aaron extends a collegial hand to Bucharest COS George, who's envious of Aaron's promotion and upcoming choice assignment. Des George is still reeling from his "sudden decision to retire." On this occasion, George lives up to his reputation as a total jackass prone to bouts of boorish behavior. With Aaron's hand extended, George turns his back and mechanically continues to stuff piles of personal items into a number of cardboard boxes placed on his desk. Aaron can't help but marvel at the sheer amount of personal crap George has managed to accumulate. He's like an oblivious fat rabbit bouncing from box to box. His jaw quivers as he picks up various items, thereby causing his large double chin to sway in comical, jerking motions.

Aaron asks Leonardi to wait exactly seven minutes then tell COS Jelly Donuts to look out of his window. "There's just one more thing I have to do before I go."

Right on time, a curious George looks through his office window and down to the sidewalk. Two stories below, Aaron is waving George's bright yellow bag of fresh jelly donuts high above his head. He takes one from the paper bag, places it carefully on the sidewalk, and, with a small theatrical jump, squashes the donut into the concrete. Red filling and bits of dough shoot out from the sides of Aaron's boots. Passersby pay little notice. A small child attempts to join in the fun before being hurriedly pulled away by his mother, who's not amused.

George watches in disbelief as Aaron slowly sets the bag on the ground before lighting it on fire. The fire soon consumes the bag, causing lumps of sugar and grease to pop in small, flaming bursts of light. In celebration, Aaron performs two laps of an impromptu victory dance around the burning bag of cholesterol, arms flailing about in Vampire childish abandon.

As a final tribute, Aaron smiles, fully extends his right arm and points his index finger up at Jelly Donuts's face, now aghast and framed in the large window. He clearly mouths the word "Capisce!" then drops his arm and walks off to the delight of his colleagues, who viewed the entire event from another window.

Elena's burst of laughter is followed by one word. "Brilliant!"

Joe cracks an inside joke. "Now I see why the Chief picked him first!"

Not to be outdone, Marlowe shoots back, "He'd never have the guts to do that if he were still human."

Aaron smiles as he recalls just how badly he wanted to piss on that fire. On reflection, it's probably fortunate for him that Vampire bodies don't produce waste.

CHAPTER 27
SERGEY POSAD

Meanwhile, the scene inside the Sergey Posad Biological Weapons facility is more reminiscent of an eighteenth-century insane asylum than the pristine bioweapons laboratory that existed before Volkov's transformation.

Volkov's assistants had the presence of mind to follow laboratory emergency standard operating procedure. Aleksander set off alarms that alerted authorities of a biohazard emergency. Grygor called the twenty-four hour Bio-alert Center and excitedly informed the watch officer of the situation. The entire facility was immediately locked down.

Several hours have passed and the assistants are reduced to pacing about restlessly in the now tomb-like facility. Aleksander peers through a narrow exterior window in an attempt to catch a glimpse of activity outside. The facility has been completely cordoned off. Other buildings in the area have been evacuated. He can faintly make out the dark silhouettes of armored vehicles positioned along the outer perimeter. The shadows of what appear to be heavily armed military personnel stealthily advancing toward the building only add to his distress. They're coming from all directions. Lights oscillate in the distant sky to mark another frenzy of activity taking place just beyond the horizon. Without emotion, Aleksander sums up their situation. "We're fucked! Seriously, Grygor, they have no plans to rescue us. We're trapped in here with the monster. We should have left him here to rot and saved ourselves when we had the chance. It's too late now."

Grygor falls limp like a sack of potatoes onto the chair at his workstation, head buried in his hands. A feeling of mutual despair sets in. "I could tell by the duty officer's reaction that I made a big mistake by providing all those details about Volkov. The phone went dead after he said he would get back to me. They cut the phone lines. But we're supposed to immediately provide even the smallest details of an emergency. We did what we were supposed to do."

Aleksander's gaze is still fixed on the activity occurring beyond the window. He's strangely calm. "Yeah. I would do the same if I were them. We're witnesses—expendable. There's no emergency response SOP for a monster trapped in a lab. Say your goodbyes, Grygor. Maybe they'll have pity on us and come up with a good cover story about how we sacrificed our lives for Mother Russia. They'll award us nice, big medals for our heroic deeds. Put wreaths of flowers on our graves. We might even make the evening news. Wouldn't that be nice, eh?"

"Fuck you, Aleks." Grygor avoids eye contact with his colleague. The young man with the boyish good looks can't stop shaking. Of the two, he has the most to lose. An index-card-sized copy of a family photo is clasped tightly between the thumb and forefinger of his right hand, taken on his wife's last birthday with her and their two young sons. Aleks, however, hasn't had a girlfriend since his ex-fiancée ended their relationship on the anniversary of their first date. Maybe he'll write her a goodbye note. She'll regret leaving him once he becomes a "Hero of the Russian Federation."

The fatalistic Russians quickly chain smoke down to their last two cigarettes and share regret at having consumed their last bottle of vodka the night before. Vodka would really come in handy right now.

Grygor finally stops shaking and manages to gather his wits about him. "Listen, Aleks, I'm not going to sit here and do nothing. It's been hours since we've heard a sound, despite all that stuff going on outside. If we're lucky, Volkov's dead.

Why should his fate be any different than all those lab rats! If he's incapacitated, we can finish him off. It's our only hope. Do you understand, Aleks?"

Aleks shrugs, feigning his best tough-guy nonchalance. His tall, lean profile is silhouetted by the moonlight as he peers through the window to see what's going on outside. It's eerily quiet. "Okay, Grygor. Let's go. Even a condemned man should get to choose how he dies."

The two assistants warily walk the long corridor toward Volkov's lab, alert for anything. The only sound is the loud echo of their footsteps against the hard tile floor. The walk seems to take an eternity, but with some trepidation, they finally reach the lab. Grygor peeks through the small window of the heavy metal door. He moves his head to various angles in an attempt to view as much of the inside of the lab as possible. They arm themselves with implements found nearby.

"Where's Volkov? Is he even there?"

After some hesitation, Grygor musters enough courage to tap lightly on the window. "*Dorogoi nash* Volkov... Dr. Volkov... Are you all right? We need to know you are yourself again. Please, Comrade, say something. We are your loyal assistants Grygor and Aleksander. We are here to help you."

Grygor's plea is met with silence. Out of the corner of one eye, he catches the fluttering movement of a large shadow on the far wall of the lab. The two assistants nervously give each other a nod to proceed. They're stuck between two boulders, as the Russian expression goes. They'd rather take their chances with the monster Volkov than face what's sure to be a death sentence on the outside.

Aleksander has armed himself with a long metal rod while Grygor inserts the large bronze master key into the door's locking mechanism. Grygor looks over at his colleague, who nervously nods for him to proceed cautiously. Tension mounts as the key is slowly turned once, twice. The third turn is completed with a metallic clunk. The door is unlocked.

The two men push inward and the heavy door slowly opens. Aleks enters the dark room first, holding the metal rod like an ancient warrior would hold a spear. A seat cushion is his shield. Behind him, Grygor is armed with a large container of hydrofluoric acid. The short stocky Grygor leans against his friend's back for psychological support. Back to back, they slowly, cautiously enter the lab.

The container lid has been unscrewed and Grygor, wearing a pair of black, heavy butyl rubber gloves, uses his left hand to press onto the top of the container, thus securing its contents, while his right hand applies upward pressure underneath. He is shaking almost uncontrollably; it's a struggle to keep the container steady. The fumes almost overpower them. Joined at the hip, the two proceed ten steps into the lab. They call out to Volkov with every few steps.

They scan the room in nervous, jerky motions. No signs of life. A pool of thick green mucous is on the floor, the spot where Volkov was last seen the night before. Aleks flips a switch on the wall. No light. No longer able to control their fear, they begin to slowly walk backward, reversing their steps. They share one common thought—to get the hell out of the lab as soon as possible.

Then it happens. First they hear laughter. A recognizable voice, but much deeper than Volkov's. Demonic. A foul, evil smell fills their nostrils, a stench so bad it stops them solid in their tracks. The booming laughter now sounds more like the roar of an approaching freight train. They're locked in the grip of fear with their backs pressed firmly against one another. A presence they can't see has them surrounded. Sight has degraded to panic-induced tunnel vision. Panic turns quickly to hysteria as Aleks uses his makeshift spear to make wild thrust at shadows dim in his periphery.

Grygor is shocked by the feel of something hot on the left side of his neck. Startled, he drops the container of acid on the floor. The unsecured lid rolls under a nearby metal table. The acid forms a bubbling pool around their feet, eating away at the soles of their shoes. Their shoes quickly disintegrate. The acid now consumes the bottoms of their feet. Flesh and bone foam up into a heavy, red-colored froth. They collapse to the floor in excruciating pain, thus more of their bodies are exposed to the corrosive liquid. When acid meets soft flesh, the resulting chemical reaction pulls in the surrounding air, resulting in the formation of large mucus bubbles. The bubbles burst and accelerate the process into a runaway reaction.

Volkov towers over his hapless assistants. The Super-Vampire's metamorphosis unfolds in front of them. They're trapped in their own agony. His huge eyes are ablaze in crimson light. A crooked smile is etched across the hideous bumps and lesions now prominent on his face. He enjoys the spectacle of his two former assistants writhing helplessly on the ground in horrible agony. Their screams excite him. The smell of burning flesh is delightful!

Volkov isn't content to yield the pleasure of the kill to an inanimate executioner. Why, when he can easily take these first two human victims for himself? The hulking figure reaches down into the goo and strikes Aleks's neck with such force that it decapitates him cleanly. Deeper satisfaction is realized by gorging on what's left of his flesh and blood. Volkov reaches again into the human muck to lift up Grygor. He places his victim into a bear hug and squeezes him tightly until a loud cracking sound is emitted from the condemned man's rib cage as its crushed into dust. The acid drips like water off the Super-Vampire's impervious body. The irreversibly blood-crazed Volkov pauses momentarily to study the unrecognizable remains of his assistants. Satisfaction gives cause to smile. In a loud, guttural exclamation, the Super-Vampire makes an announcement to the world. "It has begun. Armageddon is NOW!"

During the noisy bloodbath, FSB and OMON troops have stormed the building only to find the formerly pristine state-of-the-art laboratory facility in complete shambles. Within minutes, they warily reach Volkov's laboratory. Armed with heavy weapons and shielded by state-of-the-art hazmat suits, security forces burst through the door in well-rehearsed urban combat fashion. The sight of bubbling puddles of chemicals mixed with hair, flesh, and bones makes the hardened troops cringe. One of the younger soldiers is overcome with nausea and vomits into his respirator. Volkov has vanished. Outside, in the distance, a hunched, hulking shadow swiftly passes under the last light pole at the far edge of a cleared field, just before the tree line that borders the nearby woods. At the Kremlin, later that evening, the OMON commander reports the regrettable news of Volkov's escape to Vladimir Putin. Vampire Zero is seething. His cheeks twitch.

"You reported the facility had been sealed tight. You yourself assured me there was no possibility of anyone leaving the facility alive. Then how did Volkov manage to escape? Is Volkov alive or dead? Well, General?"

The General stands at rigid attention, his arms planks at his sides. He thinks he's prepared for the worst. "Mr. President, it was impossible to escape. We had every millimeter of the perimeter under control. Every single millimeter was under physical and technical coverage. No one could have escaped. He, Dr. Volkov, he's not human."

Putin is tired of excuses. He stands inches away from the General's face, staring intently into his non-blinking eyes. Vlad the Impaler snaps his neck like a twig.

CHAPTER 28
THE DEAD HAND

V LADIMIR PUTIN HAS CONVENED AN EMERGENCY MEETING OF THE System. The atmosphere in the command bunker, deep in the earth below the Kremlin, is tense.

Klemko briefs the ongoing operation to erase all traces of the carnage wreaked by Volkov at Sergey Posad. Damage control relies heavily on a network of trusted witting and unwitting human collaborators. The events at the bioweapons facility have forced Vladimir Putin to bring in additional support, thus increasing the possibility *Systema*'s existence could be compromised. Fortunately, leaks are very unlikely, even if someone unconnected should accidentally stumble onto what really happened. In Russia, centuries of natural selection have weeded out those who choose to recklessly defy authority.

As luck would have it, no FSB or OMON officers or first responders saw Volkov. Still secret is the fact that a Super-Vampire is on the loose in Russia. National media assets have been provided with a suitable cover story. According to the Russian media (per talking points exactly as provided by the Kremlin), Dr. Volkov and his two assistants, Aleksander and Grygor, were infected by a deadly disease during their conduct of a defensive bioweapons experiment gone awry. The three scientists heroically sealed themselves in the laboratory to ensure the Russian public would not be exposed to the deadly pathogen. The Russian government will soon share details of the accident with the public for the sake of transparency. The press will announce the details of medal presentation ceremonies to honor the heroes at their funerals.

Vampire Zero can't concentrate on Klemko's briefing. This "incident," as it is described in order to downplay its significance, has shaken him. *Systema* has withstood many challenges to its rule, but this one feels different. Has Vladimir Putin lost control? One of his Vampires has gone rogue. There's no telling what he might do. Putin reminds himself he's emerged stronger from every challenge he has faced. He relishes in the sweet aroma of power and the pungent odors of fear and intimidation. He reminds himself he is a survivor.

The Russian leader mulls over his options. Volkov's demise and the destruction of Sergey Posad have dashed any hope of a cure. To survive, he needs to find a new scientist. Someone as brilliant as Volkov, but sane. Someone to revive the program. Someone to find a cure. Vampire Zero buries his head in his hands, and exclaims, "It's hopeless!"

Without warning, Putin launches at the unsuspecting Badanov and wraps his right hand tightly around Badanov's scrawny neck. His victim's feet have been lifted several inches off the floor. His larynx makes a series of loud, crunching, popping sounds as it's slowly crushed to the width of a drinking straw.

The Chess Master's red glowing eyes search desperately for help from the assembled mass of his dumbstruck colleagues. With his left hand Vlad the Impaler slowly draws a sharp, slender wooden stake from the left inside breast pocket of his suit jacket. He eases the wooden shaft deep into the heart of his hapless victim until only the tip of the blunt end is left visible. He slowly turns the shaft like a screw. The Vampires witness Badanov's death with a mixture of horror and morbid fascination. They can't help but admire Vampire Zero's demonstration of power and authority. Long minutes pass before Badanov draws his final breath. His body then suddenly disappears in a short series of brilliant bursts of bright light. All that remains of the Chessmaster are a teaspoon of ashes and a singe burn mark on the floor.

Vampire Zero wears a curious look. Expressionless, he tilts his head to the side and announces blankly, "Now we know how a Vampire dies."

Vampire Zero adjusts his suit jacket, then takes his seat at the head of the table. The meeting is brought back to order. "We are all accountable for our actions. Everyone makes mistakes, but a pattern of mistakes is a different matter. It is inexcusable. If it were not for *Tovarish* Badanov's poor judgment, the Trust would not exist. If it were not for Badanov's ill-fated moves, *Tovarish* Kruchkov would still be here amongst us. We have all been weakened as a consequence of our dear friend's unreliability. Yes, his death is regrettable, but it was necessary. Remember, we are all expendable. His service has been terminated for the greater good of *Systema*."

Putin leads the assembled group in a moment of silence in Badanov's memory before outlining his plans to deal with Volkov. "As we gather here tonight, we confront a new threat. We must hunt down one of our own. Rubik, have you received any reports on Volkov's current location?"

Rubik rises unsteadily to address the group, employing a PowerPoint presentation. "Sir, our sources assess Volkov is most probably on his way to a ballistic missile site in Siberia. We have positioned human and technical assets at various chokepoints to track his movements. NTMs (national technical means) have been redirected to increase surveillance coverage of all nuclear sites. Aircraft, dismounted special forces, drones and satellites."

Iron Feliks interrupts the briefing. "What makes you think Volkov is headed for a missile silo?"

"There is no doubt. An analysis of his notes, journal, and diary confirm his intentions to launch nuclear war between the United States and Russia. In fact, he has left a letter personally addressed to you, Mr. President."

Rubik hands the handwritten, single-page letter to Vampire Zero. In it, Volkov apologizes for his failure to find a cure and has sworn "by his dead hand" to atone by unleashing nuclear war on the United States.

Putin is impatient. "Get to the point, Rubik. Which one?"

"Which one?"

"Which silo? Where does he intend to launch the missiles?"

Rubik hesitates before responding. "We don't know."

Mercader groans.

"Great. Determining his direction will be like peeling off the layers of a Matryoshka's brain."

Beria pipes up cheerfully. "Even if the mad scientist gains access to a missile control room, he cannot activate the launch sequence. The codes are strictly controlled. Only our president has the approval authority to launch a nuclear attack."

Vladimir Putin clears his throat. The room is dead silent. "That is a problem. Iron Feliks will explain."

All eyes turn to Iron Feliks, who leans back in his chair for effect. "Comrades, our president is right. Volkov's oath to atone for his failings 'by his dead hand' speaks to his intention to activate the top secret 'Dead Hand' missile launch protocol. Let me explain. Our intercontinental missile silos are connected to a central radar and communications system. The computers in the silo command centers are purposefully not connected to a network in order to prevent any chance of penetration via any attack, including a US cyberattack. Volkov evidently intends to use his Super-Vampire powers to trick one of the computers into thinking Russia is under nuclear attack. In retaliation, the computer will automatically launch missiles under its control against preprogrammed targets in the United States."

System Vampires respond with an audible gasp.

"If that happens—IF that happens—other silo-associated radars will pick up the launch and those computers will also assume Russia is under attack. They will automatically follow suit. Even a limited US response would trigger the launch of every active nuclear-tipped Intercontinental Ballistic Missile (ICBM) in our inventory."

Mercader can hold back no longer. "Iron Feliks, are you suggesting Volkov has the power to bypass Dead Hand?"

Iron Feliks has given the matter considerable thought. He seems pleased with himself. "Well, we are in unknown territory. The concern is his special senses will pick up on the simple line of code, in effect the password, that must be inserted into any launch computer to direct the automated system to take control. We must assume that if Volkov can gain access to a computer in any silo control center, he will succeed in initiating the launch sequence. We Vampires have special senses, shall we say, for this purpose. Our ability to sense tiny perturbations in global stability is a gift from our maker. For us, numbers are not as random as they seem to humans. For a Vampire of Volkov's supercharged sensory perceptions, I would think it would be child's play for him to decipher the pattern of numbers."

Vampire Zero takes over the briefing. "Enough information. We have awoken to our worst nightmare—an insane Super-Vampire obsessed with the need to impress by destroying the world."

Vampire Zero barks orders brusquely. "Klemko, contact the Trust's liaison representative in Moscow tonight. Schedule a meeting with Wolf in a neutral location. Only you two. Propose a temporary truce. Negotiate the terms of joint cooperation between the Trust and the System to find and neutralize Volkov. Use your discretion concerning how much information you provide the Americans. However, you are not authorized to disclose the existence of Dead Hand. Remember, the Americans are our enemies. And Klemko—obviously, there is no need to make Wolf aware of the nature of Volkov's work at Sergey Posad."

Klemko replies simply, "Understood, Sir."

Putin rises. All rise. The meeting is concluded. They stand at attention and shout in unison. "Vampires rule!"

CHAPTER 29
THE QUEST

Two days later, Wolf and Klemko meet secretly in a Russian safe house located on the northern outskirts of Vienna, in the picturesque wine country village of Nussdorf am Attersee.

Klemko has a challenge. Can he convince his archfiend Wolf the existential threat Volkov poses to the world is real? Can he allay Wolf's natural suspicions that the Trust is being lured into some sort of an elaborate trap as revenge for the elimination of Kruchkov?

After a perfunctory exchange of pleasantries, Klemko presents Wolf with a personal letter from Vampire Zero, "proposing joint cooperation to neutralize a potential existential threat to the US and Russia." Vladimir Putin "guarantees this truce between the System and the Trust by his own authority as president, and by his word."

"Well, Klemko, you have my attention. Please pass on my personal regards to Vampire Zero, but with all due respect, 'his word' will not suffice to enter into any kind of agreement with the System."

"I anticipated as much, Rainer. I'd be disappointed if you accepted our proposal at face value."

Klemko lays out a stack of photos taken of the scene at Sergey Posad. Volkov's demolished laboratory. The ravaged remains of Volkov's lab assistants. One blurry photo of Volkov snapped by a junior FSB officer posted along the facility perimeter (his memory was later erased, which saved the poor lieutenant from a positively grisly fate). "Rainer, there's something else. I was ordered to withhold information from you about Volkov's activity at Sergey Posad. You see, things went terribly wrong. He was working on a serum—a Vampire cure—using the blood of Yuriy Andropov. My bloodline. Your bloodline. We suffer from the same disease. Volkov failed Putin. He failed me. He failed you."

"Why are you telling me this, Klemko?"

"You need to know the truth, or we will fail in this joint operation. As a case officer myself, I know you would not accept our proposal just because I showed you some gruesome photos. Of course they could be fakes. Fabricated. I guarantee with my own life what I am telling you, for if you divulge what I have said to Vampire Zero, it will be my sacrifice for humanity, not yours."

Wolf pauses, then responds. "I'm not sure why I trust you, old friend, but I know you well enough to know when you're leveling with me. Have I ever told you that you're a great case officer?"

Wolf smiles. He signals his approval for the joint op, then turns sullen, lashing out at the Russian. "But you got us in this mess! Now you want us to get you out of it?"

"All of us, Rainer. All of us. Volkov is my problem, but he is also your problem. This Super-Vampire intends to initiate thermonuclear war. He's on his way to Siberia as we speak. There's no time to lose. Volkov is highly alert and can sense his fellow System Vampires. We need an edge. The element of surprise. We will work together to guide your Trust Vampires to him like a laser. We have no other choice. You think I'd be here if there was any other way?"

Klemko takes a deep breath before continuing. It goes against his nature to ask the Americans for help, even in a crisis. "There is one 'hitch,' as you Americans like to say. We have no reliable data on how to kill a Super-Vampire. We can only estimate how much more powerful he is than any of us. Eliminating Volkov is going to be a formidable task, even for teams of Vampires working together. Do you have any ideas, Rainer?"

Wolf doesn't bite. He has doubts about whether this far-fetched story is a provocation intended to elicit information about how the Trust eliminated Kruchkov and the freshly recruited Russian spy, Tom Burns. "Why are you asking me for help, Klemko? Surely *Systema* must have some ideas about how to vanquish this Super-Vampire you spawned."

Klemko reflects silently on the fireworks display of Badanov's last moments. He grabs Wolf's hand and places it over his heart dramatically. "The source of a Vampire's life force lies is his heart, and it is supported by the rich blood that flows through his veins. More so than with humans. A stake aimed at its center can potentially be fatal—IF the Vampire has been sufficiently weakened in the seconds and minutes leading up to the moment when a well-aimed strike is delivered. The Vampire's body collapses in on itself in a runaway chain reaction—like a collapsing black hole—until he vanishes in a flash. Nothing is left. Or so we think. It's only a theory."

"Klemko, are you sure you have no experience in these matters? Let me hazard a theory in response to yours. In and of itself, a stake through the heart may be insufficient to terminate a Vampire. This 'spontaneous combustion,' if you call it that, may only occur if a Vampire is compromised physically to the point cells cannot regenerate faster than they deteriorate. In other words, we think the Vampire must lose his will to live for the stake in the heart to do its business."

Klemko is pensive. "Ah… that complicates things. We've never carried weapons because, well, it has never been necessary. Perhaps we've become arrogant. Combat among Vampires is a different matter. Rainer, let's agree on this: our teams will equip themselves with weapons of their choice to confront the rogue. Agreed?"

"Agreed."

Wolf has no choice but to accept the Russian proposal. If there's even a one percent chance Volkov can succeed, then he must be eliminated. It'd be reckless to discount the possibility of nuclear catastrophe. Unbeknownst to Klemko, Wolf is privy to top secret CIA reporting on the automated Russian missile launch system, Dead Hand. The DDO can't tip off Klemko to the fact he's read in to the existence of the Soviet-installed missile launch system. The CIA's own information, obtained from sensitive Russian sources in Soviet times, is ironically the proof he needs to accept the Russian proposal. Klemko and Wolf shake on their agreement. Their Vampires will carry out a joint operation to stop a madman from initiating MAD. Who says US and Russian intelligence can't cooperate?

Klemko lays out some maps and papers on the table as he delves into specifics. "The Russian side will provide real-time intelligence on Volkov's current location and movements. We know he is headed for an area of Siberia where a number of active missile silos are located. You will have access to their locations as we narrow down the search area. The American side will dispatch two teams of two Vampires each to track down and eliminate Volkov. Two Russian teams will shadow them in parallel. It's your decision who to deploy, and to which area, based on the information we provide as the operation unfolds."

"How do you plan to minimize outside interference, Klemko? Do you plan to keep the authorities in the dark?"

"Of course, Rainer. As you must also. The CIA, FSB, SVR Headquarters must be kept in the dark. We will devise sufficient cover stories in the event of any disclosures through leaks or the media."

"Klemko, that's all fine, but I have conditions. All orders to American teams will be issued under my leadership. Under no circumstances will you tell my Vampires what to do. American and Russian teams will operate in parallel. They will not, under any circumstances, commingle. We'll carry our own weapons and gear. COS Moscow will be present in the System's command center 24/7 throughout the entire course of the operation. Only Janicke will task the American teams, and only he or I will approve all orders. My Vampires will have real-time access to the same intelligence information made available to the Moscow command center and the Russian teams. Deal?"

"Of course. Understood. Anything else?"

"Yes, one other thing. As you know, it's wise for rivals to create a disincentive to betray one another—a practice the CIA and the FBI have perfected—

as you have between your special services. We'll exchange hostages. A System Vampire will join me at a secret location from which he and I will maintain communications with my Vampires and your command center. Your Vampire will be treated in full accordance with diplomatic protections and immunities. I expect the same treatment for my Vampires."

"Rainer, you will have Beria by your side. Janicke will be our guest in the joint command center in Moscow. The American and Russian teams in Siberia will work together but separately just as you propose. Your conditions are not only acceptable, they are necessary. We cannot afford to be distracted by our blood feud if we are to save humanity from nuclear holocaust."

Reluctantly the two old enemies shake hands. When two alpha wolves cross paths in the Siberian forest, only one continues on its way. It won't take long before one double-crosses the other. Who will strike first?

They rise from their chairs and prepare to depart the safe house. It's a bitter cold Vienna winter evening outside. Despite a strong preference not to wear winter clothes, they take care to blend in with their human counterparts. As Klemko puts on his scarf and gloves, he slaps Wolf on the back. The Russian offers a parting salutation. "Trust, but verify!"

Years ago Ronald Reagan expressed the hopes and aspirations of the world when he made this remark during his unsuccessful joint effort with Soviet leader Mikhail Gorbachev to abolish nuclear weapons. Such a caveat only confirmed there was little trust when Ronald Reagan first uttered the phrase during the Cold War—and there is certainly even less trust now.

Wolf smiles. "If it were only that easy."

CHAPTER 30
THE COMMAND CENTER

COS Moscow Janicke waits outside the old American Embassy building located on Tchaikovsky Street in central Moscow, with Elena Constantin by his side. It's a cold, blustery, sunless February day. Wisps of snow fall to the ground, giving color to the gray landscape. The weather forecast calls for more snow, typical for the middle of an endless Moscow winter.

Janicke hops up and down gleefully. "What a gorgeous day! Great day for ops, huh?"

Constantin agrees with a smile. Their coats are unbuttoned to take in the cold as they wait to be picked up and escorted to the command center.

The Trust has a surprise for their hosts: the unannounced inclusion of Elena as an additional "hostage." She traveled overnight from Paris to provide backup if the Russians pull any surprises of their own. Besides the protective value of the buddy system, this operation will test Elena's oracle-like ability to divine things others can't, and, hopefully, foresee the future to anticipate the Super-Vampire's moves. Aaron's also counting on her to keep a wary eye on their enemies. Study them. Identify vulnerabilities. Pick up any scent of betrayal. Complex, interconnected, and multilayered objectives are standard Russian procedure. The KGB's appetite to prove their counterintelligence superiority borders on obsession. Like their CIA counterparts, at times they indulge themselves in what case officers call "art for art's sake"—when the operation itself becomes the objective, rather than the intelligence impact.

Elena's CIA career was not focused on the Russian target. As required of the rising generation of post-9/11 Agency officers, she served the obligatory two war zone tours followed by a traditional tour, in her case in Africa. Her subsequent assignment to Bucharest was directed by Rainer Wolf based on her sustained performance. She developed quickly to become the classic CIA case officer generalist. Now, however, for the remainder of her career, and perhaps her life, Elena Constantin will work against the hardest CIA target on earth—Putin's System.

As if out of nowhere, a small motorcade of three spotless black Volga sedans appears parked at the curb directly in front of the Americans. Klemko quickly exits from the back seat of the middle car and steps over to Aaron. He's obviously surprised by the sight of two Trust Vampires, but offers a hearty greeting, hand extended. Unruffled, Klemko introduces himself with a bit of theatrical flair. "Welcome to Moscow, Elena Constantin! I trust your flight was uneventful."

"Yes, routine. Beautiful weather we're having, isn't it?"

"Constantin, my name is Klemko. KGB chief of liaison. System Vampire. But you probably know all that already."

Elena nods in acknowledgment. She's read his dossier. They shake hands. Klemko ushers them into the middle car.

"Aaron, please ride in the back with me. If it is not an imposition, Ms. Constantin, can you please sit here?"

Klemko signals for his aide to relinquish the front passenger seat to Elena. The young officer holds the door open for her, then, once she's seated, gently shuts it before he scurries off into the rear vehicle.

The two male Vampires banter back and forth during the nearly hour-long drive to the KGB safe house, mostly off-color Vampire anecdotes accompanied by loud snorts and bursts of laughter. Vampires emit strange wheezing sounds punctuated by involuntarily gasps for air when they laugh. Thankfully left out of the conversation, Elena ignores their adolescent behavior. So much for the hope male Vampires would be more chivalrous than their human counterparts. Seems all males are the same! After she became a Vampire, Elena cut her long blond hair short in a razor cut on the sides, longer on top. She added tattoos to commemorate a succession of memorable experiences, some personal changes to give her an edge in this Vampire-eat-Vampire world. Despite the assault of loud adolescent noises emanating from the back seat, Elena remains focused on memorizing the circuitous route to the secret System command center, just in case.

The KGB safe house, purloined for this occasion, is an apartment located in a working-class neighborhood on the southern outskirts of Moscow. Hidden within a large eight-story building built in the old communist style of dull, gray slab concrete, it's an identical copy of the four other buildings erected along the row within which it stands. Amenities such as plumbing and electricity are haphazard at best in this region of Moscow, packed tightly with Soviet-era apartment buildings. Balconies, although unsafe for residents, burst outward with all manner of homemade TV and radio antennae.

The motorcade comes to a halt in front of the entrance to Building 1007. Klemko and his two guests exit the vehicle and glide briskly through the aluminum-framed glass double doors. Klemko directs his two guests to a nearby iron elevator. Once inside the small cavity, he pushes the button for the tenth floor. As the confined cage lurches unsteadily upward, Aaron feels a premonition his death match with Kruchkov on the phantom tenth floor was but a foreshadowing of terrible events to come. He takes solace in Elena's presence.

The elevator doors open to reveal quite an impressive setup. Aaron expected something along the lines of a small, smoke-filled room with blacked-out windows and antique-looking equipment. This safe house is grand by comparison. It occupies the entire quad of apartments on the tenth floor. Visitors are initially greeted by an unmarked, green diamond tuck upholstered, leather-padded door. It is quite a contrast to the overall near-ghetto surroundings.

Inside, the apartment brims with state-of-the-art technology. Large flat-screen monitors attached to black boxes wired to Cyrillic keyboards fill the space of almost every wall in the large living room and kitchen. Pieces of communications gear are stationed on tables in the living room and one wall is almost entirely consumed by a large flat screen on which is depicted an interactive map of various sections of Siberia that Volkov is known to have entered. Other screens display a multigrid composite of views taken from various sources, both fixed and mobile. One feed is displaying real-time video from a helicopter nose camera as it flies low over a portion of the Siberian forest, a massive, endless expanse of trees, snow, and wind-swept desolation.

The Russian hosts greet their Americans eagerly, one might say voraciously. Their eyes flash bright red as the Americans enter the command center. The two sides remain a comfortable distance from one another. The Russians offer no introductions, no handshakes. Not a word is spoken. In keeping with time-honored traditions of Russian hospitality, their hosts have prepared a welcoming spread of bloody meat and other Vampire-suitable *zakuski* laid out on a table nearest the living room window. A nice buffet spread, Vampire style! Hosts and guests consume a generous quantity of raw, bloody delights, washed down with copious amounts of Vodka and red wine. Vampires barely notice one another as they satisfy their primal hunger pangs.

After lunch, the group members adjourn to their respective rooms to freshen up for what they anticipate will be a fast-paced 24/7 operation. Volkov's actions will dictate if and when they get a break. The Russians return dressed for the occasion in black-on-black clothing, including dramatic billowing, black capes. Iron Feliks, the only outlier, is dressed in his standard heavily starched Chekist uniform complete with tunic.

"WTF?" Elena mouths to Aaron. He shrugs. For their part, the Americans share the same preference for black, although they opt for sleek buttoned-down shirts with black trousers and shoes.

"So American," states one of the Russians; he rolls his eyes as he speaks.

After a round of "awkward-how-we're-all-dressed-in-black" looks, Klemko escorts his guests into the conference room. A bulky oak table fills most of the space. Iron Feliks and Mercader are formally introduced. Klemko begins. "Janicke, you can start by laying out the plans for your side."

"Sure. Let's get straight to business. The Trust has sent two teams to hunt down Volkov. He'll be referred to simply as the Target."

Klemko also wants to depersonalize the hunt for Volkov. "Our side will also refer to Volkov simply as the Target. Please continue."

"One team consists of Leonardi and Marlowe. The other team is Lowell and Masterson. I think you know them. Should I provide you with additional information about them?"

"Ah, no. That won't be necessary. We know them well enough. Good choices, I might add."

"I'll oversee the deployment of our teams in consultation with Rainer Wolf. He'll monitor the operation in real time from his command center in the northern Virginia suburbs with your colleague Beria."

Mercader can't resist an outburst. "Which safe house? Does he need any equipment?"

Unamused, Klemko gives Mercader a dirty look before nodding for Aaron to continue.

"As you know, Beria is now colocated with Wolf. It's essential this operation be joint within our respective command centers. By 'joint,' I mean both sides will have access to all information. Our teams in the field have been ordered to avoid contact. If they encounter one another, they must—and I mean must—immediately break contact. Let's be professional about this: we have a job to do, but we all understand there's no trust between us. Given what's at stake, we can't allow our baser instincts to interfere with our mission."

"Why? Are you afraid?" Mercader says under his breath.

Elena suppresses a laugh. Klemko ignores Mercader's taunting and continues without pause. "On the Russian side, Rubik and Ivan will move on a parallel axis with the team of Marlowe and Leonardi. Boris will shadow Lowell and Masterson. Mercader and Constantin will be held here in reserve and will support the teams in the field. The four teams will be referred to as Team 1 (Rubik and Ivan), Team 2 (Boris), Team 3 (Marlowe and Leonardi), and Team 4 (Lowell and Masterson)."

"Brother. What freakin' gall to give themselves top billing when they need us here to take care of THEIR business," Elena mutters loudly. It's a slap back to Mercader. Vampires can't help themselves when it comes to defending their honor.

The Assassin casts a smile of newfound respect toward Elena. Perhaps he's underestimated her. She's feisty! His eyes flash red while hers return a bright amber glow. Mercader sniffs the air dramatically. There's nothing discreet about the brazen way they're checking each other out. They're case officers. It's part of their job, after all.

Iron Feliks has remained silent. He strokes his goatee, intensely observing the Americans' curious body language. His attention shifts to Klemko and Janicke as the coordinate efforts. So many wasted words. So much excessive motion. Unnecessary drama. Amateurs.

The Vampires discuss the mechanisms they'll use to exchange information in real time. On cue, a System-witting FSB technical officer is ushered in to provide a briefing on the communications equipment and protocols to be issued to the four field teams. The nondescript tech officer departs as quickly as she entered. It's Mercader's turn to brief the group. He outlines arrangements made to meet the remaining Americans upon their arrival at Moscow's Sheremetyevo Airport. Russian customs and border police will waive normal entry procedures and bring the Americans into the country "black"—with no entry stamp. Russian and American teams will be brought directly to the command center for separate operational briefings. Schedules have been arranged so the teams will have no contact with one another.

Later that afternoon, the command center is host to a surprise guest. Vampire Zero arrives unannounced. On cue, Klemko opens the safe house door, clearing the way for Vampire Zero's discreet entrance. System Vampires automatically huddle around their leader. Putin scarcely glances at the Americans on the other side of the room, but intensely sniffs their presence. His upward raised nostrils flare as he takes in scents unknown to him—exotic, rather inviting smells. He delicately wipes a bit of drool from his mouth at the thought of taking a big bite out of his *glavniy protivnik*.

The group members take their seats in the conference room. Russians and Americans are seated on opposite sides of the table. With the aid of a laser pointer, Klemko highlights a dizzying array of technical and human assets deployed to track the Super-Vampire in real time.

Vladimir Putin methodically ticks down a list of questions. "How will you prevent disclosures and media attention that we are hunting a Super-Vampire? What's the cover story?"

"Our legend is based on a threat posed by a Chechen terrorist cell planning the sabotage of a nuclear facility in Russia. Top secret. Strictly need to know. Any disclosures will be handled severely. We keep a list of any unwitting humans who come in contact with Volkov—and will handle that later."

"And our nuclear facilities? What do they know? Are they prepared for Volkov's arrival if our teams don't get to him first?"

"Nuclear installations have been placed on high alert. Russian Spetznaz (Special Forces) have been deployed in response to the cover story—the Chechen terrorist threat. Per your instructions, Sir, our forces are unwitting of the existence of the Super-Vampire."

"Is the search footprint sustainable throughout the course of the operation? How can you ensure the bubble of the Target's movements remains sealed?"

"Sir, we have triggered the full mobilization of the special services, special forces, and various security organs. The enhanced security presence in Moscow and surrounding regions will mask the deployment of our assets to Siberia. We will draw on assets as necessary as we close the bubble around the Target. That said, we will depend on our witting teams of Vampires to close in on him to limit the disclosure of the operation to non-witting forces."

"And how do you guarantee success? How confident are you that our plan will stop Volkov in his tracks?"

Klemko pauses. He has no way to know whether the Vampire teams will actually be successful, even if they can mange to put aside their animosities and cooperate. He chooses his words very carefully. "Sir, our advantage is that we hunt one of our own. We can sense his thoughts, anticipate his moves, as he can ours. This is where our American partners come in. The Target will anticipate our response to neutralize him, but not our alliance with the Trust."

Putin frowns. "'Partners'? 'Partners'? Let's not get carried away, Klemko. All wars require tactical maneuvers for the sake of expediency. This 'alliance,' as you call it, is necessary, but it changes nothing between the System and the Trust!"

Vladimir Putin stares unblinking at Aaron and Elena before turning his attention back to his side of the table. "Should anyone interfere with this operation or become aware of the real nature of our mission, they must be liquidated. No exceptions. For the duration of this activity, normal approvals to kill humans do not apply. It's open season, but only as necessary to preserve the *krisha* (cover) of the operation. Understood?"

The System Vampires rise to attention. Reflexively, Aaron and Elena stand with them. "Vampires rule!"

Janicke mouths "Vampires rule!" as he looks over at Elena. In return she mouths "Vampires drool!" then guards herself to keep from bursting out in laughter.

Vampire Zero leaves as suddenly as he arrived. In short order, all four teams report their respective positions on the ground in Siberia. They're on the move. The operation shifts into high gear. Klemko and Aaron pass initial instructions to their respective teams. Communications are up and running. The first batch of encrypted intelligence feeds is up on the big screen.

It's been a quiet morning, all things considered. Mercader is beside himself trying to figure out why Aaron has quietly filled pages and pages with seemingly random numbers. Is he trying to break the Dead Hand code? Surely he can't be aware of the top secret Russian program. Even Iron Feliks is apprehensive. Is Janicke toying with them? In fact, Janicke is simply memorizing iterations of pi. He has, however, noticed just how well this has driven the Russians to distraction—oh, the enjoyment!

After several uneventful hours, a red light flashes at steady intervals on the large interactive map of Siberia. A report on Volkov's possible location has just come in. The chase is on!

CHAPTER 31
THE CHASE

THE DEAD OF WINTER DEEP IN THE HEART OF SIBERIA IS AN EXCEPtionally inhospitable place. With an average ambient air temperature of minus 40 degrees, high winds and heavy snowfall are constant. Nature's supremacy in this region is enforced via a seemingly unending punishment by a furious rage of violent storms, including debilitating—to humans—meteorological phenomena.

Team 3, Marlowe and Leonardi, have made good time through the ice and snow toward Volkov's last known location. They've covered a large swath of ground without being overly concerned about being seen. The area is desolate. Vampire endurance exceeds even their own expectations. It seems the effects of adrenalin can supercharge Vampires.

Their encrypted KGB communication gear is bulky but reliable. Regular feeds from Elena help guide their movements. Thus far it appears the System has honored their end of the bargain via the provision of unfiltered information on a real-time basis. They stop occasionally to triangulate Volkov's last known movements against three missile silos located in their AOR (area of responsibility).

While the command center provides a steady relay of data, the Americans rely increasingly on their keen Vampire senses for midcourse corrections.

Confident they're headed in the right direction, they gain ground on their unsuspecting target. Volkov's heavy stench lingers long after he's passed and his aura hangs faintly in the air. It appears as a filthy, brown haze visible only to Vampires. Their advantage: Volkov hasn't been exposed to the scent of a Trust Vampire. Given the mission, he'll eventually alight on their unique scent, but hopefully not before they've closed in on him.

In parallel, Team 1, consisting of Terrible Ivan and Rubik, track the Super-Vampire in the wake of his filthy stench. After about an hour, the Russian team comes across the mutilated carcass of a freshly slaughtered cow lying stiff in a pool of frozen blood near the outskirts of a small, isolated village. They follow the Super-Vampire's lingering scent through the maze of an endless Siberian forest. After about an hour, they emerge into a small clearing to find fresh footprints in the snow. They're barefoot and enormous.

Rubik turns to his colleague. "Ivan, Volkov is huge—he's much larger than I expected. We need to report this."

Terrible Ivan is impressed. There's nothing he wants more than to confront the Super-Vampire. When Terrible Ivan first keys the radio to render their report, Rubik stays his hand. "Ivan, wait. We are closer to Volkov than those weak Americans. Wouldn't it be better if we took care of this nasty business ourselves?"

Ivan is perplexed. "Rubik, I can't hear you. Our orders are clear. Vampire Zero wants the Americans, not us, to liquidate the Target. There's nothing to discuss. We cannot defy orders."

Rubik snaps back. "Ivan, why should the Americans be given this honor? It will only strengthen the power of the Trust at our expense. Volkov is one of us, is he not? It is our sacred duty to deal with him."

Ivan is gruff. "Perhaps that is as it should be, but it is not for us to decide."

Rubik refuses to relent. "What are we to do when, I mean if we come across Volkov first?"

Terrible Ivan wags a disapproving finger at his comrade. Rubik jumps in before he has a chance to say anything. "Okay, our mission is to track him. So let's track him. I have no intention of waiting for the Americans to catch up to us. They're slow, soft. Unfit to go against us, much less Volkov!"

Terrible Ivan isn't known for his intellectual prowess, but he's smart enough to see the mistake in defying Vladimir Putin. He puts his right hand on Rubik's shoulder sympathetically. "Rubik, what's the big deal? Relax. The sooner we get this job over with, the better. I'd rather be dining on the Americans than working with them."

After a short pause, Rubik takes a long draw from his oversized flask of vodka. He throws his arms up in frustration and the two trudge off through the heavy snow.

Teddy and the Professor head along a preplanned reconnaissance route in the event Volkov's destination is one of the three different missile silos in this general area. As scientists, they're fascinated by Siberia's inhospitable climactic conditions. The fact that they actually thrive in this extreme cold is discomfiting to them. Psychologically, they're still in denial and refuse to embrace the less human characteristics of their species. As the Professor likes to say phlegmatically when asked how he's doing, "Well, it's been a bit of a struggle."

To make the point that they haven't changed, Teddy is dressed in a thick wool cape and hat. The Professor wears an oversized wool coat, which conceals a bag strapped to his waist. And yet they move with accelerated speed in spite of themselves, only vaguely aware of the ease and grace with which they're able to navigate these harsh conditions.

By late evening, they've triangulated the three missile silos and selected a base camp position roughly equidistant between the three locations. With sufficient advance notice from the command center, they should be able to intercept Volkov well before he's within striking distance. Base camp established, they await news of the Target's current location and destination.

Meanwhile, the pace of activity in the command center has become hectic. Information streams in from a variety of intelligence sources—HUMINT, SIGINT, IMINT, NTM. The Target's rampaging, straight-line trajectory has made him easier to track. He's on a relentless quest to fulfill his destiny. The Super-Vampire relies on a steady consumption of fresh blood to fuel his accelerate pace.

Terrified local villagers report the grisly discovery of decapitated and mutilated human bodies in hunting lodges and remote houses around their village.

In a different section of the Siberian wilderness, Boris is serene as he progresses through the seemingly endless tundra. Yet to come across any information of value, he basks in the solitude and raw beauty of the surrounding countryside. Strong Arctic blasts are but an inconvenience to the System Vampire. His body is invigorated by nature entombed in snow and ice. He stops just long enough to take off his shoes and sink his feet deep in the cold sensation of the landscape, twiddling his toes in delight.

Alone in the cold, Boris reflects retrospectively on Klemko's decision to designate him, a singleton, as Team 2. Nothing Klemko does is by coincidence. What does Klemko intend by isolating him in this way? Perhaps Klemko questions his loyalty to *Systema*. Do they know Sergey Deniken is still alive? Considering Klemko's peerless skills of manipulation and deception, it's not out of the question this joint operation is a well-conceived three-dimensional chess game designed to rid the System of three enemies in one fell swoop: Volkov, the Trust, and Boris. If so, it's a brilliant plan. Boris would be disappointed if Klemko hadn't at least considered it. Given the alternatives, Boris would rather take his chances with Volkov than twist in the wind on a dead Vampire's noose.

Exasperated, Boris lets out a guttural howl summoned straight from the depths of hell. "VOLLLLLKOV!"

His response is only the repeated echoes of his own voice. Another even louder cry is let loose. "VOLLLLLLKOV!!!"

Silence. He looks up to the heavens for encouragement. With all his rage, Boris offers a final call to summon the Super-Vampire. "VOLLLLLLLLLLKOV!!!"

Same response: only repeated echoes. A old Russian proverb comes to mind: "До Бʹога высокʹо, до Царʹя далекʹо." "Damn you both!"

In a final act of isolated defiance, Boris spits high in the air. His spit freezes before it hits the snowpack. Keep moving!

CHAPTER 32
MASKIROVKA

This particular Siberian winter is one of the most unusual in recorded Russian history. Aside from the expected extreme cold and blinding snowstorms, a rhythmic pattern of meteorological microbursts continues to rotate in series of short durations that ignite extremely violent winter storms. Unfortunately, this rare weather phenomenon plays to the Super-Vampire's advantage. He's become almost impossible to track. Human surveillance means have been reduced to the production of intermittent hits on the Target's location and activity. The command center has to rely to a greater extent than anticipated on the four deployed Vampire teams.

Terrible Ivan and Rubik react to reports now streaming in from the command center. Fresh tracks and other indications of the Target's location are being reported with increased frequency. Volkov can't be more than an hour or two ahead of them. He appears to be headed toward Silo 585B, near the village of Igarka on the Yenisey River. That critical piece of information is duly relayed to Marlowe and Leonardi, who close in on the Target's last reported location.

The responsiveness of the American team has frustrated Rubik. He pushes his partner to increase their pace. Ivan stops them in their tracks. "*Tovarish*, I know what you are doing."

"What am I doing, Ivan? Stop thinking so much. It is not your strong suit. Are we not positioning the Americans for the kill, as we have been ordered?"

"Bah!" Terrible Ivan is not fooled.

"And lay off the Vodka until this is over."

The search takes the two Russian Vampires to a remote village imprisoned away from the rest of the world by the brutal Siberian winter. This village had the great misfortune of being located directly within Volkov's path of devastation. In the center of the village System Vampires encounter a terrified crowd gathered in the old town hall, armed with old hunting rifles, knives, and other makeshift weapons. Containers of food, water, and ammunition are stacked neatly along the back wall. One villager, dressed in a large fur overcoat and fur mittens, presents a sickle affixed to the end of a long, wooden shaft he insists is razor sharp. A Russian Orthodox priest stands in the middle of the room, brandishing a large wooden cross. He shakes uncontrollably. His teeth chatter loudly.

A large bonfire burns a few dozen meters from the entrance to the town hall in stark contrast to the blowing snow. The contrast of a whiteout atmosphere against the light of a burning bonfire is quite a mesmerizing sight, reminiscent of a scene from a black-and-white Frankenstein movie.

The Russian Vampires survey the crowd. After a few minutes, the village mayor cautiously approaches them. The two strangers are obviously not from these parts. The old man is wise enough not to ask their names or question why they're not dressed for the cold. He simply motions for them to follow. Maybe they can help.

Villagers slowly gather around the mayor, who excitedly recites tales of the large, inhuman creature who swept through the village like a tempest, leaving only death and mutilation behind. Others stand in the shadows, sobbing and fearfully holding onto one another. Floorboards creak and scattered coughs resonate in the barren town hall.

Pathos and desperation smell something like wet mold to Vampires. Rubik again surveys the crowd pressed tightly against the mayor. Ivan picks long icicles from his bushy beard. The Vampires pity the poor villagers. Terrible Ivan addresses the crowd. "Which way did this creature go?"

Some peasants fall to their knees, lower their heads, and make the sign of the cross. No one actually believed the monster folklore they took delight in passing on to the next generation. Parents told their children fairy tales about nocturnal monsters, tales meant to steel them against the hardships of life. Tonight, the worst of their bedtime stories stands right there in front of them. No one dares make eye contact with the two strangers. Finally, an intrepid old woman, short and frail, with thick, gray hair and piercing green eyes, walks over to the open door. Her heavy blue overcoat is unbuttoned from the waist down and blows open as she exposes herself directly to the frigid, arctic blast. She points a long, thin, shaking finger past the bonfire toward the steppes lying beyond the village. She doesn't so much as utter a word.

Rubik puts his arm around his Vampire companion's shoulder in satisfaction. "Time to move in for the kill!"

Ivan the Terrible turns, smirks, and makes conspiratorial eye contact with Rubik. His voice shakes the rafters of the forgotten village. They shout in unison. "The Trust be damned! Vampires rule!"

With a dashing *Spasibo* and a gallant bow, the two Vampires sprint from the building and quickly fade into the Arctic white, determined to catch Volkov before the trail runs cold. Two large men armed with long-barrel hunting rifles close and barricade the doors of the town hall while the old woman remains standing in the same spot, pointing toward hell on earth.

A report of this latest development will have to wait. Rubik flips the switch on his radio to the off position. He looks over to Ivan. "Too much static. We can try to recontact the command center after we move to somewhere with better reception."

With some luck, their next transmission will report how they stumbled across and dispatched the rogue Volkov.

Marlowe and Leonardi haven't received any updates on Volkov's position for over an hour. Not overly concerned, they rely more on their gathering senses to follow the sulphur odor of danger as they emerge from the forest into a small clearing. Their direction of travel is confirmed by a trail of thin, brown mist. The snowstorm has tapered off and a light snow continues to fall. Gray clouds grudgingly part to reveal hints of a blue sky. The two Vampires push through the pristine, waist-deep snow into a large clearing and up to an old, white house.

A row of stairs leads to an open front door. No sign or scent of life. The abandoned two-story house is a precommunist-era relic of the former landowner's majestic estate. The steeply pitched roof is topped by a long spire, the only artifact still visible through the deep blanket of snow. This once elegant manor house is now entombed by the Siberian winter. The interior is completely frozen and wrapped in an iridescent mix of snow and ice. Their light footsteps emit a muted crunch as they enter the house and slowly fan out across the great room. They carefully survey the entrance to a large dining room. Joe stands erect, his ears attuned to the slightest sound. Viktor is hunched over; his nose almost touches the blanket of snow covering a floor of ice. He places his left hand palm down on the floor to sense any tremors of movement. "Mad Dog, I smell Vampires. They're not ours."

"I know, Joe. They're in the house."

They hear the unmistakable creak of a foot lightly placed on a loose plank of wood. In response, their nostrils flare at the prospect of imminent immortal combat. Ice formed around their eyes melts in the heat of a bright amber glow. Their slow breaths forms a clean, frozen mist. Communication is telepathic. Their senses are coordinated to track an unseen prey.

In the middle of the dining room, a young boy of about seven crouches on the floor, shivering, frozen in fear. He's hidden himself under a thick wool blanket while holding his pet dog, whose throat had been slashed. Joe gently lifts the blanket and the boy off the floor.

Joe and Viktor realize a trap has just been sprung. Leonardi gingerly places the boy on the floor in a far corner of the room. They move to the center and assume defensive positions, prepared for an attack from any direction. Joe whispers to Viktor. "The boy. Dog. Blood. Bait. Bait for Vampires. Here we go."

Their eyes follow the sound of footsteps coming from an entrance on the opposite side of the room. Rubik and Terrible Ivan have also tracked Volkov to this same house and are surprised to encounter the two Americans instead of their prey.

The System and the Trust confront one another face-to-face. Rubik makes no attempt to conceal his satisfaction at this chance encounter. He's been in this situation once before and is determined to write a different end to the story. He's the first to speak. "Well, well, what a pleasant surprise. It would seem we were all drawn here by the one we hunt. If we cannot claim Volkov as our trophy on this day, then we will have to settle for you!"

The four Vampires circle one another slowly. Eyes meet in flashes of red and amber. Marlowe attempts to defuse the situation. "Listen to me! We're not the mastermind of this encounter. Obviously Volkov has tricked us. He's spread this trail of crumbs to lure us into a trap. Our Target will be the beneficiary of our distraction. Can't you see that?!"

Rubik is undeterred. Terrible Ivan is growling. "A worthy adversary should be appreciated like vodka, or like the fine wine you prefer, Marlowe. I'll savor lapping the warm blood that flows through your veins!"

The Russians are in no mood to be denied. At this point, neither are the Americans. Too much bad history between them. Too much blood has been spilled between them. Ah, yes… blood! All four Vampires' fangs tingle in anticipation of a hard bite. Warm, flowing blood. With a piercing howl, Rubik launches at Marlowe from halfway across the room. They meet midair and crash to the ground in a thunderous thud.

Terrible Ivan gives a shrug before striding purposefully toward Leonardi. He'll make this quick. Items of frozen furniture break into thousands of tiny pieces as the four combatants move at flashing speed. Marlowe and Rubik engage in sword play with their razor-sharp claws. On the floor, on the walls, and on the ceiling, they exchange blows! A large, frozen chandelier is brought crashing to the floor, and still the Vampires fight on at full throttle. Thick ice coating the surfaces of the room scatters and slowly melts as it makes contact with splattered Vampire flesh and blood.

Joe slips on the ice-caked carpet and falls flat on his back. In a nanosecond, Terrible Ivan is on top of him. He strikes several vicious slashes across Joe's face followed by a barrage of mighty blows directly to his chest. Warm, dark red blood flows from deep wounds faster than Joe's body can heal itself. Terrible Ivan is close to victory. As Joe lies exposed on the floor, he spots an improvised weapon just beyond his reach.

With all his remaining strength, the wounded American Vampire knocks Terrible Ivan backward far enough so that he can regain a fighting stance. The massive Russian mounts yet another charge. Joe reaches for and breaks off a large wooden shaft entombed in a thick shell of ice. With the momentum of Ivan's lunge, Joe falls backward but with the sharp edge of the shaft pointed at his enemy's chest. The continued forward progress of Ivan's lunge attack secures his death. As they both fall backward, the wooden shaft is plunged deep into Ivan's chest at the point of his heart. Ice shatters, leaving only the wooden stake intact, which emerges several inches through the Russian Vampire's back.

Joe maintains his grip on the stake, keeping it firmly lodged in the Vampire's heart. Terrible Ivan is bewildered as he looks in disbelief at his mortal wound. Rubik breaks contact with Marlowe and runs over to his dying companion. "No, no, no, this cannot be. What have I done?"

He sobs uncontrollably, cradling Terrible Ivan's head in his arms. The red glow in Ivan's eyes slowly fades. His speech is slow, labored. He struggles to breathe. "So this is what death feels like. I've felt worse. This isn't so bad, Rubik. One last sip of vodka before I go. Tell Vampire Zero I was a warrior to the end. Goodbye old friend."

The Vampires shield their eyes in anticipation of Ivan's passing. After several rapid, intense bursts of light, he's gone. All that's left of Terrible Ivan is a few drops of water mixed with ash.

At the command center, Elena Constantin sways back and forth in a trance. Eyes shut tight, the Oracle reacts to each blow as they're exchanged between Vampires. She moans loudly as the death struggle between Leonardi and Terrible Ivan reaches its climax. Command center cadre have formed a circle around Constantin. They watch in rapt silence.

Elena suddenly cries out, "It's done!" At the very moment Terrible Ivan vanishes in a fireworks display, Elena slumps to the floor, exhausted. Even Iron Feliks is awestruck. A witness to an extraordinary scene. Instinctively, Mercader jumps to Elena's aid. He gently lifts her from the floor and places her outstretched on a nearby sofa. She looks up at him, expressionless. "Terrible Ivan is dead."

Back in Siberia, the Trust Vampires quickly exit the house. Rubik is alone and still on his knees at the spot where his friend died. Out of breath, Viktor Marlowe contacts Aaron at the command center.

"Team 1 and Team 3 crossed paths. Ivan is dead. Joe is gravely wounded. He'll heal eventually, but he's out of action for now. Fuckin' Volkov sprang a trap to distract us—set human bait. It's a misdirection ploy. He's not headed for Silo 585B. We're out of the hunt. Team 4 is our only hope. Two scientists. How ironic."

At the command center, Klemko tries unsuccessfully to raise Rubik on the radio. After several tries, he puts down the handset and hangs his head. Out of the corner of his eye, he catches Iron Feliks's wan smile. Visibly upset, Klemko walks over to Putin's deputy and pokes him in the chest with his right index finger. "We have lost a brother. Have you no soul?"

Iron Feliks is placid. "*Dorogoi Drug*, none of us have souls. I mourn for the comrade we lost as you do, but that will not bring him back. We must consider what has happened today unemotionally, with no nostalgia for the past, but with a clear eye to the future."

Klemko makes no attempt to hide his emotions. "Comrade, you're crazier than Volkov. What do you mean?"

"What I mean, *Tovarish*, is that this Super-Vampire has proven himself more cunning than the Trust and the System combined. His skill at strategic deception—*Maskirovka*—is beautiful to behold, is it not? It was an elegant move. Distract us. Provoke us. How can it be denied? Volkov is the teacher and we are his students. Our Target is the worthy adversary, the *krainy vrag* we have always sought to justify our existence. No one should doubt the need for *Systema* in Russia after this day."

Klemko resists the temptation to respond because he knows Iron Feliks is right—but for all the wrong reasons.

At the CIA safe house in northern Virginia, Wolf and Beria closely monitor the news. Volkov has eluded Teams 1 and 3. Wolf, in his capacity as DDO, is forwarded an urgent phone call from the chief of the Counterintelligence Center, Alan Tourier. Talk about bad timing! Tourier requests an urgent meeting, preferably tonight. He refers cryptically to an ongoing investigation for which he needs DDO approval to undertake certain actions. Wolf reluctantly agrees to meet. This distraction is the last thing he needs right now.

Later the same evening, they meet at a French restaurant in McLean, Virginia. Tourier is convinced the Russians have a mole in the CIA. He's also concluded this mole has some connection to an FSB officer named Sergey Deniken who walked into Bucharest Station several years ago. Tourier, known as a low talker, speaks in an even lower voice to ensure no one can eavesdrop. "Rainer, bear with me. I don't want you to think I've lost it. The walk-in, Deniken, was dismissed as a nut case. I'm not so sure. The Vampire story is ridiculous of course. But let's suppose the Russians are doing some kind of bioweapons research. That might explain the symptoms described by Deniken. We're picking up strange reports about unexplainable Russian bioresearch. Looks like they may even be experimenting on human subjects. Let me stress—unconfirmed reports. We're also getting information on a serious accident at the bio facility in Sergey Posad. What do you suppose it means?"

"Alan, that doesn't make sense. Why would bioweapons research have any connection to Russian intelligence efforts to recruit a penetration in the CIA? I'm reaching here."

Tourier can't contain himself. "Just a wild theory, but what if a bioweapon was developed that caused physical and mental changes to a target, made him or her more vulnerable to recruitment? As you well know, the KGB had a long history of dabbling in mind control. They're into all sorts of exotic drugs and substances. Maybe this is a next gen project."

"And how would that work, Alan? It sounds preposterous."

"I don't know, Rainer. All I need is your approval to investigate the possibility. I need to pull some operational files plus dig into some personnel files of active and retired officers who may fit the general description of the symptoms Deniken reported."

Wolf feels physically ill. It's hard to eat fully cooked food—disgusting. Each bite makes him want to wretch. Plus he has a splitting headache. He musters a laugh in an effort to disarm Tourier. "Alan, do you hear yourself? You need to take a break. Perhaps it's time for a vacation. Don't worry. If there's a Russian mole, we're gonna nail the bastard. I have complete confidence in you. If there's anything you need, let me know. Oh, and keep this crazy talk to yourself."

Alan relaxes disappointedly as he gazes down into his plate of half-eaten Normandy chicken fricassee followed by a large gulp from his glass of Argentinian Malbec. "I guess you're right, Rainer. It sounds crazy when I hear myself say it."

CHAPTER 33
THE RACE TO SILO 747

THE STORM HAS FINALLY PAUSED—FOR NOW. Special operations have recommenced. The atmosphere in the command center is nothing less than frantic. Progress: a Russian military helicopter carrying a team of elite, Spetznaz soldiers zeroes in on the Super-Vampire's last known location, about seventy miles east of the closest silo. Command center personnel remain glued to the interactive map TV monitor. The Spetznaz team leader reports, "We have him in our sights. We are engaging!"

Command center speakers fill the room with the sound of heavy gunfire. A reaction of cautions optimism prevails until, moments later, communications go dead. The flashing red blip tracking the helicopter's transponder is gone. Minutes later a separate report provides confirmation the helicopter was caught in a wet microburst and went down, exact whereabouts unknown. No survivors.

A report of the incident is immediately relayed to Team 4, Teddy and the Professor. After having shaken Teams 1 and 2, Volkov is headed in their general direction. Trust Vampires benefit from live data feeds of the Target's movement as he rapidly approaches the outskirts of the three missile silos in their area.

Unfortunately, the American Vampires continue to lose ground on their quarry. All Vampires possess a certain sixth sense in their ability to navigate unfamiliar terrain. This internal compass even works in places as inhospitable and vast as the Siberian wilderness. Vampires can see clearly through haze, smoke, and other weather conditions. However, the intensity of the earlier white-out blizzard has slowed Team 4's pace in comparison to the others.

Janicke decides to assert leadership, whatever that means in this situation. "God dammit, Teddy! The Target is ahead of you. You have to step it up. How can you let that Russian Vampire outrun you?! What the fuck, Lowell!"

Teddy responds, annoyed. "We know what the hell we're doing—do you? This isn't a Vampire-damn race! We need to get to the right silo before he does. There are three silos in front of us—747, 837A, and 936B. Can you confirm his destination? Until you can, we're trying to keep all three silos roughly equidistant."

"Teddy, we're not certain where he's headed. Where does that leave you, for planning purposes?"

Teddy's frustrated. "Okay, according to our calculations, Volkov's in front of us only if he's headed for Silo 936B. But we don't think that's his goal. Too linear. Too obvious. Most likely, he's headed for silo 747. Silo 747 is farthest from his current position to the east. The bastard's smarter than anyone thought, Aaron. I think he plans to surprise us as well. That's our best guess."

Aaron involuntarily laughs into the mike. "Guess?! Your fuckin' guess? That's the best you can do?"

Teddy fires back. His face flushes with anger. "What's so damn funny? The world's about to be obliterated and you're laughing? If you're done being an asshole, maybe we can get back to this saving the world from nuclear Armageddon."

Mental note, Aaron. Stop making jokes in inappropriate situations. On the other hand, can't imagine better material than a Russian Super-Vampire all hellbent on mutually assured destruction, with only Teddy and the Professor standing between him and judgment day. Kinda funny, when you think about it. Aaron puts on a straight face. *Get your head back in the game.*

"Based on the Target's last known position and assuming he's headed for Silo 747, how much early warning do you need to get there before he does?"

There is a brief pause while Teddy calculates time of travel from their current position to the silo.

"Any time now. Yeah, NOW!"

"Shit! Go, GO!"

"Got it. On the way. 4 out."

Direct and intense, a female Russian speaking voice crackles in loud, tinny resonance over one of the many radio speakers in the room. Reports confirm another Spetznaz helicopter, bound for Silo 747, has crashed in white-out conditions, which have suddenly returned. Two other choppers headed for Silos 837A and 936B will have to maneuver wide around the center of the storm before they can proceed to their objectives. Caution: each helo has only about forty-five minutes of fuel remaining.

At the command center, the three System Vampires stand semi-stunned, staring motionlessly at the main TV monitor. Iron Feliks sums up their thoughts dryly. "The Russian winter has saved us in our darkest hours. Napoleon. Hitler. Today, our cruel winter has become the agent of our own destruction."

Everyone ignores him. No one's ready to concede anything to the rogue Super-Vampire. Klemko walks over to address Aaron, standing behind the Russians. "Volkov is headed for 747. I sense it. So do you. He has a score to settle with us before he turns his attention to humanity. He'll be waiting for your Vampires at 747."

Klemko makes one more appearance on his personal stage. He's a firm believer in the philosophy that a bit of drama adds spice to any situation, but especially in dire circumstances. "Your Wilfred and Liam are our last hope. I wish them only success in their mission, on behalf of mankind." He walks away with a wave, overacted.

Elena catches Aaron's eye. She mouths the words "Drama Queen," then rolls her eyes for emphasis.

Teddy and the Professor are about to test the limits of their superhuman endurance in a desperate race to Silo 747. They need time to deactivate Dead Hand before Volkov breaches the facility. In reality, they're less sanguine about the prospect of overpowering the Super-Vampire. But they have no other choice than to try.

Klemko steps from the conference room into the privacy of an adjoining bedroom and closes the door. After a moment of reflection, he decides to take matters into his own hands. Right now the least of his worries is what Putin will do to him if he fails. A radio handset is keyed.

"Boris, proceed to Silo 747 immediately. You must get there before the Trust. Is that understood?"

Boris hesitates. "I'm shadowing Team 4, as you have ordered. I will proceed to Silo 747 immediately, but I am behind them. There is no time to close the gap unless they run into trouble."

"Boris, listen very carefully. You must take out Volkov. If you can, intercept the Target before he reaches 747. If you cannot, sprint to 747 and confront him in the facility. I will order security to delay Volkov and the Americans if they arrive before you. The Trust is too weak to complete this task. We cannot put the fate of the world in their hands. You must do it."

Boris is distant. "My understanding is the Trust has been ordered to eliminate Volkov. The Trust and the System are not to commingle under any circumstances. Has our president countermanded those orders?"

"Jesus, Boris! The world is about to explode and you're questioning orders. Yes! These are Vampire Zero's orders. Do it now! Vampires rule!"

"Message received."

Boris acknowledges the order and quickly stows the bulky communications device without returning the System's salute. He sniffs deeply for Volkov's scent through the barrier of icy crust formed on his nostrils. Red-hot eyes quickly melt the falling snow accumulated on his brow. Once more, Boris issues a blood-curdling call to his quarry. "VOLLLLLLLLLLLKOVVVVVV!"

Off in the distance, the Super-Vampire is brought to a halt in the deep solitude of the forest. The faint call from his stalker resonates familiar. It can't be. It's *Tovarish* Boris—gentle Myshkin! Volkov nostalgically recalls his days as a loyal member of *Systema*. This wasn't the way he wanted things to end. But those days are behind him now. The arrow of time points only forward. His destiny lies unimpeded before him. Very soon he'll prove his worth to Vampire Zero. Fortunately for Team 4, the Super-Vampire hasn't consumed any blood for several hours. Lack of fuel has slowed his pace.

In the chaos of his mental state, Volkov doesn't comprehend the other team of Trust Vampires hot on his trail, relentlessly determined to deny him his destiny. Boris's cry in the wilderness causes Volkov to temporarily let his guard down. The pause of nostalgic reflection has given him reason to question himself, even if slightly.

Inexplicably, the mad-Vampire Volkov makes another, brief mistake—he stops in the middle of a small clearing to take stock of himself. At twelve hundred meters overhead, an FSB drone catches his image, relayed in real time to the command center. The fact that the drone survived the last blizzard is somewhat of a miracle. The weather-besieged trackers catch another break when the clouds break just enough to zero in on the Target's fuzzy form. From the command center, Mercader has taken remote control of the drone. Elena can't help but assist. Seated next to Mercader, she helps navigate the craft toward its unsuspecting target. Aaron notes the irony of these two archfiends working together, if only in this key moment of the hunt.

Something else has Klemko distracted. He's intuitively cognizant of Iron Feliks's hidden desire for Volkov to elude his pursuers. Aside from the potential catastrophic consequences of Volkov's mad quest to destroy humanity, the original Chekist, Iron Feliks, is pondering a deep philosophical question. Are Vampires the fulfillment of a long-held socialist dream to produce a higher expression of man? Perhaps Volkov can be cured and meet his highest potential, thereby raising mankind's own expectations as a species—the fulfillment of the ideal of a new Soviet man. If only he could be captured alive.

Aaron relays Volkov's last known coordinates to Team 4. "Teddy, the drone will try to slow him down by forcing him to seek cover. Get to the Silo, lock yourselves inside the launch center, and deactivate Dead Hand before the target arrives. Erect one hell of a barrier to buy time. Be prepared to engage inside the confines of the launch room where his size may work against him. Be prepared to make a final stand in the launch center. Final stand. WTF. There are worse ways to go."

Teddy groans. He reaches deep to summon up all his courage. "Don't worry, Aaron. We've got this."

The Professor swallows hard, scratching his bald scalp. "Okay, I'm fine with that... But let's hope it doesn't come down to us."

As usual, the scrupulous scientist is just being realistic. The plan, if you can call it that, comes together. If they can get to the silo in time, Team 4 will deactivate Dead Hand. The command center will talk them through the lengthy procedure. If they can't deactivate the launch sequence, they'll have to pick the best physical location to ambush Volkov. If Volkov gets on the computer, he'll try to trick the Soviet-era launch protocol into believing the US has launched a nuclear attack. Dead Hand will then automatically launch a Russian counterattack. Mutually - Assured - Destruction!

As the American Vampires race toward mayhem, Volkov's attention is on the sound of a faint rumble high in the sky above. With Elena's help, Mercader has the crosshairs of the drone's heat-seeking missile centered directly on the target. Even a direct hit won't be enough to eliminate Volkov, but it should significantly slow him down.

Mercader's finger slowly pulls the trigger with crosshairs perfectly aligned. Volkov is, however, steps ahead of the action. His red eyes aglow, he makes telepathic contact with Mercader. The two Vampires lock in on one another. A test of wills. Within seconds, Mercader is overpowered by intense pain. The joystick falls from his hand as he collapses on the floor. Jolts of electricity contort his body. Almost a thousand miles away, Volkov pumps a knowing victory fist before he melts away in a mad dash toward silo 747.

Escape and evasion from Mercader's unsuccessful drone strike slow Volkov down, allowing Teddy and the Professor to arrive first at the silo. They slip by the phalanx of Russian military personnel guarding the perimeter. Their concentration is focused in the direction of the bright inferno of another Spetznaz helicopter crash, the victim of another microburst snowstorm.

The vacated silo entrance is locked and further secured by a tamper-proof seal. Silo security forces expect Chechen terrorists to attack them at any moment, as was briefed. But fears are spreading that something more sinister is afoot. Conspiracy theories are running rampant among the guard force that Chechen terrorists are advancing toward them with a terrible inhuman creature in the lead. Not taking any chances, they have barricaded themselves behind the thick blast-proof metal door.

The American Vampires have no intention of making a frontal assault on the facility. Once they reach the silo, they scale its outer walls to the rooftop. Based on the small scale model studied in the command center, they plan to enter the facility through a locked heavy metal maintenance door that also affords access to a tunnel that ultimately leads to the silo's launch center.

With a Vampire spider's sense of touch and his natural mechanical ability, Teddy is able to easily pick the lock of the also blast-proof maintenance door. They pull the large door open just enough to squeeze by and crawl into the musty chamber. Once the door is pushed shut, Teddy picks the lock back to the secured position.

The pitch-black silo interior poses no issues for the Vampires. Alert with eyes glowing amber, the two crawl silently through the silo access tunnel, then scale down the grails of its inner walls onto the ground floor of the facility.

The launch control center is located at the end of a long walkway framed entirely in thick slabs of gray concrete. They've made an end run of the silo's physical security. Fortunately the security force was deployed in a Maginot Line–style of defense intended to stop an anticipated frontal terrorist assault. The silo interior, to include the launch control center, was left abandoned.

One long minute later, or maybe two, Teddy has picked open the lock to the launch control room door—all with rather rudimentary, quickly improvised tools. The two Vampires enter the launch room. Lowell picks the door locked from the inside while Masterson takes position at the launch computer. Communication with the Moscow command center is established. Teddy does his best to hastily build a barrier of heavy metal objects stacked against the entrance door.

Lowell: "I really hope we don't have to fight that big bastard."

Masterson: "What do you mean we? I'm stuck here playing with this antique piece of crap Atari-like computer. Only a couple of generations beyond punch cards. This is gonna take some time."

With Aaron's assent, Klemko barks orders at Team 4 as if they're members of the System. He methodically talks the Professor through the roughly eighty steps required to disengage Dead Hand. The last line of code will shut the computer down, but it can't be entered until the machine has processed and accepted the lengthy protocol. Only then will Dead Hand disengage.

Klemko speaks deliberately, ritualistically reciting each step of code word protocol directly from the Strategic Rocket Forces launch control manual. Password accepted. The Professor, with Teddy right beside him, recites each step verbatim before executing. The margin for error is zero. If the launch computer identifies possible intrusion efforts, it will shut itself down. If it concludes an intruder has attempted to shut it down, it could initiate the launch sequence on its own.

The Professor can't contain his frustration. "This is impossible! The piece of shit computer reacts skeptically to each command. It's as if the thing is alive and doubts the provenance of the commands we're inputting."

The process is interrupted by a series of loud crashes and bangs. Volkov has announced his arrival via a full-frontal assault on the facility. The gates, guards, and guns are but a nuisance to the rampaging Super-Vampire. He's launched an all-out *Blitz Krieg* on the silo. Nothing could have prepared security forces for Volkov's fury. In the name of operational secrecy, the command center alerted the guard force to an imminent attack by Chechen terrorists. They weren't prepared to defend against a Super-Vampire. Even had they known the truth, it wouldn't have made a difference.

A visibly nervous Teddy has concentrated his attention on the massive steel door. He's brandishing a four-foot length of one-half-inch-diameter metal pipe, the tip sharpened into an improvised weapon. He's the team's diversionary effort should Volkov manage to breach their defenses before the computer is powered down.

"Uh, Liam, I don't want to worry you unduly," Teddy deadpans, "but you'd better hurry. By my rough estimate and based on the sound of Volkov's approach, we don't have much time left to do this."

They hear Volkov systematically peeling through layers of FSB and military security on his pell-mell assault on their location. Interludes of tense silence are interrupted by a flurry of automatic weapons fire, explosions, loud bangs, and bloodcurdling screams. The sounds keep getting louder and closer. Then all goes quiet. Wilfred and Liam alert to an unspeakable evil, breathing heavily. Volkov is on the other side of the launch center door.

The Professor realizes they don't have enough time to complete the arduous step-by-step disengagement protocol. With an air of resignation in his voice, he notifies the command center. "The Target IS prepared to breach our position. Hurry up, dammit! We need to speed this up!"

Klemko continues to bark orders to keep them focused. "No matter what happens, Trust Vampire 5, you must stay on the computer. The sequence cannot be interrupted. There is no way to speed it up. Vampire 4, delay the Target long enough to complete the protocol."

Teddy grabs the mike. "This is Vampire 4. Yes, there is a way to speed it up. Talk twice as fast and dispense with the bullshit ritual."

Hunched over the small screen, the Professor enters the next stream of instructions now coming in like machine-gun bursts. Instinct takes over. He stares at the computer in an attempt to form a Vampire–computer mind meld. Perhaps a coincidence, but the archaic computer's processor actually picks up speed. The Professor's fingers are now a blur on the keyboard.

Fortunately, the Professor is in his element. The rapidly scrolling numbers are quickly processed. He makes an attempt to vent the tension in the room. "Hey Wilfred. What ever happened to Viktor and Joe? This is more up their alley."

Teddy is in no mood for quips. "Focus, Liam. Focus!"

Meanwhile, Volkov has regained his strength. He hurls his body against the thick metal door, which is bent inward. The second charge buckles the door. He's in on his third try. The glow of the Super-Vampire's red eyes beacon through the metal barrier. Sheer rage. A few hundred pounds of scrap metal is all that stands between him and the computer station.

Volkov pauses long enough to size up his adversaries. He could have breached the makeshift barrier with ease, but instead chose to pick through it piece by piece, selectively heaving metal bookshelves and desks all over the place in a calculated show of strength intended to intimidate his enemy and buy some time to recharge before a final assault.

At long last, Volkov stands directly before his American opponents. His hulking presence makes the room seem much smaller. He relishes in the anticipation he'll soon dine on their warm blood. After he's taken control of the thermonuclear weapons of course. The rogue System Vampire and his Trust adversaries square off in a battle that will determine the fate of the world.

CHAPTER 34
BY HIS OWN HAND

EVEN A SUPER-VAMPIRE NEEDS TIME TO LICK HIS WOUNDS. Volkov is weakened by injuries sustained from hits by heavy weapons and explosives. A large section of his shoulder was torn off by a rocket-propelled grenade (RPG). Fresh blood mixed with chunks of flesh are smeared all over his upper body. Blood and goo mix with melting ice to form pools of water around his feet. His grotesquely disfigured, distended frame is matched only by the stench he continues to exude.

To their surprise, the American Vampires are not afraid. Likely death is met with expectant calm. It all makes perfect sense to them now. Without question, the formation of the Trust was necessary. Their mission to save the world was not a fantasy of Rainer Wolf's overactive imagination, after all. The improbable joint operation between the System and the Trust is humanity's last hope to avert thermonuclear war. There is no place they'd rather be than in this command center, trapped with a Super-Vampire.

Even while on the run, Volkov has continued to transform. He's swollen into something of a beast of mythological proportions. The constrained dimensions of the launch control center cause him to hunch over. Several gaping wounds slowly close, emitting a dark red-green viscous ooze. A large fold of scar tissue has grown to replace the chunk of shoulder torn away earlier by an RPG. Volkov glowers menacingly at his enemies while he picks out bullets imbedded in his torso. Nothing can stop him now—especially not these puny, pathetic Americans.

Teddy boldly positions himself between Volkov and Liam, assuming an aggressive stance reminiscent of the martial arts fighters he's seen on TV. The stocky, bearded Wilfred offers words of encouragement to his colleague. "Liam, I'll buy you all the time I can. It might not be long, but I'll try to keep him busy long enough for you to finish what the hell you started."

Volkov laughs at the thought that Teddy represents the last obstacle between him and his destiny. The blood-red glow of the Russian's eyes is met with an equally determined bright amber stare.

Teddy forges a plan taken straight from the annals of prizefighting. He'll dance like a butterfly, stay outside the range of the Super-Vampire's knock out punch, and tire him out until he sees an opening sufficient to put him down for the count with one well-timed sting. Okay, maybe two. Teddy barely sidesteps Volkov's sudden, sweeping right hook aimed directly at his head. Buoyed by his initial success, Teddy nimbly dodges Volkov's brutish lunges, bobbing and weaving to keep his slower opponent focused on him. Prancing Teddy is well aware one blow could end this match. The Thermopylae-like confines of this battlefield give Teddy an advantage. Volkov has to stop frequently to channel his strength in order to pursue attack in any direction.

Volkov becomes more enraged with each wild swing. He abruptly stops chasing his quarry. Time for a new tactic. He hangs upside down from the steel beams drilled into the concrete ceiling. Energized by a lustful battle cry, his right fist shakes violently at the two Americans.

His opponent's surprise maneuver catches Teddy off guard. His hands rest by his sides. Where is Volkov?

Meanwhile, the Professor has tuned out the brawl. His total focus is on the commands to disengage Dead Hand. Klemko continues to provide reassurance that the process is nearing its end.

Without warning, Volkov drops from the ceiling. His ears tune to the voice on the radio. "Klemko! Well, my friend, what have we here? All the might of the Trust and the power of the System united against me, your humble servant, Volkov? Your respect pleases me. Let me show you my power!"

In the clamor, the Professor is unable to clearly hear Klemko's frantic instructions.

Teddy looks over to Liam, confused. Shit. He's lost sight of Volkov. He looks hard to his left, then right, then behind. *Where the hell is he?* The pitch-black room is permeated only by a ringing silence and that awful stench!

By the time Teddy sees Volkov standing inches from his face, it's too late. Volkov delivers a mighty blow across his chest. He's hurled across the room like a rag doll and crashes violently into a set of heavy wooden bookshelves. He's knocked out, buried under a pile of Cyrillic-print military manuals in the corner of the room. Wood splinters and shards of torn metal are scattered everywhere.

The Professor is too focused on the disengagement sequence to take note of what just happened. Volkov approaches from behind, grabs him by the shoulders, and pulls him straight out of his chair. Liam's feet are dangling several feet above the hard, dark gray concrete floor. Pleased, Volkov slowly tightens his grip around his victim's neck. As he opens his mouth wide to sink his large, stalactite fangs into his victim, thick strands of opaque-gray saliva extend between his large, sharp teeth. At that very moment, Boris strides into the control room.

Volkov is subdued by Boris's surprise entrance. Of all System Vampires, only Boris showed him respect—and sympathy. Boris was the only System Vampire Volkov trusted. Even in his madness, faint memories of his former human self still reside within him.

"What are you doing here, Myshkin? Did Vampire Zero send you to help me complete the mission? It is our day, my brother. Our master will treat us as heroes when we return to the Kremlin triumphant. Let us fulfill our mission together. Take this Trust Vampire, Boris. He's yours to dispense with. Feast with me!"

Boris gives the Professor a long, hard look. His eyes glow bright red. His lips form a devious smile. "Yes, Brother Volkov. Let's finish them off! I will feast with you."

The Super-Vampire's eyes pulsate in alternating crimson red and deep black flashes. "Yes, Boris. I will squeeze this miserable wretch until his puny head pops. You will have the honor of plunging the stake through his soft American heart."

Boris walks over to the shattered bookshelf, breaks off a large shaft of wood, and, with his hands, rubs one edge into a sharp point. By the looks of the gaunt Professor still squirming in the Super-Vampire's grip, this weapon should easily do the trick.

Volkov can hardly contain his zeal. "Do it, Boris. Do it now. Now!"

Boris carefully aims the stake at the center of his squirming victim's heart. Although unable to move, the Professor remains defiant. In a flash, Boris whirls around and plunges the stake deep into Volkov's chest. The wound is just to the left and below his heart. Volkov screams in shock. A thick, deep red-green ooze flows openly from his chest like hot lava from a volcano.

The wounds of betrayal are more painful than the weapon lodged in his chest. Enraged, the Super-Vampire places both palms over the exposed portion of the stake. He presses hard, pushing it cleanly through his back. Weakened by the trauma to his body, Volkov lunges unsteadily at Boris, shrieking in pain.

By now, the Professor has helped a groggy Teddy to his feet. He survived, but just barely. "Forget about me, Liam. Get back to work. Finish the sequence. We'll take care of Volkov."

Teddy searches for a suitable weapon to finish the fight.

With his back to the Americans, Volkov pins Boris to the wall with both hands wrapped tightly around his neck in a death choke hold.

Teddy approaches Volkov from behind. The Super-Vampire senses a threatening presence. He drops Boris to unleash a mighty back-handed blow, knocking Teddy to the ground. Volkov repeatedly stomps on the upper torso of his defenseless victim in an effort to finish him off.

The Professor tries to finish the disengagement process, but can't just stand there and watch his buddy's demise. He pulls a crossbow from concealment under his heavy overcoat, takes careful aim, and fires the spring-loaded device. The thick iron shaft hits Volkov in the center of his heart. The force of the strike propels him backward, pinning him firmly to the wall. Stunned, Volkov looks down at the stake penetrating his body, then over to the crossbow with a mixture of scientific curiosity and bewilderment.

"You only get around to using this now?!" Teddy exclaims.

"I didn't think it was gonna work," the Professor replies meekly, admiring his invention.

By now, Teddy and Boris have each ripped a pair of long, metal rebar rods from the back wall. In a coordinated motion, the two Vampires plunge the rods completely through Volkov's weakened body near the middle of his abdomen. Penetration continues deep into a nearby concrete wall, firmly anchoring the Super-Vampire. Volkov screams in suspended agony. Somehow the, Super-Vampire musters enough strength to slowly push himself forward. He steps unsteadily away from the wall and slides his midsection free of the rebar rods. Chunks of flesh and red-green ooze remain stuck to the rebar. Opaque bubbles form, then pop to release a putrid odor.

His grievous wounds have taken a serious toll. Seemingly in slow motion, the dying Vampire falls to his knees. His chest emits a deep, gurgling sound matched only by the excretion of a thick, viscous red-green colored oozing substance.

Armed with a large splinter of wood in the rough shape of stake, Boris assumes a position towering over Volkov. As he prepares to strike the final blow, he hesitates. The reluctant executioner weighs his loyalties. To whom does Boris owe allegiance? To Vampire Zero? Or to Mother Russia—and all life on earth?

The silence is broken by the Professor's jubilant exclamation. "We did it! Dead Hand is disengaged. I've entered the code. The computer has powered down."

"Now you tell us," is all Teddy can offer. He's spent.

Still on his knees, Volkov stirs. His survival instincts have not been extinguished. His grievously damaged body attempts to heal itself haltingly. Volkov's personal war is over. For the first time since becoming a Vampire, he's beset by feelings of humanity, a melancholy retreat to the better days that once were fine and noble, despite everything that has transpired since then. With repurposed feelings of conviction, he grasps a discarded stake with his left hand and takes Boris's hand with his right.

"Finish it, Myshkin, or I swear I will finish you."

The two American Vampires flank Boris and Volkov. Teddy unconvincingly motions for Boris to step aside. Boris waves them off. He harbors no doubts as to what he must do. Myshkin helps Volkov to his feet, gently resting him against the gray, concrete wall. He looks compassionately into the Super-Vampire's flickering red eyes. Telepathically, he bids his old friend a final, emotional goodbye. Volkov nods before raising the outside of his arm, just behind the elbow, so Boris can position the metal stake toward the center of his heart. Volkov places the palm of his right hand around the end of the stake. Boris, in turn, places the palm of his right hand on top of Volkov's. A final telepathic message: "Do it now, Myshkin. Now!"

Boris's eyes flash a brilliant red, nodding his final approval. The pressure exerted by his right hand assists Volkov's effort. The stake is slowly pushed deep into his heart. The Vampires watch Volkov exhale his final full breath. The red glow in his eyes quickly fades to deep black. The Vampires instinctively look away from the brilliant flash of light and cringe in expectation of the intense heat wave that rumbles through the room, marking the Super-Vampire's passing. They turn back to find a large pile of ash on the spot where Volkov last stood. Black burn marks are etched into the nearest concrete wall and into the ceiling above them. The screen of the launch computer has melted, exposing its burned interior of electrical components. Volkov is gone.

Teddy contacts the command center. "It's done. The Target—Volkov—has been eliminated. He's dead."

Klemko is on the radio. "How did it happen?"

Teddy offers Boris the radio. "By his own hand."

Teddy takes the mike. "Boris arrived on the scene shortly after Volkov self-terminated. He confirms the Super-Vampire took his own life in the launch control center of Silo 747."

The Moscow command center shifts into full damage control mode. Teams are ordered to clean up any Vampire evidence. A special team will arrive to sanitize the scene and plant evidence to support the cover legend. The national media will report an unsuccessful attempt by a Chechen terrorist cell to perpetrate nuclear sabotage. Vampire teams will report to their assigned rally points for transport to Moscow.

In Washington, Beria fights hard to suppress an urge to scream out loud at the news of Volkov's demise—and by suicide?! He doubts the report's veracity.

Back at the command center, Aaron offers the Trust's condolences over the loss of the Spetznaz teams, helicopter crews, and Silo security personnel. He and Elena pack up and hastily prepare to depart. A sense of relief permeates the room. However, working bilaterally to save the world changes nothing. A zero-sum game of war still exists between the two sides.

Late evening in the Kremlin, Putin privately entertains a young lady in his office. They're positioned comfortably next to one another on an oversized, yellow-and-white regal sofa in the large seating area. Rich, dark, fresh-brewed Kona Hawaiian coffee is served from a porcelain pitcher into two beautiful coffee cups, complete with saucers, all part of a larger antique china collection that once belonged to Czar Alexander I. The tick-tock of an antique grandfather clock can be heard in the background.

Putin is relaxed and enjoying himself when his aide, FSB Colonel Petrov, knocks on the door and abruptly enters the room. The longtime aide walks directly over to Putin without averting his eyes to steal a glance at the attractive young woman also seated on the couch.

Putin takes the note from his aide's hand. After a lingering pause to savor what he's just read, he smiles in satisfaction at the report of the successful liquidation of the Target. He casually refolds the note and places it in the inside left breast pocket of his suit jacket. Colonel Petrov leaves the room and, with a formal bow, pulls the floor-to-ceiling double doors closed behind him.

Vampire Zero relishes a surge of a supercharged energy like high-voltage electricity coursing through his veins. The exquisite joy of revenge! He casually mulls over candidates to replace his three lost Vampires: Badanov, Terrible Ivan, and Volkov. Their loss is unfortunate, but it presents a prime opportunity to place new pieces onto the chess board. He is surprised by the Trust's ability to dispatch Volkov. Like Iron Feliks, however, he's not entirely convinced Volkov died by his own hand. He resolves to solve that mystery in due course.

Vampire Zero admiringly eyes his new love interest, young KGB junior officer Ana Svetlova. Why not?

CHAPTER 35
BERIA'S OPERATION

SYSTEM VAMPIRE BERIA IS ON A MISSION. New information. An FSB source in Romania reported that Beria's colleague Boris met with Sergey Deniken in Transylvania. The large cash reward offered for any information leading to the whereabouts of former FSB officer Deniken has paid off. Beria was tasked to stop in Romania on his way from Washington to Moscow to meet with the FSB source.

Beria delights in this newfound success. The source's information is correct. He dutifully counts out the cash reward and sends the source, a corrupt Romanian police sergeant, on his way. The low-level asset is given strict warning to keep his mouth shut under penalty of death.

In short order Beria finds Deniken hiding in a CIA safe house in the outskirts of a Roma (Gypsy) encampment in the village of Orsova, located near the border with Serbia. On his own initiative, Beria decides to eliminate Deniken without consulting the System. Permission is a formality easy to ignore under the circumstances.

Easily overpowered, Deniken is brought to an old, abandoned industrial warehouse. The Sadist indulges in several gratifying rounds of torture designed to loosen his victim's tongue. His determination to extract a full confession is evidenced by the pedestal-mounted video tape recorder set to preserve the encounter.

"Sergey, you dog, you will die here today. The choice of how much you suffer is in your hands. Tell me about your relationship with Boris Smertsov. Confirm this to me, and your suffering will mercifully end. I promise." Deniken is barely conscious.

"What can I say to convince you" I have not seen Boris since the bastard cut all ties with me, many years ago. Fuck him. And fuck you!"

Deniken screams out in excruciating pain as the Sadist makes meticulous incisions along carefully chosen parts of his body. Various steel implements chosen specifically for this purpose are employed. The hapless victim is tied to a steel gurney with heavy knots of piano wire. His body is positioned right at the mouth of a large furnace burning hot in the center of the warehouse.

Beria takes care not to kill his subject prematurely. As an experienced purveyor of the art, he knows anyone will confess to anything given enough torture. People will say anything to stop the pain. Therein lies the problem. Even a Vampire with his extensive experience can't divine whether information extracted under extreme torture is true or false. Beria, however, isn't just any interrogator. His skills, honed over many years of satisfyingly comprehensive experience, give him unique insight into his victims' agony. The Sadist knows Deniken's confession doesn't add up.

"Why do you torment me? Kill me now and be done with it. I will confess. I am meeting with a CIA officer."

"Ah, much better!"

Beria gives Deniken another chance to come clean. The Russian Vampire wasn't expecting this revelation. The condemned man confesses that his handling officer tasked him to provide information on the Russian exile community in Romania. He claims not to know the true identity of the CIA officer. But based on Deniken's physical description of his CIA handler, it is surely the Trust's second in command, Aaron Janicke.

Beria assumes the traitor wants most to protect the details of his CIA handler. Somehow, Deniken finds the strength not to compromise his friend

Boris. Further efforts at "elicitation" convince Beria his victim has no further information to offer. It is Sergey's final act of defiance against his tormentors.

"You have done well, Sergey. You have suffered enough. I will now ease your pain."

With that, Beria opens the furnace doors to expose the raging inferno inside. With a satisfied smile, he slowly rolls the gurney, with Deniken hoarse from screaming, into the flames.

In Moscow, Putin convenes another meeting of the System. It's almost midnight. The atmosphere in the command bunker is one of subdued celebration. Vampire Zero is in an uncharacteristically good mood. High praise is lavished on his Vampires. They eliminated Volkov, averted nuclear war, and restored order.

Klemko reports. Rainer Wolf has requested an after-action meeting in Vienna. Putin sniffs a whiff of danger in the air. "Yes, be careful in Vienna, *Tovarish* Klemko. The Trust has tasted our blood. They feel powerful and will seize any opportunity to strike if we let our guard down."

When his turn arrives to speak, Beria reports only select details of his mission to Romania. "I have established without a doubt that the traitor Sergey Deniken is dead, as Boris has reported."

Vampire Zero interrupts him. "My loyal Beria. Good news, indeed! See me after the meeting. Iron Feliks and Klemko, remain behind for Beria's briefing."

Panic-stricken, Boris manages to keep his emotions under control. Surely Beria managed to extract the fact that Boris didn't kill his friend Sergey but instead warned him to flee. Why didn't Beria disclose this incriminating information about Boris?

After the meeting breaks up, Beria walks casually over to address Boris, privately. "We need to talk about your old friend Sergey Deniken."

Boris smells the bitter odor of blackmail. It smells a bit like carrion to a Vampire.

A few days later, Beria testily calls Boris out for a late night meeting in Gorkiy Park in central Moscow. "Meet at 10:00 p.m. at the top steps of the majestic column entrance."

Boris fully expects to be ambushed and arrested by an FSB surveillance team when he greets Beria in the park. He has come prepared to kill Beria if he gets the chance. Since the Volkov affair, all Vampires now carry weapons. All that's left is a nostalgia for the good old days when their only natural enemies were humans.

To Boris's surprise, Beria has come alone. The two Vampires stroll casually down a tree-covered path in the deserted park. Boris wants nothing of the affectations of Beria's condescending small talk. He gets straight to the point. "What do you want, Beria?"

"It's simple, Boris. You bring me the man. I'll find you the crime. I smelled a rat with your man. And I was right. Wasn't I?"

Boris nods, expecting the worst.

"I don't know why you lied about killing Deniken, Boris, but it doesn't matter. I completed the task for you. The dirty little traitor is dead. Oh, it felt so good to 'work' again."

Boris gathers his wits about him so as not to betray any emotion for the loss of his friend. After all, he warned Sergey to leave Romania. Deniken has no one to blame but himself for his demise.

"So, how do you propose to properly atone for your lapse in judgment, Boris? I see no way out of your situation. No, wait! Before you respond, there is a small favor you can do for me in exchange for not betraying your secret to Vampire Zero."

"What is it?"

"Your friend was a double agent. Before he expired, and mercifully I must say, he confessed the CIA has been handling him for several months."

Boris is visibly shaken.

"Don't look so shocked, Boris. Betrayal is much easier the second time around. You should know that."

Beria laughs, pleased with himself. He emits a sound reminiscent of the noise a weasel makes when grabbed by its tail and hoisted off its feet. The slight-framed Vampire's crooked, tobacco-stained front teeth are on full display. Boris resists the temptation to slash out impulsively. He knows he must keep his cool.

In an attempt to provoke a reaction, Beria lustily relates the gory details of Deniken's final moments interspersed with short bouts of weasel laughter. "Before I put the miserable wretch Deniken out of his misery, he confessed that he scheduled a meeting with Trust Vampire Janicke in a fortnight. I'll be standing there in the traitor's place to ambush him."

"And how does this concern me?" Boris is genuinely perplexed by this turn in the conversation.

"You, Boris, will be there to assist me. If I can't bring back the American's head, I'll wipe his remains off the floor and bring them back as my trophy. Together, we will avenge the loss of our comrades at the hands of the Trust. In exchange for your cooperation to eliminate Janicke, I'll protect your secret. You will have only this chance to redeem yourself. You will help me become a hero in our master's eyes. What do you think of my plan?"

Boris smiles. "Brilliant!"

CHAPTER 36
THE MOLE HUNT

B ACK AT CIA HEADQUARTERS IN LANGLEY, VIRGINIA, WOLF HAS TO take care of some rather unpleasant business. CI chief Alan Tourier's investigation has come too close to the truth. He's too smart for his own damn good. Tourier reported his analysis up the chain of command in the form of highly classified spot reports. Paranoia driven, he withheld the names of CIA officers he considered to be mole candidates.

Fortunately, the list of recipients was limited to only the director of central intelligence, the DDO (Rainer Wolf), and the director of national intelligence. The CIA learned the hard way to strictly compartmentalize sensitive CI information. This of course, runs counter to the "duty to share" culture of the intelligence community. A spy warned is a spy who will never be brought to justice. History is replete with stories of spies who fled to Moscow—and in reverse, resettled in the West after their identities were compromised.

Fortunately, Tourier keeps his deepest, darkest theories to himself, owing to an obsession about the possibility his mole hunt could be compromised. The irony isn't lost on Wolf. Even though the former CIA counterintelligence chief, James Jesus Angleton, suspected basically everyone of being a spy, he didn't suspect his close friend Kim Philby. Philby, the British SIS (Secret Intelligence Service) "Head" assigned to Washington, DC, defected to Moscow and announced he'd been a Russian spy for decades. Tourier's paranoia is about to fail him. He keeps too much information to himself. Tragic.

It's late in the evening when Wolf stops by Alan's office within the Counter Intelligence Center vault. Tourier regularly works late nights. Wolf enters to find the bookish CI chief completely absorbed in a stack of files piled high on his desk, some of which overflow onto his couch.

Tourier looks up apprehensively, startled by the sound of an unexpected visitor clearing his throat. He quickly closes the file he's reading. Wolf attempts to relax his colleague with an air of nonchalance as he surveys the disheveled office.

"Alan, I've never understood how someone with such a meticulous mind can have such a scatter-brained office. What are you working on?"

"Oh, it's nothing." Tourier is terrified.

"No, please show me, Alan. I do admire your work. Been reading your spot reports. You might be on to something. Can you give me an updated assessment of your leading mole suspects?"

"Sure, Rainer," he stammers. "How about if I get you something first thing in the morning?"

Wolf lifts the file from the center of Tourier's desk. It's his "soft file" of likely mole candidates. Janicke's name is at the top of the list. C/CIC has connected Janicke to a number of anomalous events, to include the suspicious circumstances behind two separate Russian walk-ins in Bucharest. Both sources disappeared mysteriously. To the well-trained mind of a CI professional like Tourier, the circumstances just don't add up. As taught by his mentor, Rainer Wolf, "In Russia, there's no such thing as coincidence."

"Alan, you know how much I enjoy brainstorming about moles. Aaron Janicke? Come on, you really think Janicke's a Russian mole?"

"Rainer, did I say Janicke's a mole? I hardly think we're there yet. Just touching all the bases like you taught me."

Tourier abruptly rises to his feet, turns around, and attempts to reinsert another file back into the top drawer of his gray, USG standard issue five-drawer combination safe. Wolf notes the tab on the file labeled "Wolf." Tourier is unable to face his uninvited guest. All he can do is hope Rainer Wolf will walk away.

Wolf drops a file on Tourier's desk. It lands with a thud. "Alan, there's nothing more unforgivable for a case officer than to create false information to discredit one's colleagues. How do you intend to atone for this lapse of integrity?"

Wolf has no interest in hearing the condemned CI Chief's response. Tourier's head drops, expecting the worst.

"Alan, I'm sorry. Not what you deserve, but you should've left well enough alone. You've left me no choice."

Wolf grabs Tourier's neck from behind and violently twists it to the left until it snaps. A pain-free death is the least he can give his former protégé. He places the body gently on the sofa, displacing several stacks of files. It is harsh justice. But necessary justice. The world has only gotten meaner and the CIA has only gotten softer.

Well after midnight finds the Headquarters building deserted. Wolf gathers up the collection of Tourier's soft files. His protégé's analysis was spot on. Before departing the CI vault, Rainer collects every scrap of paper related to Tourier's mole hunt. Wolf places the file he put together on the deceased CI chief's fabricated information about his CI colleagues squarely on the desk facing the chair, where it will be found in the morning. Alan Tourier's body, along with a burn bag full of his complete "soft" files, was disposed of in the Agency's basement incinerator, the place where classified cable traffic is routinely destroyed.

CHAPTER 37

BORIS'S REVENGE

Aaron Janicke is in his Moscow office lost in thought and twirling a fountain pen between his fingers. He's developed an affinity for old-fashioned pens. Perhaps the black ink reminds him of warm blood as it spills across the paper with each stroke. He takes a pause from the tedious daily review of incoming cable traffic from Headquarters. Not much at all in the way of substance. Way too much gutless rhetoric about staying safe and how not to offend our "Russian hosts." State Department diplomats are worried CIA activity will damage US-Russian bilateral relations. Blah, blah, blah. COS Moscow channels his professional disgust by talking out loud. "Liaison equities, hah. Every fuckin' liaison service in the world will steal us blind if we let them. And we should do the same to them. What utter and complete bullshit!"

About the time Aaron turns his attention to the computer screen, the Station counterintelligence officer enters his office. The officer hands Aaron a note discreetly passed by an unknown Russian volunteer. Junior Station C/O Kristina Kosewell found the envelope resting on the driver's seat of her locked vehicle this morning when she left her apartment for work. The unopened envelope was addressed to "COS Moscow—Eyes Only." An x-ray determined it contained no hazardous material—or readable fingerprints. It's safe to open.

Aaron carefully tears the seal on the back flap of the envelope and extracts the note, a single sheet of paper from a standard issue, yellow legal-sized notepad. He thanks his Station colleague, who departs the office.

Aaron can hardly believe what he's reading (in Cyrillic print).

Dorogoi Drug,

Beware of Vampires! You will be ambushed at your next scheduled meeting with CIA agent Sergey Deniken in Romania. Deniken has been compromised. The case is blown. Deniken is dead. Am I clear? The System is aware of the time and place of your upcoming meeting. Be prepared or be eliminated.

Vash Drug.

Trap? Janicke tries several times to contact Deniken via their emergency communications plan. No success. He sends an immediate COVCOM message to Rainer Wolf requesting guidance.

To: The Chief

Request guidance in response to a volunteer note received today from unknown write-in source in Moscow. Volunteer note was dropped in a Station officer's car. Substance is a warning addressed to me, as COS Moscow. Stated Deniken case is compromised and I will be ambushed at my next scheduled meeting in Romania. Note is signed "Your Friend."

Despite the eight-hour time difference between Washington and Moscow, the Chief's response arrives within about fifteen minutes of Janicke's message #6402.

To: Vampire 2:

I am concerned this is a trap. That said, the only way we will know for sure is by taking the bait. Proceed with the meeting as planned, but bring Constantin, Marlowe, and Leonardi to provide countersurveillance. If circumstances permit, combine forces to eliminate any System Vampire who shows up for the meeting. Plan for the best, but prepare for the worst. Report results ASAP.

Wolf

In subsequent COVCOM exchanges, Rainer and Aaron speculate on the volunteer's identity and motivation. Fortunately, Wolf had shared with the Trust the contents of the dossier provided by the volunteer while on the train to Vienna. Unfortunately, Agent Nul went silent after he clandestinely brush passed the dossier on System members to Wolf on the train. Was this new volunteer in Moscow one and the same person as the train volunteer? Wolf and Janicke sense their battles with the System are nearing a climax. They "hear" faint disturbances in global stability, like the grinding sounds of tectonic plates of shifting continents.

CHAPTER 38

A PERSONAL AFFAIR

Rainer Wolf makes a decisive move. He intends to take full advantage of the relative calm while the Trust and the System retreat to their respective corners before the bell sounds the start of the next round. The implied truce is over.

Wolf calls Klemko out for another meeting in Vienna. His decision is driven by an ulterior personal motive. His wavering loyalties must be reconciled. The physical signs of his tormented mind are unmistakable. Migraines have become unbearable. He's frequented by images of a noble, enchanted, innocent Russia. They relax his spirit, but disturb his mind.

His secret counsel with human allies Flynn O'Donovan and Father John has convinced Rainer to sort out his true feelings. Just as Alzheimer's disease ravages a healthy mind, Rainer understands his disease will eventually claim him plus rob whatever remains of his soul—if it hasn't already.

He's tormented by the question of which cause he truly serves. The pin has been pulled to initiate the end game of this personal chess match. As he did the day he exhorted the Russian mole Abel to "bite me," he must know who he really is and what he truly stands for. No guts, no glory.

As agreed, Wolf and Klemko meet in a former CIA safe house located in the town of Heilegenstadt on the northern outskirts of Vienna. The plain wooden house is located about a half hour's drive from the Russian safe house in Nussdorf am Attersee, the venue of their previous meeting. The Trust reactivated the safe house after the Agency dropped it from its inventory. The CIA within the CIA is slowly building a secret infrastructure to support its growing stable of assets. Trust Vampires work overtime from their posted locations to wire the world with a global network of human sources. Their spies are recruited mostly in a kind of false flag operation. Sources believe they work for the CIA when in fact they work off the books for the Trust. Since the CIA and the Trust both serve US national security interests, the Vampires see no conflict in this approach.

Rainer Wolf requested the private meeting with Klemko on the pretext of wrapping up loose ends after the "Chechen nuclear terrorism case," as the joint operation between the CIA and the FSB is referred to by their respective headquarters. The System's cover legend succeeded beyond Vampire Zero's wildest imagination. Russian national media reported the liquidation of the terrorist threat as a major success for Putin's get-tough policy on Chechnya. The US president hailed the US-Russian cooperation to thwart the threat as "proof that our common interests coincide on the most important issues, such as combatting nuclear proliferation and nuclear terrorism." Politicians on both sides hailed the joint success. However, Vampires—on both sides—are galled by the official rhetoric about the great lesson learned and how liaison cooperation benefits both countries. What bullshit!

After an exchange of phony pleasantries between two Cold Warriors in the twilight of their second careers, Wolf gets down to business. "Klemko, the Volkov operation has proven once more what's possible when we can actually cooperate with one another. Perhaps we should extend our truce in an effort to identify more areas of common ground. Our presidents are happy. Well, mine certainly is. Also, my DCI is currently very pleased with the DO. Hasn't always been the case."

Klemko knows his nemesis well enough to know when he's being sarcastic. On more than one occasion Wolf joked that whenever Klemko decides to retire, he should take up acting as a second career. The next Bela Lugosi, perhaps.

"Rainer, Rainer, Rainer. Don't bullshit me, old friend. You didn't drag me to Vienna to regale me with some fairy tale about brotherhood and cooperation. If I didn't know you better, I'd say you lured me here to pitch me."

Klemko moves his pawn to King-4. Wolf makes his opening move. "I did. I came here to recruit you, dear friend. And why not? We share the same blood. We're not so different, you and I."

Klemko reacts with satisfaction. "You are so right, Rainer. We do share the same blood. We cannot escape who we are. You, Rainer, are one of us. I am here alone. That's how much I trust you. Mother Russia runs like a river through your veins. The torment you feel will end only when you accept the reality of who you are. No man or beast can betray his true nature for long. Not even you, Rainer Wolf. We're too old to waste one another's time. We arrived here today with two masters. We depart as one—on the same side. Agreed?"

"Agreed."

The Russian case officer's skills are admirable. He's as smooth as they come, authentic. Wolf needs to hear the Russian's pitch. He needs to resolve how he (Rainer) will react. Klemko continues. "My friend, let's share a good bottle of wine so we can settle in for a nice, relaxing evening. This doesn't have to feel like work, does it!"

As host, Wolf is obliged to make the opening toast. The archfoes raise their glasses, lock eye contact.

"Whatever the results this evening, let's toast to an outcome that serves not our selfish interests, but the higher values we fight for and live by."

After clinking glasses, Klemko is subdued. He picks at the bloody amenities laid out on the coffee table between their two Austrian Empire baroque-style chairs. Several minutes of contrived silence later, Klemko makes a reciprocal toast. "Rainer, we once played a game a long time ago when we were human. I asked you one question, and you asked me one question. The game has only one rule. We must answer truthfully. Are you willing to play this game again as Vampires, for old times sake?"

"I remember it fondly. Okay, I'm game."

"I'll go first, Rainer. Transport yourself back in time to your assignment in Moscow. You like to say you were in the belly of the beast—the Soviet Union. You met a young Russian mother pushing a baby stroller in a park. You were on your surveillance detection run for an operational outing. I know, because I was on the KGB surveillance team watching you. You stopped in your tracks to look into the young mother's big, round, innocent eyes. You seemed lost in thought. I've always wanted to know—what were you thinking?"

Rainer responds without hesitation. "At that moment, Klemko, I came face-to-face with the reality it would be no less tragic if a Russian mother and child were to perish in a nuclear holocaust than if an American mother and child perished. At that very moment of my young career, I understood we couldn't trust our masters to save us. We couldn't just assume they'd make the right decisions. Neither yours nor ours. Our people would be served better if you or I had the power to make these decisions, and not those in power."

Klemko leans forward and moves his chair an inch closer to Wolf. "Do you feel the same today?"

"Is that your question?"

"Yes. Let me rephrase. Wolf, do you feel the same now as you did when you were human?"

Wolf responds again without hesitation. "More so. I trust you and not Vampire Zero. I've seen your master's ambition with my own eyes. Even though you're Russian and I'm American, our ambitions have limits. We share the same humanity. If anything, being a Vampire has strengthened our convictions. We see things more clearly now than we ever did as humans."

Klemko didn't expect Wolf to unburden himself. Surprised, he returns to his script. Perhaps he's the better case officer. "That's all fine and good, Rainer, but you have not answered my question. Do you still have Mother Russia in your heart? The affection you described for the Russian people remains, no? Do you feel the blood of Andropov surging in your veins?"

This time Rainer pauses. "I like the way you're answering the question for me."

The Russian Vampire leans forward again, eyes glowing red, boldly sniffing for signs he's worn down his American target. He has the advantage of preying on the debilitating effects of his target's tainted blood. Klemko's soothing, melodic, even-toned, low-pitched voice tests Wolf's susceptibility to hypnosis. Vampire-on-Vampire hypnosis doesn't work unless the target willingly submits. Wolf has no intention of surrendering his free will to Klemko.

Wolf smells Klemko's devious intentions and preempts him. "You've asked your question. Now let me ask mine."

Klemko shifts back in his chair. "Of course, please do."

"What happened to us, Klemko? What have we become? Is there no end to our machinations? Have you not risen above it?"

"Rainer, if I may be so rude as to press you to answer my question, I sense the pain of your second metamorphosis. The first occurred when Abel bit you and you formed the Trust. The second occurs now. When at last you come to our side, you will be complete, both man and Vampire. Relief will come only when you submit to your true self."

Klemko's words ring true. They soothe Wolf like an old favorite folk song from distant Russian villages, far from the purposeless hustle and bustle of American life. The American Vampire fights the unwelcome nostalgia by reminding himself that all countries have folk songs. The innocence he craves is a virtue of all peoples. "Klemko, I'll answer your question now. You see, I'm unreliable in my own skin. I can't reason with myself. Unfortunately, there's no transfusion to replace my tainted blood. You've helped me to understand. I now know what I must do. It's clear."

In the intimacy of the conversation, Klemko abandons his instinctive cautiousness. Russians have a cultural habit of drawing in close during conversation. Guided only by his instincts, Wolf draws closer to Klemko. Klemko's face is but a whisker's length away. Wolf captures Klemko's eyes. "Old friend, I know what I must do now."

Klemko smiles approvingly. His body slumps. The victor. He places a reassuring hand on Wolf's shoulder. Slowly, imperceptibly, Wolf draws a sturdy wooden cross, with the shaft sharpened into a point, from a brown leather sheath hidden on his belt tucked away in the small of his back. The American Vampire plunges the sharpened end of the cross into deep into Klemko's chest, penetrating his heart.

The System Vampire gasps in mid-sentence, his mouth agape. Wolf holds the stake firmly in his chest, keeping him upright. Klemko's hands gently move to his sides. The stricken Russian Vampire can only mouth one word. "You?"

Wolf's tone is empathetic. "Klemko, we agreed only one of us would leave this room alive. Neither of us has won today. We arrived here with two masters. We depart here with none."

Klemko nods and squeezes Wolf's hand.

Wolf delivers a short eulogy. "Rest in peace, my friend. On this day, neither of us can claim victory. Maybe it's for the best. We will meet again in some other place."

The stake is removed and to Wolf's surprise, Klemko's body still lies undisturbed before him. No flash of light. No fireworks display.

No time to contemplate the meaning of Klemko's delayed ascension to Vampire Valhalla. Wolf walks over to the opposite side of the room and sits at an antique roll-top desk. He rolls back a concealment device in which a COVCOM system is hidden. Wolf unceremoniously bangs out his final message to the Trust in his signature two-finger style.

Old school reporting. Give me the facts, and dispense with the drama. The objective is clarity, substance, not an imitation of John Steinbeck. Stick to details as if they were typed on a manual typewriter with five carbon copies. Short and sweet. Most important, clear final orders for the members of the Trust.

After a brief hesitation, Rainer can't resist adding just a pinch of color to his final report. "I take comfort in the idea there remains something essentially human in me, despite what I've become. As a human, I could never take my own life. I must end my Vampire existence for the sake of all that remains good in me. There has never been a war in which both sides didn't believe in the righteousness of their cause. As a Vampire, I have learned that belief itself isn't enough to justify war. One must know the difference between good and evil. Make that your quest. One day, God willing, a Vampire will return to the living—redeemed."

In Trust. The Chief"

A push of the transmit button and his COVCOM message is sent. It'll be there waiting for Janicke when he returns to Moscow. At this very hour, however, Janicke is indisposed. He is leading a team of four Trust Vampires to a rendezvous with the System in Romania.

Rainer Wolf peers wistfully out of the living room window. The sky is bathed in baby blue with white wisps of cloud. The branches of a nearby tree sway back and forth in a gentle breeze. His migraines are gone, replaced with clarity and purpose. At ease with himself, he looks down at the stake clutched loosely in both hands. It's time. After one last deep breath, he positions the sharpened end of the cross, still stained with Klemko's blood, directly at his heart.

With complete resolve and acceptance, Rainer Wolf plunges the stake through the center of his heart. The pain is welcomed, cleansing. A faint smile graces his face while the amber glow in his eyes slowly extinguishes.

Meanwhile, in the town of Brasov, in Transylvania—the place where it all began—four American Vampires lurk in the shadows of the interior of the safe house where Janicke had scheduled his meeting with the deceased Deniken. They await the arrival of the System Vampires. It's 11:30 a.m. The Americans are well positioned, but nervous. Beria should be here by now. Fortunately, it's a cold foggy day, complete with drizzling rain. Is this a setup? An ambush of our ambush?

Elena repositions herself next to Aaron. "Do you feel it? I feel a loss. Hear a rumbling sound. An instability. It's big. It's Rainer, isn't it?" Aaron can't bring himself to look into Elena's eyes.

"Yes, it's the Chief. No time now. After the op."

Aaron confirms Elena's intuition. From his window viewpoint he catches a glimpse of a lone, shadowy figure approaching the safe house from a block away. "Elena, cover the back entrance in case the Russians come at us from different directions. Viktor, Joe, and I will cover the front."

Thirty minutes prior to the anointed meeting time, Beria makes contact with Boris at a staging area one block south of the safe house. He paces nervously back and forth, having doubts whether to proceed with his rogue operation to ambush Janicke. "Boris, am I acting rashly? Perhaps we should discuss this with Vampire Zero before we take matters into our own hands."

Boris now has the upper hand. "*Tovarish*, why do you doubt yourself? We may never get another opportunity to eliminate THE deputy chief of the Trust. If we don't follow through today, he will suspect the traitor, Deniken, has been eliminated. What will Vampire Zero think of us when he is informed about this?"

Beria's face turns ghostly white. In his obsessive scheming to curry favor with Putin, he never considered what his master would do to him if he bungles this operation. "You're right, Boris. Let's get this over with. We'll be feasting on American blood within the hour."

The two Russian Vampires warily approach the safe house. All is quiet. No sign of life. Beria is first to walk through the door. The entrance leads straight into the living room. What's that scent? Not human. A shadowy figure is seated in a tall-backed, plush chair in roughly the center of the room. Beria's instincts kick in. Alarm, danger.

"Is someone here? Announce yourself, now!"

Aaron Janicke swivels the chair around to face Beria. The American rises to his feet, joined by Marlowe and Leonardi who emerge from the shadows to his left and right. "Have you ever heard the American expression 'high noon,' Comrade Beria?"

Beria snarls.

"Does this dog bite?" Leonardi mockingly mimics the voice of Chief Inspector Jacques Clouseau from the *Pink Panther* series, whose antics he finds amusing.

The Russian Vampire ignores the taunts. To his credit, he has no intention of backing down. Besides, he has help. "Today, we defend the honor of the System! Boris, join me!"

Beria looks around frantically for his companion. Boris is nowhere to be found. He swiftly departed the scene once Beria walked into the safe house. The Russian Vampire doesn't stand a chance against his four Trust opponents. Left with no other option, he's determined to go down fighting. In a final act of defiance, Beria launches himself across the room at the American Vampires. His teeth firmly clenched, eyes drenched in a rich red glow.

The Americans came armed with special garrotes, custom made and sharpened specifically to cut through bone with minimal effort. These weapons were designed to be used like whips. In response to Beria's charge, Aaron aims his garrote high, at the soft nape of the neck. Viktor crouches, aims low at the soft part of the back of the knees. Joe swings his garrote in a mighty arc at the hapless Vampire's fleshy waist. Three swift blows, perfectly timed, just as they rehearsed.

Beria's ferret-looking face is expressionless as his body is sliced cleanly in thirds. Three perfectly sliced sections of his body tumble like dominos to the floor. Limbs spasmodically twitch, trying to reattach to one another. It's difficult to watch those discombobulated Vampire's body parts try desperately to reconstitute themselves. When each body part loses its life force, the spastic motion ebbs and finally stops. Beria's decapitated head faces upward with a puzzled expression on his face. His eyes glow red only for a few seconds. The three pieces of Beria disappear in a short flash of light. It appears the Trust has engineered an execution method tailored to Beria's exquisite specifications. Talk about customer service. Poetic justice.

CHAPTER 39
ODE TO THE CHIEF

Trust Vampires are among the many gathered to bid farewell to the Chief, Rainer Wolf. His funeral is held at National Cathedral in Washington, DC. The weather is very appropriate for the occasion; cold, blustery, with heavily overcast skies. A light, steady rain is accompanied by intermittent claps of thunder and streaks of lightning. Couldn't ask for better conditions for a Vampire send-off.

Flynn O'Donovan leads with a heartfelt eulogy in which he praises Rainer Wolf as a man of wisdom, purpose, and destiny. A life dedicated to fighting evil in the name of good. To the American Vampires, it's all a bit much and more than a little disingenuous. Rainer Wolf wasn't even human, after all. There are, however, many attendees preoccupied with their own ulterior motives. Unfortunately, the CIA has well earned its reputation as a den of intrigue rife with professional and personal rivalries. As the eulogies continue, whispers within the crowd grow louder. What an odd coincidence Wolf was with Christopher Kringle when he died of a heart attack. How could Alan Tourier simply vanish into thin air? What really happened to Rainer Wolf in Vienna?

The mystery of Rainer Wolf has assumed an "Elvis" cult-like quality. Some observers question the official explanation of how Wolf and Klemko died in a motorboat explosion while on a liaison outing on the Donau River. At senior Agency levels, speculation is rife that Tourier was recruited by the Russians to sow disinformation by falsely accusing officers of being Russia moles. There is a growing concern that Kringle, Tourier, and Wolf were assassinated by FSB hit teams. It is, after all, well known that Putin reinstituted "wet operations." Indeed, after Wolf's death a special liaison channel between CIA and Russian intelligence was opened to discuss ending the age-old practice. Killing or drugging one another's agents just doesn't bring the same return on investment anymore. Some interpret this as tacit admission by the Russians they physically target CIA officers for harm, breaking with civilized behavior and traditions established over decades of wars in the shadows.

Rumors also abound about fresh CIA and FBI investigations into Russian penetrations of the US intelligence community. Perhaps the three CIA officers were assassinated because they uncovered the truth about Russian spies in the US establishment. At least the speculation serves to deflect attention from the Trust.

Long after the funeral has concluded and late into the night, each Trust Vampire offers a short, blunt, impromptu farewell to Rainer Wolf. They stand in a half circle at the edge of his fresh grave, heads lowered in solemnity, eyes bright amber. Actually, Vampires don't do solemnity very well, despite the need to try. There is, however, solemnity in humor.

Aaron tries his best to eulogize. "The hour of a Vampire's death will chime for each of us. It's the day the Vampire departs the second life with honor, dignity, and respect."

"Amen."

Muffled laughter.

"Ashes to ashes."

Marlowe: "Why do Vampires leave only a teaspoon of ashes?"

Murmurs. Giggling.

Masterson: "Immortality is a gift for the living, but a curse for the Vampire."

Leonardi: "Damn straight."

Lowell: "Rainer, you son of a bitch. You just had to get to the next world before us to check it out, didn't you?

Leonardi (again): "I'say Fuhgetahbout coming back here to bite me again! That was Aaron, Chief, in case you can't see us."

More laughter.

Constantin: "Did I ever tell you Aaron was the shittiest choice you could have made to replace you?"

Much more laughter.

Aaron: "I think we're done here."

Janicke closes out the proceedings. "Rainer would have liked this tribute. He'd never admit it, but he most wanted our love and affection."

They bow their heads in a moment of silence.

"Who am I kidding?!"

Raucous laughter.

As a final gesture, Aaron passes on Rainer's last instructions. Each Vampire is given their new assignment. "Rainer requested that henceforth, all members of the Trust freely choose this fate and not have it imposed on them. As you all know, the boat explosion death thing was a cover story. He died in our safe house, along with Klemko. What I haven't told you is that we recovered his body. We also delivered Klemko's body to the System. They were appreciative. I don't know how or why it happened, but at death, their Vampire bodies reverted to human form."

Aaron points to the freshly dug grave. "Rainer Wolf rests here. May he rise again. Or maybe not."

In Moscow, Vladimir Putin works alone, late into the night in his Kremlin office. The Americans have forced him to raise the ante. Force must be met with a greater force. Vague disturbance in global stability resonates. He leans back in his black leather executive chair and places his feet up on the expansive, antique oak desk. Huge, red velvet curtains covering three massive windows have been drawn shut. The lights in this grandiose office are off. His reflective mood is registered via an intermittent red glow in his eyes, the only light in the room.

Vampire Zero is interrupted by a familiar knock at the door. Enter Iron Feliks, who walks softly over to one of the two large, ornate chairs positioned across from Putin's desk. With a wry smile and subdued red tint in his eyes, Iron Feliks places a wooden box, about the size of a small jewelry case, on the center of Putin's desktop. He pushes it to within his master's easy reach. Vampire Zero's eyes invite an explanation.

"Vladimir, an extraordinary event has occurred. One of the workers cleaning up the mess in Volkov's laboratory found this box. The message delicately carved into its top reads, "To Vladimir Putin. From Your Most Dedicated Servant—Dr. Volkov. The worker had the presence of mind to turn the box over to one of our loyal servants in the FSB unopened."

After careful study and a good sniff, Vampire Zero slowly opens the box. The yellow tamper seals affixed between the bottom edges of the lid and the upper portion of each side give way. The contents reveal a sealed laboratory test tube surrounded by cloth padding and a handwritten note from Volkov. The note is composed in the familiar Russian form of speech used between parents and children, or between close friends. Clearly Volkov was mad when he wrote the note.

Vampire Zero—Dear Father,

I cannot begin to express my profound grief for failing you in my duty to produce a serum. I am convinced I have uncovered the secret that explains the physiological flaws in the DNA of Vampires that accelerates the aging process of body and mind. I have included in this box the refined formula I developed in order to reverse this process.

If you are reading this note, then I have failed you in finding a cure. By now you know I used the serum on myself in my attempt to save us both.

However, all hope is not lost. I have one final offering for you from the grave. As you know, I drew the blood of Yuriy Andropov from which all Vampires owe their existence. I offer you my own blood, which was drawn immediately after I injected myself with the serum.

In the event the experiment failed to reverse the process in me, this gift of my blood is intended to provide the basis for my successor to perfect. I remain convinced, even in the presumption of my own death, that I stand on the threshold of a cure.

May this sample help cure you, and serve as the basis for vanquishing our main enemy, the Trust.

Your loyal subject. Dr. Volkov

Vladimir Putin and Iron Feliks look at one another. Neither says a word.

CHAPTER 40

THE SYSTEM STRIKES BACK!

THE SYSTEM'S NEXT GATHERING IN THE KREMLIN BUNKER BRIMS WITH tension. Vladimir Putin has just been informed of the deaths of Klemko in Vienna and Beria in Romania. The remaining System Vampires are very concerned about being trapped in an underground bunker with their unhinged master.

And Vampire Zero is unhinged. The heavy oak conference table vibrates with each repeated strike of his tightly clenched fist, delivered in successive waves of rage. System Vampires are numb, silent. Heads tilted forward, eyes cast down. Putin struggles to regain composure, an act of immense self-discipline given the circumstances. His Vampire emotions are off the charts. His physical faculties are challenged by the effects of accelerated aging.

"What was Beria doing in Romania? On whose orders was he acting?"

Putin raises his head and sweeps his arms accusingly. "Any of you… tell me!"

Silence. Beria kept his plans to ambush Janicke a secret from everyone. Awkward pause. Putin hurls a look of disgust at the assembled group and absentmindedly stares up at the ceiling. His hands pressed tightly together and still staring upward, he addresses Mercader. "Who but you, my dependable Assassin, can I rely on to carry out my orders, and precisely AS I ORDERED!"

Vampire Zero looks away, wiping red tears from his cheeks. The tenor of his voice returns to an eerie calm. He wags a finger at Rubik accusingly. "These series of setbacks we suffered were set in motion by your impulsive decision to attack the Americans against my authority, and on Russian soil."

Rubik shrinks, fearing he's about to suffer Badanov's fate.

Just as suddenly as it began, Vampire Zero drops his harsh line of inquiry. He can't afford to further weaken the System. "For that act of insubordination, we lost Terrible Ivan. For now, I need you, Rubik, but I challenge you. Are you prepared to redeem yourself?"

Rubik faces straight ahead with a look of sheer Vampire defiant pride. "Yes, Sir!"

Iron Feliks maintains his icy cold demeanor. In trying times, he's always ready with words of wisdom or consolation. He summons up the best of his Bolshevik rhetoric. After all, the privations they've recently suffered are a fraction of what they've suffered in the past. It's a perspective lost on the modern reincarnation of the KGB. Iron Feliks inhales deeply before offering his history lesson for the occasion. "The enemies of the System calculate the heavy loss we have borne will lead to disorder, confusion, perhaps even dissension within our ranks. I tell you now, their expectations are in vain: bitter disillusionment awaits them. Let them think we are weak and close to defeat. He who is not blind can see that our collective, during its most trying days, is closing ranks still more closely. It is united and unshakable."

Iron Feliks's lectures often annoy System Vampires other than Putin. Today, his revolutionary fervor serves as an elixir to raise their flagging spirits. Vampire revenge-lust has replaced shame and embarrassment. Heads rise proudly. Eyes fill with a misty, nostalgic, red glow. A paranormal energy only

Vampires can sense permeates the room. This invigorating energy has taken the form of a thick, opaque, electrostatic cloud hanging low over the conference table.

Iron Feliks sees opportunity in every disaster. Danger invigorates him. Tragedy revitalizes him. Putin's mentor mouths the Chekist motto once more. Over and over, he repeats the motto just loudly enough for the others to hear. "Clean hands, a cool head, and a warm heart!"

All eyes, red and glowing brightly, focus on the mythical, mystical Iron Feliks. They join in a rhythmic chant, repeating the Chekist motto over and over. Vampire Zero's spirits are buoyed by this dramatic show of loyalty. His energy swells into an arc of inner strength that sweeps through the hearts and minds of his inner circle. As so often happens in Russian history, they are united by adversity.

In response, Vladimir Putin reminds them of their humble origins, present challenges, and future aspirations. He's unflinchingly honest about what must be done in order to succeed. In Putin's words: "The Trust may have the upper hand for now. For all we have suffered, we will be back stronger than before. It is no coincidence we have often, at the price of our own lives, stopped all global injustices to our clean conscience, to our vision of history and, I would say, to God's own truth. Such was Napoleon's injustice, such was Hitler's injustice. We will stop the American injustice as well."

Iron Feliks claps his hands in a slow cadence. The others follow suit. The tribute lasts for several minutes. Finally, Vampire Zero cuts them off like an orchestral conductor halting a performance. Putin gets back to business. "There is one other order of business we must take care of tonight. We must get back to full strength without delay. They (the Trust) are now six. There are four of our original number. We must become ten once more. We have lost Klemko, Kruchkov, Ivan, Badanov, and Beria. And Volkov. Yes, even the mad scientist was one of us. We must never apologize for who we are and what we have to do for our country. I have an announcement to make. This is our new order of seniority.

"Vampire 1: Iron Feliks."

"Vampire 2: Rubik."

"Vampire 3: Mercader."

"Vampire 4: Boris."

Vampire Zero hesitates briefly and smiles.

"Vampire 5: Ana Svetlova."

"Vampire 6: Dima."

"Vampire 7: Ilyan."

Putin introduces the initiates, gathered together for the first time as members of the System. "We diversify our numbers. We will mirror our enemy. The Trust has a Vampiress—and so shall we. Our Russian flower is not only more pleasing to the eye, but she is smarter and more cunning than her American counterpart. Dima and Ilyan, they are among my oldest and trusted friends. If I have learned a lesson from our adversity, it is that I prize loyalty above all. They will serve us well. They will serve Russia well."

The Vampires clap in delight. After the formality has ended, Vampire Zero takes center stage among the attendees, drinking vodka and dining on a dizzying array of *zakuski*. Boris is dutifully attentive, but can't focus on the conversation. He waits anxiously for the meeting to end. He relishes the thought he's done Vampire Zero a favor by helping create room for Ana Svetlova. Perhaps one day his own love interest, the Bolshoi lead ballerina Katerina, will join them.

Myshka is haunted by questions. Why was Beria such a fool to think he could blackmail him? The irony that he could betray Beria by exploiting the System's one unshakable virtue, their loyalty to one another. What possessed him to give up Beria to the Americans? Nothing's changed about his feelings toward the Americans. He had no choice but to betray Beria in order to save himself. Down to the core of his Vampire DNA, Boris is loyal to the System. At least that's what he tells himself. Boris hides a secret he's unwilling to admit, even to himself. He enjoyed passing the dossier to Rainer Wolf as agent Nul. To dangle himself as a spy was exhilarating! He also wrote the volunteer note to Aaron Janicke dropped into the CIA officer's car. It felt so satisfying, the manipulation of both Beria and the Americans to eliminate Beria. Pay him back for killing his friend. What more could be accomplished if he continues to use, no manipulate, the Trust? How long can he survive playing this dangerous game, living the life of a double agent? Does it even really matter?

Early morning and the room finally clears. Putin is semi-reclined on a plush couch, lost in thought. Iron Feliks is seated quietly across from him. Iron Feliks clears his throat. "Vladimir, we have three more vacancies to fill. Who do you have in mind for them? I am sure you are giving this much thought. Our future depends on the choices you will make."

Vampire Zero has anticipated this very question. "Ah, yes. Who, indeed, my dear Feliks? For now, that will remain my secret. I will announce the new System Vampires soon. I have not yet taken the opportunity to, shall we say, recruit them. But I tell you this. We have gained access to penetrate the US at the highest level. How would you feel if we had a System Vampire in the White House?"

Iron Feliks extends a congratulatory hand.

APPENDICES

Vampire Physics 101 Frequently Asked Questions

SECTION 1

FAQs: Basic Laws of Vampire Physics

Vampires of the intelligence world are special creations of the espionage profession. As such, these mutations have been produced from the peculiar circumstances of spycraft and are not identical to the vampires of fictional lore. Questions about their nature and instincts are best addressed within the context of Vampire Frequently Asked Questions (FAQs.) We, the authors or, dare I say, investigators of this Vampire phenomenon, have consolidated the questions most often raised by events we ourselves have witnessed, and endeavor herein to faithfully describe.

There is still much about the Vampires of our journal we simply don't understand. Although it's well known Vampires innately comprehend what makes themselves tick, both individually and within the context of their collective, they don't share their knowledge with regular humans.

On the contrary, Vampires express a certain embarrassment about what they've become. Half-human, half-animal, these unfortunate mutants don't belong fully to the world of man or beast. They exist well aware of the tragedy of their deteriorating mental and physical condition. They live moment by moment, never sure when—or how—the end will come.

As previously noted, there are no Vampire archives to consult. The entire encyclopedia of Vampire knowledge is contained within each Vampire. Simply put, there are gaps in our overall Vampire knowledge.

To the best of our ability, we've attempted to provide the following answers to FAQs.

How does someone become a Vampire?

There are no accidental Vampires. Selectees are chosen based primarily on their intelligence, bloodline, psychological suitability, and personal qualifications that will pass over to their Vampire being. For obscure reasons, the bloodlines (which a Vampire can smell) are an essential trait necessary to ensure both the power and survivability of the Vampire collective. This purity of the bloodline can be traced to the qualities that make for a strong intelligence officer, be he or she of the Russian or American tradition.

Psychological suitability is the most reliable assurance the selectee can survive the transition process and will be able to contribute substantially to the goals of the collective while still maintaining the cover of a normal life, or whatever is considered normal for a CIA or FSB/SVR (KGB) case officer.

Vampires were all once humans who represent every known blood type. Both the CIA and the FSB/SVR screen their case officer candidates against a rigorous set of eligibility criteria. The necessary qualities required to be a case officer are found in perhaps only 1/100th of one percent of the population.

It's these very unique qualities that also provide the best stock from which to derive Vampires.

Of note, besides being pure of blood and psychologically suitable, there is a Vampire ethic of sorts that surely must sound monstrous to the reader. The ethic places a strong preference on the unmarried, childless candidate, one without any deep emotional attachments or significant others. There are also other Vampire selection biases, such as eschewing obese candidates or people with debilitating medical or mental conditions.

Although it's now known to what extent such exclusions can be considered Vampire biases, there are practical reasons for selecting physically strong humans: physical weaknesses exacerbate the Vampires's propensity to deteriorate over time physically and emotionally. In addition, fewer emotional attachments create fewer complications and reduce possibilities for compromise from the human world.

Interestingly, there are no known ethnic, gender, or racial biases in Vampire selection. This tends to confirm that people of all backgrounds are considered fully qualified to be Vampire selectees. Vampires appear to be equal opportunity biters! A Vampire selectee is chosen as result of an innate comprehension by the host Vampire, that a particular person possesses the necessary criteria to contribute to the overall power of the collective to which he or she belongs. Once someone is chosen, circumstances are manipulated to place Vampires from the collective in position to exploit the human's vulnerabilities.

There is a saying among Vampires: "The key to success in Vampire recruitments is carefully orchestrating the circumstances of the initial bite." As is common in the spy profession, much attention to detail is a requirement. Vampires strive to establish a recruitment venue with a high degree of privacy, along with a low probability of interference from outsiders, known as "casuals."

Once the selectee has either accepted their fate or the Vampire has grown weary of debate, the Vampire delivers a special bite to back of the neck. If the bite is aimed correctly, it will occur near the base of the skull where it meets the spinal column.

After the fateful bite, the fledgling Vampire is in a state of physical and emotional shock for up to forty-eight hours, depending on unique characteristics of the host body, as he/she experiences painful bodily and emotional changes. Even as the tormented human is dying and in the process of being reborn, it is then told exactly what will happen, why he or she was chosen. It is vital to stress the positive—namely, there is absolutely no choice in the matter, in light of the cosmic forces at play vying for the world's fate.

The Vampire who delivered the bite becomes a mentor for the Vampire apprentice throughout the transition process. Not all who are bitten survive the arduous transition. There is as of yet insufficient data to determine what factors enhance the selectee's prospects for survival, although it is clear that reliable prescreening produces the best results.

Each member of the collective can feel the pain the selectee endures. The Vampire-in-becoming slowly develops a deep psychological attachment to each member of the collective, and more importantly, a fixation on their mission in the afterlife. It is their mission that justifies what will transpire from this day forward.

A fledgling Vampire is in one sense a babe in swaddling clothes, weak and vulnerable. Unlike a newborn, however, it is endowed with a lifetime of knowledge of each member of the collective. Each Vampire internalizes the qualities their comrades have contributed to their overall collective. The new Vampire feels its individual consciousness is being absorbed into the collective consciousness of their fellow Vampires and is strengthened by it.

Describe the physical appearance and capabilities of a Vampire.

Externally, Vampires look no different than the average reasonably fit person. The quality and color of their skin, hair, and eyes and basically every facet of their external appearance is indistinguishable from the ordinary human being. A real Vampire's smile does not disclose large, protruding fangs. Although Vampires do have fangs, we don't know exactly when or how they're physically engaged and assume this process to be controlled by the individual Vampire.

Because a Vampire's body functions essentially as a science experiment in which the laws of natural physics are placed on hold, or, more appropriately, slowed way down biophysically, their core temperature tends to hover at around 42 degrees.

A real Vampire's heartbeat is usually between two to six beats per minute, even when engaged in activities such as strenuous combat. While Vampires can't actually fly or tele-transport, they are gifted with physical abilities that well exceed the limits of human endurance. For example, the average Vampire can run at a sustained world class sub-four minutes per mile pace for something like twelve hours or more at a time.

This is especially useful for crossing large, uninhabited places such as the Gobi Desert or the vast winter wasteland of Siberia—all without producing even one drop of sweat. Your basic real Vampire can, with modest exertion, lift the rear end of a standard mid-sized car sufficient to raise the rear wheels off the ground by several feet.

Besides the psychic connection to their respective collective, Vampires also have very acute senses of sight, touch, hearing, and smell. They have limited powers of hypnotic suggestion over most humans, used mostly to make someone forget what they just saw or did.

With intense effort and for short periods of time, Vampires can accelerate their body physics to age their appearance. They do feel some physical pain, but are immune to the negative effects of intense heat, cold, and all human diseases or physical maladies.

Although they do enjoy sex, they cannot reproduce. As one can imagine, there are few humans who possess the exceptional sexual acumen required to "hang" with or satisfy a Vampire. Besides, the human sexual partner is induced through a form of Vampire hypnosis to "forget" the encounter.

It may sound odd to suggest that such an unholy creature has a moral code of ethics, but these Vampires have developed a code of ethics of sorts to not abuse their potentially abusive powers over humans. It is strictly forbidden in the Vampire "code" to abuse or manipulate a human for one's pleasure or for personal revenge or satisfaction. The comprehensive ends of the "altruistic" collective justifies each Vampire's individual actions.

In this sense, Vampires see the boundaries of their morality as lying beyond human bounds. For you see, the Vampire self-perception is that he/she is a noble savage who has sacrificed everything, including life itself, to serve a greater cause. It is only fitting a Vampire must act in a superior way to the banalities afflicting basic human behavior.

What is the life span of a Vampire?

Unknown, even to Vampires. A Vampire's life span could be a day, week, months, years, or theoretically hundreds of years. The Vampire life force is crudely analogous to cosmic black holes in space. We can measure and observe their unique physics of space and time, but we cannot calculate under what circumstances they will violently expire. So it is with a Vampire. Vampires themselves believe their existence comes with an unknown expiration date, even if they are not susceptible to the diseases and ailments to which humans succumb.

The natural laws are presumed to regulate the birth and death of a Vampire's existence, just as black holes expire by releasing massive amounts of stored energy in the form of gamma ray bursts. It has been theorized that Vampire life spans are regulated and ultimately terminated via the natural phenomena of a spontaneous and relatively spectacular release of their stored energy.

In observed death experiences of Vampires, they vanished in a flash of several brilliant nanoseconds. The only remnant of their existence is a small burn mark of roughly three inches in circumference etched into the ground and roughly a teaspoon of ash. This factor of instability, with regard to the length of their existence, is considered the driving force behind the urgency they place on their all-consuming race toward absolute victory.

What is clear is that Vampires are utterly relentless in the pursuit of their psychologically programmed mission. Victory, of course, necessitates the complete elimination of their adversary Vampire collective, to include the destruction of the potential for any future resurgence of the vanquished bloodline.

Given what we have learned about these Vampires, they seem to feel something akin to an internal alarm best described as a sixth sense their time is about to expire, like the sands of an hour glass. When any individual feels such a pall of death coming over them, the dying Vampire sends something akin to vibrations to the member of his/her collective. The other Vampires will begin to grieve for their dying comrade. It is also a warning to take immediate action to replace one of their number who is about to fall.

Given the shared bloodlines of the opposing American and Russian Vampire collectives, it is perhaps not surprising that the expiration of a Vampire on either side is "felt" by the other. Indeed, when a Vampire dies, the hypersensitive instincts of the other Vampires can feel the resulting perturbations in the geopolitical balance. Thus is the significance of the shift in the balance of power of a single Russian or American Vampire.

While most humans are able to enjoy the prospects of a certain life expectancy, no Vampire enjoys any such peace of mind. No matter how powerful they become, these creatures don't know what they are, and are much less able to reconcile their two natures into one. A Vampire might find satisfaction in fulfilling his destiny. It might find enjoyment in exercising a Vampire's special powers. But a Vampire will never find happiness as humans experience it. These denizens of the night are often tormented by the fading memories of their past human existence.

KGB Vampires, whose existence was derived from the terrible Yuriy Andropov blood experiments, are even more unstable as they were unnaturally conceived and originate from a contaminated bloodline thought to have been long eradicated. A substantial portion of the ongoing Russian experiments is, therefore, focused on forestalling the expiration of individual Russian Vampires until Vampire Zero (Vladimir Putin), has personally deemed their services are no longer required.

Do Vampires really drink blood? How do they sustain themselves?

Vampires require only small amounts of human blood, perhaps the equivalent of several shot glasses consumed on a regular basis to fully sustain themselves. They don't indulge in states of frenzied bloodlust preying on hapless human victims. To the Vampire, human blood, regardless of blood type, is like a super-concentrated high-energy source and can only be taken in relatively small quantities over an extended period of time.

In lieu of human blood, Vampires can sustain themselves on the blood of live animals, but need to consume greater quantities and more frequently in order to remain fit. A Vampire whose mojo has been substantially weakened might well try to acquire human blood to quickly regain full strength.

Blood, especially human blood, can have an almost addictive effect on the Vampire, thus increasing its natural bloodlust. Vampires have to learn early how to control their bloodlust, lest it turn into an addiction and take control of them. If such were to occur, we believe the collective would quickly eliminate the Vampire from its ranks.

Vampires require only small amounts of blood and on a daily basis. With occasional exceptions brought on by physical or emotional trauma, these creatures don't find themselves in states of frenzied bloodlust preying on hapless human victims as depicted in the annals of fictional movie Vampires.

Is there such a thing as Vampire fitness?

Yes. Vampires, like every living being, must partake of regular practices to "stay fit." Their practices, however, are quite different from those of ordinary humans.

These Vampires are hidden deep within the ranks of the CIA and FSB/SVR. Their real identities are hidden from even their colleagues. As such, they need to be able to participate in regular activities and at varying times of the day in order to appear perfectly normal. Vampires can and do attend outdoor events in direct sunlight.

When among unwitting colleagues, they can and do consume food and drink—some even smoke the occasional cigar or cigarette. So, when appropriate, a Vampire can attend the office picnic, eat a plate of barbecue, and drink a few beers. This does come at a cost. The effects of prolonged exposure to direct sunlight, and/or the consumption of food, drink, or the occasional cigar or cigarette equate to a temporary numbing of the senses, the degree of which depends on the amount of exposure and/or consumption. Vampires refer to this as a "loss of mojo!"

Vampire fitness is achieved largely through the psychic connection with the collective supplemented by an aversion to the conditions that cause "loss of mojo" as much as possible. Vampires don't require daily exercise in the traditional sense and never require a trip to the restroom.

How can a Vampire be killed?

As much as is known, a Vampire can only be killed by another Vampire. However, a human has not yet had an opportunity to, shall we say, experiment on methods of killing Vampires. In time, humans will surely be tested in confrontations with Vampires.

Methods such as direct exposure to sunlight and wooden stakes inserted through the heart are mere fiction. We don't know exactly how Vampires kill one another. We also assume that should either the Trust or System collective ever be fully eradicated, the surviving collective will remain in a semi-dormant but still vigilant state as a means of insurance their world status quo (good or evil) will remain.

How can you tell if someone is a Vampire?

It is difficult to tell if someone is a Vampire without being able to measure their pulse rate and body temperature. Not an easy thing to ask a Vampire! Even this is inconclusive as medical monitoring equipment has to be applied somewhat precisely to provide an accurate reading. Any deviations will yield way off or inconclusive results. It should be noted that Vampires have the ability to adjust their measurable physical parameters sufficient to yield normal human results for short periods of time. This does have an effect on their individual mojo. A Vampire's alternative is to use his or her limited power of hypnotic suggestion to produce normal results within the mind of the equipment operator (doctor, nurse, medical technician, etc.)

An outwardly normal person you know or suspect is a CIA or FSB/SVR case officer: someone who appears reasonably physically fit, is unmarried and childless with no significant other, who consistently consumes comparatively little food and drink when dining with friends, plus rarely goes to the restroom (except maybe to wash his or her hands and to appear normal) should pique your interest as a possible Vampire.

What exactly is a Vampire collective?

Vampires are organized into two collectives hidden deep within the CIA (the Trust) and the FSB/SVR (the System) respectively. The System collective is a product of terrible and dangerous experimentation initially implemented to raise/reanimate the deceased former general-secretary of the Communist Party of the Soviet Union, Yuri Andropov.

This experiment failed, but a portion of the blood extracted from Andropov was processed into a serum that was injected into KGB Lieutenant Colonel Vladimir Putin. Putin thereby became the first Vampire of the new order.

The CIA collective known as "the Trust" consists of strictly seven Vampires while the current KGB (FSB/SVR) collective known as "the System" consists of ten Vampires. Vladimir Putin is not counted among the ten System Vampires. As the father of all modern Vampires, he is known as Vampire Zero. The two Vampire collectives are engaged in a pitched battle of good versus evil over the future of the human race.

This Vampire war is carried out via brutal acts of espionage, the results of which influence world geopolitics and our everyday lives. It's only natural that in this battle between good and evil, each side sincerely believes it serves the cause of good. The CIA Vampires, "the Trust," believe Vampire Zero and his Vampire henchmen are bent on subjugating all of humanity to their evil System.

The Americans see the Russians as nostalgic for a world in which dictators and autocrats suppress civil liberties and democracy. For their part, Vladimir Putin and his Vampire comrades believe American hegemony is leading the world to ruin. They see Western liberalism as the cause of social decadence and moral decline. They're determined to bring the US down to size by restoring Russia to the status of superpower.

The American Trust Vampires seek to shift global geopolitics in the direction of American leadership and exceptionality. The Russian System is just as determined to check every US move and establish the Russian model as a brighter future for the planet.

The total number of Vampires on earth at any given time is eighteen—no more, no less. The logic behind the specific numbers of Vampires within the respective collectives is a mystery. Even the Vampires themselves don't know why they must maintain the 1 + 10 + 7 balance. There is a theory being researched about Vampire numbers. In part, the numerology hard-wired into the DNA of the undead must have a relationship to their survival in evolutionary terms. A key to their coexistence with humans lies in being undiscovered. Adherence to a strict small number of collective members helps ensure they can walk undetected among humans for much longer than would be the case if they were on a perpetual crime spree to "recruit" new members. Although their physical properties are almost certainly governed by the laws of nature, their functional parameters are parallel to the science that makes and controls black holes found at the edges of every galaxy.

The natural laws of physics regulate the optimal collective size and adjust, via a weakening effect, whenever that optimal number is exceeded. Russian President Putin has ordered intense experimentation intended to vastly increase the numbers of KGB Vampires with the ultimate goal of placing select Vampires within the ranks of chosen elements of the Russian military and the state's political hierarchy.

What is the purpose of the individual Vampire as a member of the collective?

Simply put, to triumph good over evil through a complete victory over its adversary collective. Each Vampire adds their respective unique qualities to the collective consciousness and thereby increases the collective's composite power as well as adding elements of those unique, individual qualities to the skills inventory of each Vampire within the collective. Each Vampire understands the whole is stronger than each of its parts. Vampires see themselves as the foot soldiers of a team, without which they are lost as individuals.

An individual can't win this game unless the team accomplishes its mission of vanquishing its archenemy and thereby ruling the world. Their bloodline will survive only through the extermination of their natural enemy. The tools of the intelligence craft, spying, intrigue, manipulation, and betrayal, represent brutally effective means to this end and nothing more.

Each Vampire on both sides of the struggle can feel the slightest trembling, shakes, and shifts to the global geopolitical balance of power. When they manage to move this force, the Vampires experience ecstasy that, crudely speaking, can only be compared to an orgasm.

What, if any, are the environmental impacts of Vampire activity?

As you can imagine, the individual Vampire has a very small carbon footprint. The real environmental impacts of Vampire activity are a result of their influences on world geopolitics. When these influences create the optimal circumstances for things such as regional instability, wars, arms races, the hoarding or waste of vast amounts of natural resources, the creation and migration of large refugee populations, international monetary, banking, and finance disputes, added stock market volatility, etc., the result is usually a substantial negative blow to the environment.

CONCLUSION

THE BAD NEWS IS THAT VAMPIRES REALLY DO EXIST IN OUR WORLD. The good news is they have not yet mastered their powers, and their numbers seem to be strictly controlled, up to this point anyway. Their impact on the world may be greater if their numbers increase over time, either through natural, but accelerated evolutionary principles at work, or through Vampire intervention. Up to now, there appears to be some sort of natural barrier to the full exercise of their gifts. These creatures do have free will, after all.

Although their physical properties are governed by the laws of natural physics, their functional parameters are parallel to the science that makes and controls black holes found at the edges of every galaxy. The two Vampire collectives are engaged in a pitched battle of good versus evil over the future of the human race. This Vampire war is carried out via brutal acts of espionage, the results of which will surely impact the course of world history.

Our only hope is that good will ultimately prevail over evil.

SECTION 2

VAMPIRE MYTHS VERSUS REALITY

Over the years, mankind has been conditioned by an understanding of Vampires derived and presented wholly by the fertile imaginations of the Hollywood movie-making machine. This cinematic interpretation has provided us with a rather complete picture of what Vampires are and why you should spend your valuable time and money in movie theaters, locked spellbound to the horror these supernatural beings mercilessly inflict on their victims.

The Vampire legend begins primarily with Bram Stoker's *Count Dracula*, conceived in 1890 and based on the legend of the mid-1400s bloody exploits of the infamous Romanian nobleman known as Vlad Dracul, aka Vlad the Impaler. Impalement on large, wooden spikes was his favorite method of executing captured Ottoman prisoners. Hollywood's embellishment of this folklore into the realm of the supernatural includes certain rules about how Vampires, as supernatural beings, function in the physical world. The rules that govern the limits of human capability simply don't apply to Vampires and thus the issue of cinematic Vampire physics versus the natural laws of physics. Moviegoers are more than willing to suspend a bit of disbelief to indulge in the movie version of Vampires.

Vampires as depicted in movies, television, and books are utter figments of imagination. In the world of fiction, Vampires are not bound by the laws of physics, with the notable exception of some common elements, such as their reaction to the effects of sunlight and wooden stakes through the heart. Indeed, certain similarities between fiction and the real world gave rise to the classification of creatures in the real world as Vampires. As even a blind squirrel can occasionally find an acorn, Hollywood does, by pure coincidence, get some things right. With this in mind, dear reader, do not confuse fiction with reality!

Vampires really do exist and have probably roamed the earth for a thousand years or more. The facts are obscure; unfortunately, there are no genuine Vampire archives to study. What is known is that Vampires are able to survive only in very small numbers. These real Vampires are bound by the same laws of physics that govern all life and matter in the universe. The difference, especially with regard to Vampire capabilities, lies in the circumstances of their creation. For a layperson, let us imagine a Vampire functions something like the earthly equivalent of an interstellar black hole—something astrophysicists are still struggling to understand. Real Vampires are constructed of the same building blocks that created all life on earth, including humans, but they interact in dynamic and explosive chemical reactions we don't fully understand.

THE MYTH

The fictional mystique ascribes certain characteristics to Vampires: undead, sociopathic evil, and at their supernatural best when under a full moon. These cruel entities rest during the hours of daylight, usually within the confines of a velvet-lined coffin, then wreak mayhem on a terrified local human population during the hours of darkness. While exposure to direct sunlight often causes them to melt or burst into flames or both, these beings can remain on earth for thousands of years as animated, yet nonliving, intelligent beings driven to perpetuate their existence though the consumption of large quantities of human blood, usually ravaged from unwilling, terrified victims.

In fictional accounts of Vampires, humans are valued primarily for their blood and are therefore categorized as a food supply to be harvested. Humans also have redeeming values such as enslavement for the Vampire's personal entertainment or to carry out menial chores during the hours of daylight. Mythical Vampires survive solely on human blood, acquired via the delivery of a bite to the victim's neck, complete with deep penetrations made by the formerly human creature's two large, protruding fangs. This bite to the neck can easily mean death if the Vampire decides to gorge him or herself and consume too much of the victim's total blood volume. Movie/TV Vampires generally exhibit extreme self-control issues with the aftereffect of their uncontrollable blood gluttony leaving the victim a mere skeleton surrounded by a skin sac.

Some myths would have us believe a bite to the neck from a Vampire automatically turns the poor, hapless human victim into one of those despicable creatures, while more modern, primarily TV series perpetuated myths present a slightly different case. In the modern TV Vampire genre, a Vampire has to purposefully intend to make the human into a Vampire, otherwise the bite to the neck, or any other part of the human's anatomy, is merely a means of direct access to a nice, juicy blood supply so the Vampire can "feed," or as it is more popularly known, "suck blood."

Regardless, select humans are "turned" or made to endure a short evolutionary period during which they become Vampires. The process is always initiated via a bite to the neck and places the new Vampire in a bond of blind obedience to his or her host. These physically superior yet supremely evil beings are all derived from basic human stock. They maintain their original human form, but being dead renders their complexion pale and them cold to the touch. The Hollywood-evolved precepts for Vampire physics dictate they can only be killed by exposure to direct sunlight or the passage of a solid wooden object, usually a sharpened stake, through the heart or the area of the chest cavity where the heart is found on a living human.

To make matters worse for their would-be human adversaries, Vampires possess superhuman strength, speed, and agility, plus are gifted with animal-like acute senses, to include the gift of extrasensory perception (ESP.) To render humanity an even more hopeless condition, movie/TV Vampires have the power to hypnotize and control humans via a concentrated gaze affixed directly into the human's eyes. This gaze, when locked into position, can also drain information from the human's brain much like a computer hacker downloads data from a target victim's hard drive.

The horror of almost unspeakable evil unleashed on our near-defenseless humankind, complete with the attraction of being able to join in the human side of the horror experience from the safety of a movie theater seat or living room couch, was pure Hollywood, highly-profitable genius. The other side of the equation: your complete faith and trust in the knowledge that Vampires are only a myth; that they exist only for the entertainment of willingly terrified ticket or cable TV- purchasing viewers; that they exist only in the minds of the movie creators and; that they can only come out on the movie or TV screen is just that—a myth!

THE REALITY

Vampires have the same carbon-based building blocks as you and I, and, therefore, they are governed by the natural laws of physics. The existence of Vampires in the real world establish the limited boundaries of human comprehension of the laws of physics, biology, and chemistry and the fundamental processes that create the universe and all forms of life. While each human being is an anonymous star in a vast and endless universe, each Vampire is akin to a black hole. Vampires begin as stars and exist at the edges of each galaxy throughout the entire universe. Humans are circumscribed largely by the laws of Newtonian physics, whereas Vampires are subject to the special physics of black holes.

As a metaphorical comparison of a human-to-Vampire transition, imagine a star turning into a supernova, slowly being overcome by its own gravity, until it collapses in on itself to form a black hole, a rip or tear in the fabric of the universe with an inescapable gravitational pull. Something so dense and powerful that even light, or objects traveling at the speed of light, can't escape. Spacetime is deformed and, within the black hole, time itself is slowed way down and perhaps stopped. Whole planets, and sometimes whole galaxies, are sucked into the black hole, made incredibly dense and crushed, before being swallowed.

To extend this analogy of Vampires as analogous to black holes, astrophysicists have not yet discovered the fact black holes come in two varieties: negative (evil) black holes exist only to consume and destroy entire galaxies, thereby increasing their size and power. Positive (good) black holes oppose the aforementioned variety via the countering forces of their own immense gravitational pulls.

It is in this counterbalance of forces the universe is held in its proper rotations, down to galaxies, planets, and so forth. The harmony of forces holding the universe together makes all life possible. Real Vampires are perpetually struggling to balance the forces of good and evil, manifesting themselves in the global geopolitical or strategic balance.

In the tiny scale of our earthly realm, in comparison to the heavens, Vampires are our black holes. They exist here on earth in varieties of good and evil. Humans who become Vampires are selected because of, among other characteristics, their individual biophysical human suitability, often actually stemming from a particular bloodline.

Purity of blood and psychological suitability are the two must-have characteristics. When these biophysical and psychological parameters are met (it's a bit more complicated than a simple bite to the neck) the human is made tacitly aware they are on the threshold of a metamorphosis they're in no position to comprehend. A special bite to the back of the neck is then quickly delivered.

The selectee is closely mentored through a process, the physical equivalent of a star going supernova, followed by the actual transition. If he or she survives this process, they will emerge as an earth-bound black hole, a Vampire. There are no accidental Vampires. The club is by invitation only. We have no idea what percentage of victims, or better put, selectees, survive the transitional journey.

The universal struggle between good and evil is barely visible as a small, almost indistinguishable speck registered deep in outer space. Even the best of today's earth-bound or earth-launched astrophysics technology can but capture glimpses of the greater battle. Our interstellar visual acuity isn't yet sharp enough to appreciate how the survival or destruction of the entire universe hangs in this delicate balance every moment of every day. We also don't have the earthly acuity to appreciate how the same dynamic is played out here on our planet, every moment of every day. The survival of humankind hangs desperately in the balance.

Suffice it to say, as the current end result of the massive gravitational pulls of competing black holes in space has, until now, kept whole galaxies in their proper rotations and, at the lower end of the astrophysical food chain, made human life on earth possible, the good and evil Vampires on earth are decisively engaged in a directly parallel battle.

Also unknown is exactly why the success of good over evil on earth is connected to its parallel good over evil interstellar success. We must, therefore, assume that everything in the universe really is connected and the success or failure of evil on earth will cause a similar, if not parallel, effect in the greater interstellar metaphysics. Although we may lack the intelligence as humans to register the dynamics of the greater battle, here on earth reverberations of the good versus evil Vampire struggle play out via its impact on the world's strategic stability.

Why is the earthly battle between good and evil Vampire collectives concentrated largely on the playing field of geopolitical events? The reason is rather straightforward: the easiest and most assured way to destroy mankind is through the manifestation of the conditions suitable to cause mankind to destroy itself.

The quickest way from point A to point B is to manipulate ideal conditions for global thermonuclear war. This is why Vampires are, heretofore, only known to exist buried deep within the premiere intelligence organizations of the two largest and most traditionally adversarial geopolitical camps, the CIA and the KGB (now FSB and SVR).

The "game qua game" is best described as an all-out life-or-death duel of global espionage between these two seasoned adversaries. The Russians' dangerous experiments with Andropov's blood have, unfortunately, kick-started the most recent and most dangerous phase of this battle. The fate of mankind now rests under a dark cloud as the Russian Vampire collective continues to put points on the board while the good guys are proverbially caught with their pants down as they struggle to play catchup. The points in this game are directions of geopolitical influence.

Victory is partially marked by either the initiation of global thermonuclear war or the destruction of the ability to cause global nuclear annihilation. Contemporary Russia, which has been more aptly described as more of an intelligence service with a country, has the initial advantage.

FINIS